REFINING FIRE

Books by Tracie Peterson

www.traciepeterson.com

BRIDES OF SEATTLE
Steadfast Heart • Refining Fire

LONE STAR BRIDES
A Sensible Arrangement • A Moment in Time • A Matter of Heart

LAND OF SHINING WATER
The Icecutter's Daughter • The Quarryman's Bride • The Miner's Lady

LAND OF THE LONE STAR
Chasing the Sun • Touching the Sky • Taming the Wind

BRIDAL VEIL ISLAND*
To Have and To Hold • To Love and Cherish • To Honor and Trust

STRIKING A MATCH
Embers of Love • Hearts Aglow • Hope Rekindled

SONG OF ALASKA
Dawn's Prelude • Morning's Refrain • Twilight's Serenade

ALASKAN QUEST
Summer of the Midnight Sun
Under the Northern Lights •
Whispers of Winter
Alaskan Quest (3 in 1)

BRIDES OF GALLATIN COUNTY
A Promise to Believe In • A Love to Last Forever • A Dream to Call My Own

THE BROADMOOR LEGACY*
A Daughter's Inheritance • An Unexpected Love • A Surrendered Heart

BELLS OF LOWELL*
Daughter of the Loom • A Fragile Design • These Tangled Threads

LIGHTS OF LOWELL*
A Tapestry of Hope • A Love Woven True • The Pattern of Her Heart

DESERT ROSES
Shadows of the Canyon • Across the Years • Beneath a Harvest Sky

HEIRS OF MONTANA
Land of My Heart • The Coming Storm • To Dream Anew • The Hope Within

LADIES OF LIBERTY
A Lady of High Regard • A Lady of Hidden Intent • A Lady of Secret Devotion

RIBBONS OF STEEL**
Distant Dreams • A Hope Beyond • A Promise for Tomorrow

RIBBONS WEST**
Westward the Dream • Separate Roads • Ties That Bind

WESTWARD CHRONICLES
A Shelter of Hope • Hidden in a Whisper • A Veiled Reflection

YUKON QUEST
Treasures of the North • Ashes and Ice • Rivers of Gold

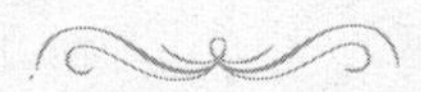

*A Slender Thread • All Things Hidden*** • House of Secrets*
What She Left for Me • Where My Heart Belongs

*with Judith Miller **with Judith Pella
***with Kimberley Woodhouse

BRIDES *of* SEATTLE,
BOOK TWO

REFINING FIRE

TRACIE PETERSON

a division of Baker Publishing Group
Minneapolis, Minnesota

Published by Bethany House Publishers
11400 Hampshire Avenue South
Bloomington, Minnesota 55438
www.bethanyhouse.com

Bethany House Publishers is a division of
Baker Publishing Group, Grand Rapids, Michigan

Printed in the United States of America

Library of Congress Cataloging-in-Publication Data

Peterson, Tracie.
Refining fire / Tracie Peterson.
pages ; cm.— (Brides of seattle ; book 2)
Summary: "In 1889 Seattle, Washington, Militine and Thane meet while serving the local poor. Though both carry a dark history and a sense of haunting pain, they begin to grow closer and wonder whether God can build something new and beautiful from the debris of the past"—Provided by publisher.
ISBN 978-0-7642-1303-8 (cloth : alk. paper)
ISBN 978-0-7642-1062-4 (pbk.)
ISBN 978-0-7642-1304-5 (large-print pbk.)
1. Man-woman relationships—Fiction. 2. Seattle (Wash.)—Social life and customs—19th century—Fiction. I. Title.
PS3566.E7717R44 2015
813′.54—dc23 2014048264

Scripture quotations are from the King James Version of the Bible.

Cover design by LOOK Design Studio
Cover photography by Aimee Christensen

15 16 17 18 19 20 21 7 6 5 4 3 2 1

To Greg Lange at the King County Archives in Seattle, Washington

Thank you for all your help with the history of King County and Seattle. Your patience and willingness to dig up obscure historical detail are greatly appreciated.

1

Seattle, Washington Territory
January 1889

There was no easy way to move a dead body. Militine Scott had this on the best authority.

Abrianna Cunningham cocked her head to the side. "I suppose we could just leave him right here." She gazed down at the man on the floor and tapped a finger to her chin. Apparently the matter was not easily resolved in her mind.

"I don't see why we couldn't just drag him off." Militine moved to the head of the body while her dearest friend in all the world walked around him squinting her eyes.

Abrianna knelt again. "Yes, that could be the irony of it all. For all his heroics and the gratitude of his peers, to just drag him off for burial would leave the audience with a sense of longing." She took hold of the man's lifeless arm. Picked it up and dropped it back to the floor. "You play the murder victim so well, Wade."

The dead man came to life and sat up. "Honestly, Abrianna, I don't see why you need a dead body in the play anyway."

She planted her hands on her hips. "Of course you don't. You aren't the playwright—you're a wainwright." She giggled. "Goodness, but I'm becoming poetic. Do you suppose that's how other poets started? I could just imagine Keats or Lord Byron having a regular conversation and suddenly words and rhyme would just flow from their lips."

Militine couldn't help but smile at the way Abrianna's mind worked. She'd never known anyone to complicate a simple matter as quickly as Abrianna. "I think, however, Wade is right. We could just reference the dead body. That way we wouldn't have to figure out how to move him."

Wade jumped up and dusted off his clothes. "When is this play to be performed?"

The floor had seized Abrianna's attention again. No doubt she was still trying to decide about the body's placement. "It was supposed to be next Saturday, but at this rate we'll never have it ready."

"We could just recite poetry, as we usually

do." Militine had no great fondness for the monthly receptions held at the Madison Bridal School. The entire point of the gathering was to introduce men to the young ladies of the school, and she had no interest in that. Which begged the question as to why she remained in residence. Better still—why she had ever come.

Most women she knew, which had been very few, having been raised in a trading post in Canada, had longed for marriage and children. Militine, however, longed for peace of mind. Something she wasn't sure she'd ever find. How she longed to be more like Abrianna. Happy-go-lucky, full of life and trust. Trust was definitely something Militine lacked.

Her friend looked rather confused for a moment and then nodded. "Perhaps you are right. We shall simply put it off until I feel confident about where the body should be."

"Now, what about those cookies you promised me?" Wade looked past both young ladies toward the hall.

"They're in the kitchen." Abrianna pointed. "You know the way."

"Indeed I do." He gave Militine a wink. "I believe I could get there with my eyes closed."

"No doubt."

"He's always willing to help for cookies. If only the entire world were satisfied as easily. I mean, just imagine the wars that would be avoided. For example, had President Lincoln offered the Southern states large quantities of cookies, perhaps the Civil War could have been avoided altogether. After all, mothers have been resolving battles for years with the promise of cookies."

Abrianna headed for the door and paused to once again return to their original discussion. "I suppose we could memorize Scripture. That always seems soothing, and I'm certain it pleases the Lord."

Militine didn't really care if it pleased God or not. They hadn't exactly been on speaking terms since heinous nightmares had taken over her sleep.

Walking to the window, Militine hoped to say something that would take Abrianna's mind off of God. She pulled back the curtain and looked out on the dismal day. "I hope it's not going to snow again today."

At one time she had thought God to be a loving Father, but over the last few months a hardness had wrapped itself around her heart. If God did care so much—if He was loving—then why had she been given such a terrible life? "I think I'll go rest. We've had a grueling day, what with all that quilting we did earlier, and besides, I'm chilled." She let the curtain fall back in place.

Stopping at the door, Abrianna gave a sigh loud enough to be heard downtown.

Militine closed her eyes and counted to ten. Waiting for what was sure to come, she sank onto the settee and crossed her arms. For whatever reason, her friend felt it necessary to worry and fret over her spiritual life. It wasn't that she didn't appreciate Abrianna's concern for her immortal soul, it was that Militine wasn't at all convinced that people *had* souls.

Father never had a soul. If he did, it certainly was in hell by now. If he was dead.

Abrianna returned and eased onto the cushions beside Militine as if approaching a wild animal.

"Militine, I know we've discussed this before, but you really mustn't turn your back on God. I thought there for a while you were coming around. I remember you saying that you thought God was a loving Father who would see all of His children safe and happy. What happened?"

Life had happened. The past and all its haunting nightmares had turned a part of her heart to stone. The sermons she'd heard about God and what He could do and what He didn't do had come together to breed bitterness. Surely an omnipotent God, a truly loving God, wouldn't allow evil people to thrive and have their way.

She didn't expect Abrianna to understand, nor did she feel that she had to explain. Militine's past wasn't something she needed to describe to anyone. Fate had allowed her to stay here at the Madison Bridal School. And in time, no doubt fate would rearrange her life again and she'd live elsewhere.

"Not everyone thinks like you do, Abrianna. Some people struggle to accept that there really is a God. Others are wounded by Him so much that they are either terrified or go out of their way to avoid Him."

"And which are you?" Abrianna looked at her innocently, but the question nevertheless stirred ire in Militine.

"That's a very personal question." If it hadn't been so cold and damp outside, Militine might have jumped up then and there and gone for a walk in the garden. She found the solitude of the flowers and shrubs to be most soothing. But it was January and nothing was blooming. In fact, snow had come in the night and now the entire world was shrouded in white. But one glance at Abrianna reminded Militine that her friend was being just that—a friend. In an effort to soften her words, she patted Abrianna's knee. "I suppose I've simply had a change of heart."

"I thought we were friends. Goodness, we've told each other all of our deepest secrets."

"No we haven't." Militine's statement was matter-of-fact. Abrianna had relayed a great many secret wishes and desires—about the death of her mother and adoption as a toddler by the old ladies who ran the bridal school. Abrianna had even let Militine in on her clandestine trips to help the poor and needy in the less desired parts of town. In turn, Militine had shared very little.

And she had no intention of sharing anything more.

But at the shocked looked on Abrianna's face, Militine worried that she'd hurt her friend's feelings. And friends weren't exactly plentiful in her life. "Some of my secrets need to remain hidden. They are ugly and painful, and I wouldn't burden anyone, much less my dearest friend, with such things."

"But that's what friends are for," Abrianna countered. "Think of Jesus with his friends Mary and Martha. Their brother Lazarus had died and—"

Militine held up her hand. "Please. No more, Abrianna. I'm trying to be patient, but my head is starting to pound."

"You're just feeling frustrated," Abrianna said, patting her hand. "And frustration is something I know very well." She flipped back a mass of unruly cinnamon-colored curls. "My hair alone is a trial to me. Most women I know have beautiful straight hair. Just look at your own dark hair. It's lovely and straight. I will never know why the Lord thought to burden me with such a mess, and with freckles, but we all must bear our crosses."

"Oh, for goodness' sake, Abrianna. Do you honestly think that curly hair and freckles constitute a cross to bear? You've lived such a sheltered and easy life that you have no idea of real need and trial, if that is your opinion."

Abrianna's mouth dropped open. For a moment she genuinely seemed silenced, but Militine knew it wouldn't last. Warding off further protest, Militine got to her feet. "I don't want to argue with you, Abrianna. Neither do I want to be hounded about issues of such a deeply personal nature."

"But I thought you wanted my honesty. I specifically recall your saying the other day that you—"

"Let it go, Abrianna. I do want honesty between us. That's why I'm going to be honest with you. If this constant talk about God is required for our friendship, then I will have to release you from further obligation."

Just let me get out of here without saying anything more. For once, please just keep your thoughts to yourself. Militine reached the door. Just a few more steps and she would be able to put the matter behind her.

"Do you truly want to go to hell?"

There it was. The one question Abrianna imposed on a regular basis. It was also a question that Militine could not answer, because she wasn't sure there was a hell . . . except for this life.

Militine turned, determined once and for all to put aside the issue of God. "Abrianna, I most seriously appeal to your good nature. Let this subject go. You once told me that a relationship with the Almighty was a thing of a personal nature. If that is so, then please allow me to figure it out for myself. It's bad enough I have to attend church every Sunday and listen to boring sermons about how much God cares for each of the sparrows."

"It's not just the sparrows," Abrianna interjected. The volume of her declaration rose. "Goodness, Militine, did you doze off? Pastor Klingle went on to say that if God cares for each sparrow, He surely cares even more for you and me. And while I do believe we have far more seagulls than sparrows, the point is still that nothing is overlooked by God."

"Say nothing more!" Militine held up her hand, and Abrianna got up from the settee. "Nothing. I don't want to discuss this again. I've tried to be tolerant. I've tried to be interested, but now I demand you leave me be!"

Brisk footfalls echoed in the hallway.

Abrianna braced herself. She knew those footsteps all too well.

Aunt Miriam entered the room with a grim expression. "What in the world is all this yelling about?"

Abrianna frowned. Militine had already raced out of the room, leaving Abrianna alone to answer.

The older woman gave Abrianna a look that could not be misunderstood. She expected an answer and expected it now.

"I was trying to share God's love with Militine, but she wanted nothing to do with it. I'm afraid I'm to blame for the loud voices. I was rather . . . well . . . pushy."

"You? I can't imagine." There was a tender teasing in her aunt's voice that did nothing to reassure Abrianna. "Nevertheless, sharing God's love is seldom done in a screaming fashion."

"I don't want her to go to hell. It is my dearest wish that no one suffer the fires of hell, and especially not Militine. She's become a dear friend. I cherish her as much as I cherish any of my friends, including Lenore. Now that Lenore is married I suppose I lean on Militine's friendship more than ever." She paused only long enough for a quick breath. "Do you think that's wrong?"

"I think it's wrong to badger a person about salvation. You know that the good Lord has the ability to bring His sheep into the fold."

"Yes, but He also told us to go into all the world and preach the gospel." Abrianna put her hand to her heart. "I do long to serve Him in that capacity, but how can I do so when I can't even win converts here at home? When Militine first came here, she told me that she believed in God's goodness, but now I can tell she thinks Him cruel."

Aunt Miriam smiled and took hold of her arm. "Come sit, child."

Obedient to her wishes, Abrianna took her seat once again on the settee. The older woman joined her, never once letting go.

"Abrianna, it is not our job to win converts. It is our job to show people the love of God and share the truth of the gospel. You can hardly do that hitting them over the head with the cross."

"But that wasn't my heart. I only wanted Militine to take serious the fires of hell."

"I'm certain that in time God will allow Militine the knowledge she needs to make her own choices. God only desires that you see to your own soul and pray for others. He wants you to seek Him and know Him for yourself. Then, by this knowledge you must live a life that reflects His mercy."

"I wasn't very merciful," Abrianna admitted. "I suppose once again I allowed my enthusiasm to get the better of me. Honestly, I don't know why God gave me such a passion for the gospel if He didn't expect me to get excited about it. Do you know that Pastor Klingle said the end of all time is quickly approaching? He believes God will soon come back to judge us all. What if I didn't do all that I could to see that everyone heard the gospel message?"

Aunt Miriam showed unexpected patience. "Abrianna, do you suppose God would allow even one person to die without having a chance to hear the gospel message? He wouldn't be a very fair or loving God if He only allowed for some to hear the message but then required all to respond to it. I cannot believe our Father in heaven would play such a trick on His children.

"I believe, however, that He has a plan for all of us—not just for Militine or the other girls here at the school. You know that I want each of the young ladies here to have a strong faith in the Almighty. I take them to church every Sunday, rain or shine, as you know. I do what I can to live a godly example before them, and I pray for each one. Perhaps you could spend more time in prayer and less in badgering."

A heavy sigh escaped. Abrianna sat back, nodding. "You are right to correct me, Aunt Miriam. I haven't been at all charitable. I do try. Honestly, I do." She lifted her gaze to the ornate ceiling. "I suppose I am one of the worst of God's messengers, but my heart is truly fixed on Him."

"I believe that, Abrianna. I think Militine knows that, as well. Give her some time. Be a living witness of Jesus, not just a vocal one. Let her choose for herself." Aunt Miriam gave her hand a quick pat and then got to her feet. "And I want you two to make up. I won't have you letting the sun go down on your anger. I'll call Militine to join us."

"Yes, ma'am."

When Militine returned with Aunt Miriam, she looked none too happy. Abrianna bolstered her courage. If she was ever going to be a godly woman who shared the gospel and helped the lost, then she would have to get over worrying about how to apologize and just do it.

"I'm sorry, Militine." She got to her feet quickly and extended her hands toward her friend. "I was wrong to allow my enthusiasm to overrule my good sense. Your friendship is most dear to me, and I do not wish to act in such a way to suggest otherwise. Please say that you'll forgive me."

Militine hesitated for a moment and then clasped Abrianna's hands. "I do. I'm sorry, too."

"I forgive you." Abrianna pulled Militine close, but she remained stiff and did not return Abrianna's hug. "I never meant to hurt you." The embrace lasted only a moment, but it was long enough to realize Militine was still guarding herself.

Aunt Miriam gave them a smile. "It is never right to argue about God, girls. He loves you both and desires that you come to Him willingly. He only wants the best for you."

"Well, I don't think God is the best for everyone."

Abrianna was surprised to hear Militine say such a thing in front of her aunt. She looked to Aunt Miriam for confirmation of this being the most scandalous thing a person could say, but the older woman only nodded.

"That is a decision that you must make for yourself." Aunt Miriam did the unthinkable and excused herself to oversee supper.

A protest rose in Abrianna's throat, but Militine spoke before she could make her thoughts clear. "Aren't you going to tell me how awful I am to think that way? Aren't you going to try to force me to read the Bible and see where I will die for all eternity without accepting Jesus as my Savior?"

It was exactly what Abrianna had hoped her aunt would do, although it was a shock to hear Militine state it so unequivocally.

Aunt Miriam paused in the archway. “Child, Jesus came for all the world to be saved, but He already knew that many would reject Him. Even so, I cannot call to mind a single time when Jesus shared the love of His Father with someone and demanded they accept it. Even when a rich young man came to Him and asked what he needed to do to be saved, Jesus told him to sell all he had and follow Him. When the man walked away unwilling . . . Jesus let him go.”

It was true. Abrianna knew the story well. It vexed her to admit that perhaps she had caused more harm than good. It was clear that Militine was not nearly so offended by Aunt Miriam’s words as she had been with Abrianna’s.

“I won’t demand you listen to me nor will I argue the points of what I believe to be true in God’s Word,” Aunt Miriam concluded, “but I will pray for you.”

The two young women stood in silence for some time after Aunt Miriam’s departure. Militine seemed to be considering what the older woman had said, while Abrianna was dealing with her conscience. Would matters of spirit and heart ever be simple?

Thane Patton marched his checker piece all over the board, cleaning Wade’s meager

showing off the board. "I think that's enough for tonight, don't you?"

Wade leaned back in his chair. "I suppose it better be, or I'll owe you my entire stash of cookies. Thank goodness Miss Poisie thought to send me home with extra."

Laughing, Thane picked up another of the oatmeal cookies and popped the entire thing into his mouth. The buttery sweetness met with his approval. He washed the cookie down with the last of his coffee. However, cookies didn't fix the fact that he was unhappy with his job of mending boats for Davidson Taylor. Nor did it give him the raise that Mr. Taylor had refused.

"So have you decided what you're going to do?"

Thane looked up from his cup and met Wade's gaze. "I suppose I'll just go on working as I always have. I don't expect Mr. Taylor to understand my need for a raise. He doesn't care that I intend to do more with my life than just mend boats."

"Maybe they will hire you into a paid position at the fire department. After all, you did say they were doing more of that these days."

"Yes, but you have to know someone to get those jobs. I might one day find a sponsor to help me get one of the lower positions, but that will still take time. This city has so much to do regarding fire safety, and it has little money to spare. The City Council has its hands full trying to figure out how to get a better water flow throughout the city."

Thane pushed his hand back through his wavy red hair. He'd lived in Seattle for ten years and in all that time had worked for Mr. Taylor, learning to repair small sea craft. His real interest had changed, however, when one of the customers convinced him to become a volunteer fireman. There was something about working in that capacity that made him feel alive—worthwhile. Almost like the past would never matter, even if the truth were told.

Wade returned from pouring them both more coffee. "I read that the pressure isn't enough to reach all of downtown. Sounds like a major problem waiting to happen."

The protests had been many, and Thane had been known to raise his own concerns. "The wooden mains are too small and feed too many hydrants. That makes the water pressure unreliable. If there is more than one fire at a time, there is never enough water." He got up and pulled on his coat. "You'd think being a harbor town would resolve all issues for extinguishing fires, but when the tide is out, there are very few streets from which the pumps can reach any substantial amount of water. It makes working as a volunteer fireman quite a questionable adventure." He drank the lukewarm coffee in one gulp.

"I can see that." Wade wrapped Thane's winnings in a section of newspaper and handed the package over. "I'm just glad we have men like you on the force."

Thane tucked the cookies under his coat. "Well, they won't have me or anyone else for long if the council doesn't figure out how to resolve some of these issues."

He left Wade's and started back to his small apartment not far from the docks. The cold air nipped at his bearded face. Maybe it was time to leave Seattle. Maybe go south. He'd heard great things about Portland and even San Francisco. The latter would surely always need another fireman.

He noticed a couple of old men hunkered over a small fire. They were wearing ragged clothes, and from the look of it hadn't bothered to groom themselves in some time. Was that all that Thane had in store for his future? What about family? Surely there were happy ones out there somewhere.

"Hey, fella, got some change for a pint? Need a bottle to help ward off the cold," one of the men said as he passed.

Thane handed him the only change he had. "Better to get a meal, friend."

The old man smiled a mostly toothless grin. "Gin goes down easier. Thank ya kindly."

Thane shrugged. It was the old man's business what he did with the money . . . and with his life. Just as it was up to Thane to decide his own future. Unfortunately, the past weighed heavy against him, and he did well just to survive the present.

2

By Sunday Militine felt able to once again deal with church and the idea that God existed and cared for her well-being. There were certainly worse things to ponder, and today was a day of rest. There would be no tiresome cooking and sewing classes, nor studies on table settings and flower arrangements.

Abrianna arrived at her door just as Militine secured a warm wool bonnet. "Goodness, but it's cold outside. I'm not looking forward to walking to church. Aunt Miriam told Aunt Poisie and Aunt Selma that the weather has given her a great determination to purchase one, possibly two, carriages."

"That would be quite an expense. Carriages aren't cheap. But I would prefer them to traipsing through the snow. I hope she will buy them immediately. As tiny as you are, you might well disappear in a snowdrift."

Abrianna put a hand to her breast. "To ne'er be discovered until spring thaw."

Militine smiled and pulled on her gloves. She seriously doubted her friend could keep quiet that long. "I suppose we shall just have to walk arm in arm and help keep each other warm. Shall we?"

Abrianna wrapped her hand around Militine's. "We shall."

Their sense of ease had returned, letting their previous argument about God wait for another day. Militine liked that about Abrianna. The young woman could get so very passionate about various subjects, but her love of those around her always helped to temper her outbursts. At least after the first two or three times.

Abrianna's friendship meant a great deal, however. Militine had never had a friend before arriving at the school. Coming to Mrs. Madison's had been an act of desperation, but surprisingly it had proved to be a blessing. But she doubted it would last.

As they did every Sunday, Wade Ackerman and Thane Patton arrived early to walk with the ladies to church. This had been a common practice for as long as Militine had been on the premises, and Abrianna declared it to have gone back much further than that. Mrs. Madison and the other ladies considered it inappropriate for women to travel unescorted by a male. The city was a dangerous place, and unaccompanied females were asking for trouble, according to the matron of the bridal school. But Militine had found more danger from a violent-tempered father than the strangers in Seattle.

Abrianna once asked about her parents, and Militine hadn't known how to respond. She could lie and say they were both dead, as Abrianna's parents were, or she could tell the truth and risk someone learning about her past. The lie seemed easier.

"Come, ladies," Mrs. Gibson directed. "Let us form a proper line for our sojourn." Mrs. Gibson was a dear friend to Mrs. Madison and her sister, Miss Poisie. Together the trio kept the school running in an orderly fashion, training each student on the details of how to better prepare themselves for matrimony.

Mrs. Madison and Miss Poisie appeared bundled from head to toe in navy wool. "It is quite cold today, and with the snow there are bound to be accidents. I implore you to walk slowly and in pairs. Hold fast to one another so if one slips, the other may help her up, just as Ecclesiastes says."

"Or both will end up on their backsides."

Abrianna was well known for her comments, and while she barely whispered this to Militine, Mrs. Madison's frown made it clear she'd overheard.

"We will practice care," Mrs. Madison stressed.

As they journeyed, Militine noticed the shoveled path. It didn't go unnoticed by the older women.

"I suppose we have you two to thank," Mrs. Madison said, looking to Wade and Thane.

They grinned and shrugged. "Might have been angelic beings making sure you could get to church on time," Thane commented.

"Angelic beings, eh?" Mrs. Madison smiled. "Or decent young men. Either way, we are thankful."

By the time they reached the small stone church, the girls around her were chatting and giggling up a storm as they did every Sunday, despite Mrs. Madison's suggestion that the walk be spent in reflection and prayer. However, once they entered the church, the ladies were all respectful and silent. Militine followed the others inside and took her seat. Only a moment later one of the elders rose to the pulpit.

"I am sorry to say we have suffered a great loss in the life of the church. Pastor Klingle has gone home to be with the Lord."

The old ladies of the Madison School gasped. "God rest his soul," Miss Poisie declared.

"Amen," Mrs. Gibson and Mrs. Madison murmured, their usual response to the younger woman's blessing of the dead.

Gasps, sniffles, and whispered words were heard throughout the sanctuary. Militine exchanged a glance with Abrianna, whose expression suggested deep sorrow. She pulled a handkerchief out of her reticule and twisted it between her hands. Militine's thoughts and emotions floundered. Should she say something? Perhaps wrap an arm around her friend? Abrianna and the old ladies had always spoken with great love for the aging pastor. No doubt this would hurt them deeply.

"We know our dear brother is in a much better place," the elder continued, "however, our pain is certain. Pastor Klingle was a solid man of God who did much to lead this congregation in truth. We will miss him." The man coughed as if to clear the emotion from his voice.

Militine glanced around the room. She felt uneasy with her own lack of emotion over such sad news.

"The funeral service is scheduled for Wednesday. I know we will each want to say our final good-byes. The church will be open at noon and the funeral held at three o'clock. That will give time to view the deceased prior to the service. The elders and deacons met and it was agreed to ask the Reverend Swanson from the Lutheran church to officiate at the service, as he and Pastor Klingle were the best of friends."

Murmurs of approval traveled throughout the congregants. "The pastor will be buried beside his wife in the church graveyard. However, there will be no outdoor services due to the cold."

After this another man led the congregation in several hymns and then they had a time of silent prayer before church was dismissed. Militine knew the loss of the pastor and the upcoming funeral would be the topic of discussion for the day. The older ladies of the church barely waited for the final amen before coming together to make plans for their part in the arrangements.

"I am grieved to the depths of my soul," Abrianna declared. She had taken out a handkerchief shortly after the announcement, but only now did tears come. "I will sorely miss Pastor Klingle. I've known him all of my life. Why, there has never been another man in the pulpit while I've come to this church. How will we ever find anyone so kind and knowledgeable? The man was a paragon of godly love and wisdom."

Wade joined them, Thane close on his heels. He patted Abrianna's shoulder. "I know you'll miss him. We all will. Pastor often came by the shop just to see how I was doing."

She sniffed. "He was so good to help me with the friendless and old sailors. They trusted him, you know. But of course, who *didn't* trust him?" Tears streamed down her cheeks.

Militine marveled at the sense of loss felt by the parishioners. Abrianna wasn't the only one crying. Some of the men, pillars of the community and church, were also damp eyed. It was hard to understand the impact of one man upon so many.

Wade put his arm around Abrianna. "They'll learn to rely on another. God will surely send us another pastor. It might take time, but trust can be earned. Right now we need to focus on what we can do to be useful to the church."

"Of course." Abrianna wiped her eyes. "I will endeavor to be brave and strong."

"I've never known you to be anything else."

Wade was right. Militine had never known Abrianna to be anything but a rock of strength. Maybe that was what troubled Militine at times. Abrianna seemed to have a clear understanding of how to face life's challenges in a bold and sure manner. No doubt the redhead would declare this had everything to do with her faith in God.

Militine shrugged. Maybe it did.

"What was that for?" Thane asked.

Militine met his blue-eyed gaze. His handsome face rather startled her. "What?"

"You shrugged. I just wondered what that was for."

"I don't suppose it really matters. Sad thing for the pastor to die. I know there are many who will miss him."

"But you aren't one of them?"

"I don't feel that I knew him all that well. After all, I've only been here a little over a year. Frankly, some of his sermons left me feeling . . ." She shook her head. When did she become so blunt and opinionated? "It's not important. I won't speak ill of the man. I'm sure he did his best."

"But at times you felt God more a tyrannical judge than a loving Father? Someone to be avoided rather than embraced?"

She looked at Thane and marveled he could be so astute. "Why would you say that?"

He stroked his neatly trimmed red beard. "I don't know. I guess I've seen something in your eyes—a look that reminds me of myself. Maybe that's why I enjoy your company so much."

Militine's face grew hot. *He enjoys my company?* She wasn't used to this kind of attention, and the few times Thane had singled her out for conversation at the receptions or dinners at the school, Militine had thought he was only being gentlemanly.

Mrs. Madison signaled to her ladies that it was time to depart, so there was no chance of pressing the matter. Militine fell into step beside the other silent women, her arm looped with Abrianna's. Their attitudes were vastly different than on the journey there.

"But at times you felt God more a tyrannical judge than a loving Father? Someone to be avoided, rather than embraced?"

How very strange that Thane should so clearly speak her heart. Her own father was exactly as Thane suggested. Especially when it came to avoiding rather than embracing. She shuddered, almost feeling the blows of her father's belt upon her back.

Coming to Seattle a year earlier had been a risk for Militine. She had actually hoped to put a greater distance between her and the life she'd hoped to forget. Her father and mother had settled about sixty miles northeast of Vancouver some thirty years ago to set up a trading post. Her mother ran the post most days while her father trapped and journeyed out for supplies. Other children had been born to the couple, but only Militine had survived. Much to her father's displeasure, for he saw little value in a daughter.

It hadn't been easy to convince Mrs. Madison to take her on at the school. Apparently she liked to have references and detailed accounts of her students. Militine could offer neither. Finally she threw herself on the mercy of the elderly trio and begged for their help. She confessed a sad and tragic past that included the death of her mother and her father's descent into alcohol. She hinted at the brutality she'd received but nothing more. They would have rejected her for certain had they known everything. As it was, they told her that there would be strict rules to adhere to and a great deal of work to accomplish. Militine agreed to do whatever was required, and it hadn't been easy.

She knew that the purpose of the school was to teach household management skills to young ladies with the intent of making them better prospects for marriage. However, for Militine that had never been the reason for attending. The Madison Bridal School seemed the perfect place to hide, especially if you were a woman who had no intention of marrying. No one would have expected her to seek refuge in a place such as this.

Abrianna had let Militine know early on that the way to progress to the place where suitors were allowed to court you was to be accomplished in your various duties. There were lessons in etiquette and elocution, French, sewing, cooking, and of course household arranging and cleaning. Militine could hold her own at most of the basic things, but she didn't want anyone to know, and early on had taken on the pretense of extreme clumsiness. This, coupled with her genuine lack of knowledge where etiquette and speaking were concerned, seemed to vex Mrs. Madison and her cohorts. She had heard them whisper that next to Abrianna, she was their greatest challenge.

She smiled, content to be exactly that. For however long she could make this situation last, Militine intended to be very nearly untrainable and greatly lacking in bridal qualities.

"Thank you for agreeing to meet with me," Abrianna declared, appointing each of her confederates to their appropriate seat around the table. "I know the others are busy discussing the funeral dinner and such, but this is also of utmost importance."

Militine had no idea what her friend was up to, but feeling sleepy after a large Sunday dinner, listening to Abrianna lecture might well lend itself to dozing. On the other hand, with Abrianna, a person could count herself lucky if the lecture didn't involve a dead body or a socially unacceptable exploit. Only time would tell if good fortune had smiled on them.

Wade and Thane sat opposite the two ladies and looked at Militine as if she might have answers. She shook her head and turned to Abrianna, hoping the vivacious woman would shed light on the subject quickly.

"I know I've kept you all in the dark about my new venture," she began. "I wanted to make absolutely certain I had the proper funding in place before coming to you for help."

"Great," Wade said, nudging Thane, "she's got a new venture, and she needs our help."

Thane nodded. "And she has funding."

"Oh, don't sound so forlorn." Abrianna squared her shoulders. "It's not like this will be surprising to any of you. You know my passion for helping the poor?"

"I know your passion for stripping years off our lives as you sneak around at night when you think no one knows. Good grief, Abrianna, is this going to be more of that?"

Militine smiled at Wade's question but ducked her head so that no one would see her reaction. She felt just as he did. Abrianna was never one for obeying the rules of society, but it would have helped everyone's peace of mind if she would have at least given those rules a brief nod.

"No, and that is why I believe you will fully support me in this endeavor. As you know, I have long felt God's calling on my life to assist the poor and needy. I believe God made it clear in the Bible that this is the responsibility of all mankind—not just the few who are seeking His calling on their lives. Though I do realize not everyone wants to hear God's calling lest they have to do something about it." She paused and appeared thoughtful.

"I suppose there are those who don't want to know for fear they will not be up to the task. Honestly, I don't mean to sound harsh and judgmental. I do sympathize with those who are fearful, but—"

"Abrianna," Wade interrupted, "could you just get back to the subject at hand? What is your new venture, and what does it have to do with us?"

"Well, Wade Ackerman, if you'll just give me time, I'll get to that." Abrianna folded her hands and rested them atop the table. "God has provided a means for me to be truly helpful. I've been working with Lenore and Kolbein." She paused and looked to Thane. "You remember them, don't you? Lenore has been my dearest friend for many years, and Kolbein Booth is the man she married last September. He's a lawyer."

"I remember." Thane exchanged a glance

with Wade. "Honestly, Abrianna, it's not like I live in a cave somewhere. Just because I'm not always hanging around here doesn't mean I don't know about things. Besides, I helped with the move here and know that the Booths live just down the street. I've encountered you and Mrs. Booth on many occasions."

"Good. I'm glad you recall them. Sometimes it's been my experience that men are less observant about such things. I don't understand if it's because they have a great deal on their minds or they simply don't care." She looked at Militine. "Remember, I was mentioning the other day how Kolbein has trouble remembering the names of the young ladies here at the school and how that really surprised me? After all, he is a lawyer and you would think such a duty would require a good memory. Of course, Aunt Selma says it's probably because he came to us by way of Chicago. She's absolutely certain that town is full of degenerates and ninnies, although Kolbein truly seems to be neither."

"Abrianna, please!" Wade's exasperated tone made it clear he'd reached the limit of his patience.

"I apologize." She offered Wade a sympathetic smile. "I am given to the details, you know. Anyway, as you all may know, Lenore and Kolbein both come from money.

And both have tender hearts when it comes to helping those in need. I have managed to convince Lenore that, with proper funding, I could extend considerable help to the poor of Seattle."

"In what way?" Wade's expression showed great concern.

Militine held her breath. With Abrianna a person could never be certain as to what would come next, but no doubt it wouldn't be a simple matter.

"Lenore is giving me a substantial sum of money so I can rent a little building down near the wharf. It is quite close to where you work on the boats, Thane." She hurried on, not waiting for any comment or protest, as was Abrianna's fashion. Militine had come to expect this as much as the others and didn't try to stop her.

"I have already spoken to the owner. He will allow us to paint it and fix it up in order that I might run a food house for the poor. Given its location, the old sailors will find it quite convenient, and it won't be that far removed from the more destitute parts of town. Those folks might also find it easy to locate. All that is required is some cleaning and mending.

"That's where you three come in. I will need help preparing the place, and then, of course, I know my aunts would feel better if

I could have one or both of you men present when I'm actually there feeding the poor."

"Is that what they said?" Wade fixed her with a stern look. "Or is that what you're hoping will be the case?"

Abrianna had the decency to squirm a bit in her chair. Militine had seen the young woman manipulate situations and cajole people to accomplish most anything she desired, but she didn't seem to be able to push Wade around.

"I feel confident," the redhead began, "that your presence will assure them of my safety. They truly trust you, Wade. You, too, Thane, and I figure you both have to eat lunch just like the rest. I plan to serve only the noon meal, you see. And—"

"Abrianna." Wade's tone was one of an insistent father with a child.

Militine smiled at Abrianna's reaction. She crossed her arms against her chest and sat back in the chair. "All right. I haven't told them yet. I wanted to make sure I had your support first. If I don't have your help, then I'll need to find someone else, and given the fact that Pastor Klingle has just died and his funeral will be the focus of our attention for this week, I wanted to secure your assistance before things got out of hand."

For a moment silence fell on the room, something most unusual when Abrianna was present. Militine could see that Abrianna was fighting the urge to say more. Instead, she toyed with a loose curl and kept her eyes lowered.

"A food house," Wade finally said.

"On the docks," Thane added.

Militine laughed aloud. "So much for keeping it socially acceptable. Nevertheless, I'm happy to help. Anything that gets me out of here and away from the grueling work of setting a proper table and hosting tea parties is fine by me."

"I suppose she'll do it with or without our help." There was resignation in Wade's voice. "I'm guessing too that you'll do it with or without your aunts' approval."

Abrianna surged forward. "Oh, but I'm sure they will approve if you are at my side. Aunt Miriam has always supported helping the poor. She is the first one to say it is our duty. I think that is why she doesn't chide me for taking extra food from the larder for the destitute. Wade, you know that you have always been my aunts' most trusted confidant. If you were to show your support and stand at my side when I share the news, I believe they would quickly rally to the cause."

Thane nudged Wade. "You do know she's not going to drop this. We might as well give in and consent. Otherwise she and Miss Scott here will just sneak out in the dead of night to fix the place up, and then instead of a noon meal, she'll be feeding folks at midnight."

Wade gave a heavy sigh, and Militine almost felt sorry for him. Once again Abrianna had created chaos where they might otherwise have had a dull and peaceful life.

"Very well. We'll help you fix the place up and come for noon meals. However—" Wade paused and pointed his finger for emphasis—"you are to do nothing without speaking to me about it first. Promise me."

Abrianna jumped up from her chair and hurried around the table to hug Wade. "Of course I promise. I'll speak to you about everything."

Militine could see the doubt in his eyes. They both knew Abrianna well enough to know that this was just the beginning of what might well turn out to be a most arduous and complicated endeavor.

3

The day of Pastor Klingle's funeral dawned cloudy and then cleared as the day progressed. Militine supposed Abrianna would say it was God's way of honoring the old man. By the time the service started at the church, the weather was actually quite nice. Of course the warming temperatures had caused the frozen ground to turn to muck and slush, but no one seemed to mind.

Militine sat sandwiched between Abrianna and a young lady named Tabitha Cooper. The latter was a slim blond-haired woman with a rather plain face. She hailed from New York and talked with a funny accent that Militine found amusing. The best thing about Tabitha, however, was that she was shy and said very little.

Brother Mitchell, the head elder of their

church, addressed the crowd. "Today we are celebrating the life of our dear Pastor Klingle—a man of uncommon generosity and wisdom." The elder lowered his head, coughed, and shifted his weight from one foot to another.

"God rest his soul," Miss Poisie declared loud enough for all to hear.

Murmured amens filled the sanctuary.

Another cough from the elder, his emotion sincere. "We thought it only appropriate that we ask one of Pastor Klingle's good friends to speak on this occasion, therefore I will now turn the service over to the Reverend Swanson." He took his seat as the older man approached the pulpit.

The man smiled down on the flock. "Let us pray. Father in heaven, we thank you for the life of our good friend Jefferson Klingle. We thank you for his work on earth and the many souls he touched. May we celebrate his life in the reflection of your glory. May we bring you honor and praise as we consider the joy and encouragement this man gave to his congregation and to many strangers on the street. We join now, although with heavy hearts at the loss we suffer, in joy of our brother's journey home, where he will forever worship you with the saints. Amen."

Militine raised her head as Reverend Swanson began sharing a comical story of when he and Pastor Klingle first met. How strange it seemed that such happiness should be shared on such a dismal occasion.

"Jefferson was not much for the cold damp of our climate. He preferred the sunny Georgia coastal land of his youth. But God called him to Seattle, and Jefferson boldly answered the call. So picture if you would the first day of May with a light drizzle falling on our fair city. But for Seattle it was otherwise a beautiful spring day. I was walking down the street heading to a meeting when Jefferson came bursting out of his hotel. He was wearing a heavy raincoat, a winter coat, and a suit coat, and I believe he might also have had on a sweater. I thought I had been attacked by some wild animal. The collision was such that it knocked us both to the ground, whereupon Jefferson promptly landed in a huge puddle of water." Many in the congregation snickered.

"I righted myself and extended my hand to Jefferson to help him up. He looked up at me with the most forlorn expression and, before accepting my help, asked, 'Is there nothing warm and dry to be had in this town?' We became instant friends in that moment. I shall always remember him fondly, often huddled by the fire on days I thought quite hot." The man paused and held open his arms. "I think it would be most fitting if others would share their stories. Just stand up and tell us what Pastor Klingle meant to you or what he might have helped you through."

Without delay several men rose to their feet. "I'll tell you what," one began, "Pastor Klingle helped me forgive my brother after he did me wrong. My brother didn't even care that he'd robbed me blind. He took everything I had coming to me from our pa and never once asked forgiveness. There was a powerful anger in me, and it was tearin' apart my insides. I was sick both from the rage and from the bottle I used to ease my misery. Pastor Klingle came to tend me when I was in the worst of it. He prayed with me and spoke to me from the Bible. He even told me of times when anger had got the best of him. He told me he had learned a hard lesson about forgiveness and that a man needs to forgive more for his own sake than for the sake of the other feller.

"I thought a long time on that. After I sobered up, I took Pastor up on his offer to come to church. That Sunday he just happened to preach on Jacob and Esau and told how Jacob stole Esau's birthright and all the trouble it caused. Made me realize my brother and me were just like that." He gave a sheepish smile as he glanced around the sanctuary. "I tell you, I had to sit tight until I heard how that all turned out."

Abrianna giggled, as did most everyone else. The man was so intense in his telling that Militine, too, longed to know how the story resolved.

"Well, in the end old Jacob had a lot of troubles. My brother, too. Jacob even knew that at one point Esau was plannin' to kill him. God knows I wanted to get revenge on my brother. Anyhow, Pastor Klingle told how God used even the deceptions and evil dealings of one brother to turn things around where it benefited them both. I can't say that's how it happened for me and mine, but I remember Pastor told of the liberty that came for both brothers in forgiveness and how they could lay the past to rest. I wanted that as much as I thought I wanted another drink. So I got down on my knees and prayed that day. It made all the difference, and Pastor Klingle was the one who brought me to where I could see that my own hatred was what kept me all bound up."

Ahead of her in the next pew, Militine saw Abrianna's three aunts nod and wipe away tears. Another man told of his love for Pastor Klingle and how the man had once given him his last dollar to help him buy bread and meat for his family. Still another mentioned the way the pastor lent a helping hand with cutting firewood when the parishioner had broken his arm.

"He wasn't all that good at chopping," the man said with a twinkle in his eyes, "but he was so entertaining, I all but forgot the pain."

Other stories spilled from parishioners, and by the time the funeral concluded, the congregants wore beaming smiles and continued sharing laughs, accounts of the past, and their love of this great man. A sadness washed over Militine. She hadn't bothered to know Pastor Klingle as anything more than the boring old man who tormented her every Sunday with his boring old teachings from a boring old book. It would seem there was far more to the man than she'd realized. This puzzled and troubled her greatly. What had she missed?

A dinner was offered after the service, and Militine did her best to be open and friendly with others in the congregation. However, she soon tired of trying to be someone she wasn't and was grateful that the dinner passed quickly. Finally, with most everyone occupied with dessert and conversation, Militine took the opportunity to slip away. No destination called to her, but by the time she reached the church graveyard, she knew her real desire was to be absent from so many people.

Taking a seat on a small stone bench, she drew in a deep breath. The sunlight seemed muted but strong enough to offer a slight warming to her face. For several minutes she simply relished the silence, but then her mind began to wander.

Her expectations for the day had been nothing like what actually happened. She'd imagined episodes of sorrowful mourning and had steeled herself for such. But these people seemed quite joyous through their tears. Reverend Swanson had even said they were there to *celebrate* the life of Pastor Klingle. It seemed absurd that a funeral should be a celebration. A party to honor the dead?

"I saw you slip away. I hope you don't mind if I join you." Thane's strong voice settled over her like a warm blanket.

She looked up and gave him a smile. "Not at all. I hope that my escape wasn't noted by anyone else. I'd hate for everyone to come seek me out."

Thane shrugged and sat down on a stone bench opposite her. With nothing but the small rock path between them and sentinels of marble and granite around them, the flesh and bone couple seemed oddly out of place. Militine, however, found comfort in the isolation and solitude of the moment.

"I needed to think." He hadn't asked for an explanation, but for some reason she felt she needed to offer one. "I'm not used to so many people in one place."

"I kind of figured that. You never seem real comfortable at the school's gatherings."

"Well, that's for an entirely different reason." She met his compassionate gaze. Perhaps he already understood. "I don't really feel accepted. I've always been . . . well . . . rather clumsy and ignorant. I never know what to talk about, and when I do speak, it always seems to come out wrong."

"I think you talk quite eloquently."

She laughed. "Only because of the elocution lessons. Goodness, but I do weary of proper etiquette and speech."

"So why bother then?"

Folding her hands together, Militine hoped Thane might accept her simple explanation. "I had nowhere else to go. I have no family, and marriage seemed impossible given my inability to do much of anything."

"I don't have any family, either. They're all dead." Thane picked a piece of lint from his coat. "I suppose I ought to sound more grieved over it, but it's been a long time."

"Were you . . . were you close?" The words came hard.

"No." He offered nothing more, and knowing the need for privacy Militine didn't pry.

"Sometimes," she said after a great pause, "I feel I have more in common with the dead than the living."

He nodded, his gaze never leaving hers. "Me too. I suppose when there's been a lot of death and dying in your past, it's that way. I never quite got past it. Never have talked to anyone about it except Wade, and sometimes I wish I'd kept it from him, as well. I don't need anyone feeling sorry for me."

"Exactly. I don't want that, either." She shivered, but not from the cold. "I just want to forget."

"Yes."

She didn't know what else to say. It seemed strange that she should find a kindred spirit here in the graveyard on the day of a good man's funeral. How odd that they would find themselves together, each sharing such an obviously painful past. "Do you think God really cares about each of us?"

Thane cocked his head to one side and then stroked his beard. "I know He's supposed to. Wade talks about God like that. I can't say that I've ever known that for myself. Seems if He cared so much, a whole lot of bad things wouldn't happen."

"My mother taught me that God loves everyone. I tried to hold on to that all my life. I figured if God was real and loved everybody, no one should have to worry about things like hell and heaven." She could see nothing but acceptance in his gaze. "Abrianna talks about hell and losing my soul. I can't say for certain that I understand or believe—especially that God loves everybody."

"What changed your mind?"

Militine paused but hoped he might understand. "The evil in this world."

"There's a lot of it."

It wasn't the reply she'd expected. It seemed funny that this normally passive young man should speak with authority on such a dark topic. She found herself looking deeper into his eyes. The pain that stared back at her was almost startling. "Yes." The word came out in a whisper.

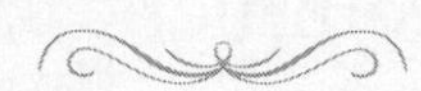

The day after the funeral Abrianna once again took charge of getting her mission accomplished. If only her friends could be as passionate about these things as she was. No matter. She would carry on as planned. They just needed the right push. "I know you'll see the potential," she told Wade and Thane. "It's perfect for what I want to do. Come on, boys, pick up your feet or this will take all day."

Wade offered a weak protest. "Grief, Abrianna, it's not like the building is going anywhere."

Nevertheless he did increase his speed. "I realize it's not going anywhere, but Mr.

Layton might. He promised he'd be there at ten o'clock, and it's nearly that now. Although why he picked ten and not noon, I cannot say. I suggested we meet there at the dinner hour so I wouldn't have to drag you two away from work. I do apologize for that."

"Do your aunts know you're down here?" Wade asked and Thane gave a muffled laugh.

She didn't like being so predictable, but there was nothing to do but be honest. "They don't, but I will tell them in time. You know how it is, Wade. Aunt Miriam believes there is danger on every corner."

"And so there is, especially where you're involved." His comment caused Thane to laugh out loud.

Abrianna fixed Wade with her fiercest glare, but that only seemed to make matters worse.

"I think the danger is on the part of anyone who messes with our Abrianna," Thane announced. "Just imagine it. Someone dares try to assault her, and she launches into a speech on why it's not only unacceptable on their part, but they are delaying her from important business elsewhere."

"No doubt," Wade agreed. "And then she'd offer them cookies."

"See if I offer *you* any cookies again." She turned to Thane. "Or you."

"Now, Abrianna, don't get your ribbons in a knot." Thane came to her left and took hold of her arm. "You know I'm not trying to be mean. We just worry about you."

"It's a full-time job." Wade took hold of her right arm and sandwiched her between them. "I swear I spend more time keeping up with you than I do my woodworking. I have three orders I'm behind on, and all because of these kinds of escapades."

She stopped in midstep. Contrition mingled with her guilt. "I am sorry for that. I had no idea. I can be so unthinking. You know that I never meant for that to happen. Aunt Miriam always tells me that a man's worth is tied up in his job. I hope I've not damaged your self-worth, Wade. You either, Thane. You are both very worthy men, and it grieves me to think I might have caused trouble for you in this manner.

"If your self-worth is in question, I would have suggested speaking to Pastor Klingle, but since he has passed on, that would obviously do no good. I suppose you can pray about it. I certainly will." She looked from one puzzled expression to the other. Neither man seemed to understand her words. "Am I not making sense?"

Wade laughed and tightened his hold on her arm. "You seldom do, but that hasn't stopped me from participating in your exploits. Just rest assured our self-worth is doing just fine."

"Oh good. Look, there's Mr. Layton. Come along." She pulled the men forward as she hurried to greet the older man. "Mr. Layton, thank you so much for agreeing to see me here."

"I had my misgivings," he said as he tipped his hat. "Are these your brothers?"

Abrianna laughed. "In a way. They both seem to pester me as a brother might a sister. Sometimes I feel they do so just to vex me into silence or inactivity, but I do not yield to such games."

"I'm sure you don't." Mr. Layton nodded his head toward Wade and Thane. "I'm James Layton. I suppose you know from Miss Cunningham that I own this building."

Wade and Thane nodded and followed the man's gaze. Abrianna could tell by their expressions they didn't think much of the dilapidated shack.

"It needs a great deal of work. You did say I could alter it. These gentlemen will assist me in that endeavor."

"You may do anything you like so long as it is an improvement."

Wade shook his head. "I think even knocking it down would be an improvement."

"Nonsense." Abrianna took a pencil and

pad of paper from her coat pocket. "I'm not afraid of a little work. Now, Mr. Layton, you named a price that I felt was a bit high. I propose to reduce that amount by ten percent. Also, because I will be putting a great deal of money into the repairs, I expect my first month's rent to be waived."

"I never agreed to that!" The man's face reddened. "I knew it was trouble dealing with a woman."

"You have no idea," Wade muttered under his breath.

"You may not have agreed to it yet," Abrianna said, reaching into her pocket once again, "however, I am prepared to improve your building above the cost of what one month's rent will total, and I will pay the second month in advance." She held up the cash. "Now, have we a deal or not?"

The man looked to Wade and then to Thane, as if for help. Abrianna waited patiently for him to fully weigh the proposal. The shack had been empty for months, and no one else seemed at all inclined to benefit this man with either repair or rent.

"I feel as if I have no choice in the matter. No say whatsoever," Mr. Layton declared.

Wade nodded. "It's better that way. If you don't give in, she'll just go into a long lecture on why she's right and you're wrong. It could go on for hours and hours. This way, if you agree, you'll be on your way and we can be on ours, and maybe all of us will manage to have a hot lunch. Otherwise, I fear we might be here until well into the afternoon."

The man shuddered, as if the very thought were too much to take in. Abrianna didn't care what argument Wade used, so long as the man was swayed to see things her way. It really seemed much too simple a matter to complicate for long.

Finally, with a mutter of unintelligible words, Mr. Layton nodded. "Very well. I shall accept your offer."

Abrianna handed him the money and then fished out two pieces of paper from her pocket. "Sign these. You'll see that I already have signed my name at the bottom."

"Excuse me?" The man took the paper and scanned it.

"It says that we have an agreement for the amount of rent and the repairs. It also states that I will lease this building from you for one year without any increase of rent."

Again the man looked to Wade, then shook his head. "I will sign it." He did just that and handed her back one of the pages and a key to the building.

Abrianna smiled. "I appreciate doing business with you, Mr. Layton." She held up the key. "Come along, gentlemen, and we will assess what is to be done."

Mr. Layton hurriedly dismissed himself, almost seeming afraid he might be forced to participate. Meanwhile, Wade leaned down and whispered in her ear, "Why would anyone put a lock on the place? A good wind could knock it down."

She paid him no attention. It was better not to give in to his theatrics. Goodness, but men seemed to make much ado about nothing.

She unlocked the door and pushed it open, very nearly pushing it off its hinges. "I shall put that first on my list." She glanced around the room, chiding herself for having forgotten the lantern. "I know it's dimly lit and has only one window, but we can remedy that. I propose we add an additional window."

"You propose that, do you?" Thane said, touching one of the exterior walls. "You want us to put a window in this paper-thin wall?"

"We can reinforce it," she said in complete exasperation. "Honestly, must I think of everything? I brought you two here to be helpful. Now do your jobs." Fearing her statement had come out too harsh, Abrianna turned to face them both and smiled sweetly. "Aunt Miriam and the girls are making Danish pastries today. The dough is light and flaky, and there are a variety of fillings. Cherry and berry and apple. Oh, and peach. I know how you like peach, Thane. The sooner we get this list of supplies figured out, the sooner you two can walk me back and just happen to get in on an early lunch. I figured you'd especially like that, Wade."

It was always easy to talk Wade into helping when food was involved. It was a wonder the man didn't weigh as much as old Mr. Phinster at the apothecary. It was rumored his girth made it impossible to climb the stairs to his abode, so he just set up a bed at the back of his shop.

Wade crossed his arms and sighed. "All right, Abrianna. What exactly do you have in mind?"

4

"You very late," Liang announced as Abrianna crept through the back door.

The small Chinese girl put her hands on her hips and shook her head. "Mrs. Madison, she not happy when I not find you."

"What in the world is so important that I was being summoned? Usually everyone is busy with classes at this time of day." Abrianna shed her coat and hung it on a peg by the door.

"Three new girls come," the fifteen-year-old explained. Liang had become a member of the household when the anti-Chinese riots a few years earlier had driven her family from Seattle and left her without kith or kin. "You know Mrs. Madison talk to everyone when new girls come."

"I know. I just didn't know they would

be here so early. Goodness, but I know Aunt Miriam's speech so well I could give it myself." She sighed. There was nothing to be done but go and face the music.

"You go now before she come again." Liang pushed Abrianna toward the door.

Making her way to the back drawing room where such lectures were given, Abrianna slipped into place behind Militine. The other girls pretended not to notice, but Abrianna could feel their gazes. More than this, however, she could feel Aunt Miriam's disapproving stare.

"As I mentioned earlier, our three new students hail from Kansas City," Aunt Miriam announced. "Elizabeth tells me that she can cook quite well and has done so for many years." The young woman in question stood and smiled. She was just a bit plump with a fair complexion and brown hair that she had neatly plaited and pinned atop her head. "Elizabeth, tell us a little about yourself."

The girl nodded and turned to face the other students. "Living in a big city, I had to do what I could to help my family. There were ten of us, so I went to work serving tables at one of the restaurants. Eventually I worked my way up to cooking. I really like to cook." She looked to the older woman.

"Thank you, Elizabeth. You may take your

seat." Aunt Miriam motioned to the next girl. "This is Josephine. Tell us something about yourself."

Josephine, a tall lanky soul with a homely face and mousy brown hair seemed mortified at the thought of public speaking. She stood looking at the floor for several seconds before murmuring, "I like to garden." She hurried to retake her seat.

"Thank you. Josephine also mentioned in our interview that she can sew quite well. Our final new student is Clara."

The young lady stood. She, too, was fairly tall, but where Josephine was plain and willowy, Clara was curvy and pretty. "I'm just so happy to be here. We three read about this school in the newspaper and decided we would apply together. We knew each other from Sunday school. Just imagine our excitement at all three of us being accepted." She paused and looked around the room.

"I play four musical instruments and have taught lessons to others, so I'm happy to teach if the need arises. I play piano, organ, flute, and guitar. I used to play for church. Oh, and I often led the choir."

Abrianna liked the girl's enthusiasm. She felt that Clara was most likely a kindred spirit who would be bold and generous with her talents. The other two seemed equally nice, although Josephine's painful shyness was something of an annoyance. Shy people were always twice as hard to get to know and seemed easily offended. Although because they were shy, they would seldom say anything on the latter. Instead, Abrianna knew them to usually withdraw into themselves, leaving her feeling responsible to draw them back out.

"Ladies, I want all of us to be welcoming and kind to our new students. As you know, I have a list of rules posted for all to see in the hall upstairs. You three should memorize the rules and adhere to them. There are very few second chances, as we are all adults and should be able to obey the rules given." Aunt Miriam looked to Abrianna as if to drive home her point.

Abrianna gave her a sweet smile. She would not allow Aunt Miriam to get the best of her. She loved her aunts but knew they would not understand the reason for her tardiness, nor would they approve of her plans. At least not until she had a chance to make them understand that Wade and Thane would be supervising the entire operation.

"The rules consist of several important issues that we will discuss here and now," Aunt Miriam continued. "I insist that so long as you are a student here, you will conduct yourself as honorable young ladies. You will attend church services every week unless you are ill or have an injury. You will dress and arrange your hair in a modest manner befitting your age and station. You will keep yourself properly groomed at all timcs. You will attend classes every day, and when and only when all three of your instructors agree that you are ready to receive callers, will you be allowed to attend the receptions and other social events as potential bridal applicants."

She paused for a moment as if to ensure everyone was listening. "There are strict rules about outings. You are not to leave the building unescorted. By that I mean that one of our approved gentlemen or one of the instructors will accompany you. There are no exceptions." Again she looked to Abrianna.

"There is an established curfew. None of you are to be out after six in the evening unless you have a prior approval from me. This is for your own safety. The city is full of smooth-talking men who seek innocent victims. Taking the responsibility for you here at the school means that I must provide for your safety. On Sunday I will introduce you to Wade Ackerman and his friend Thane Patton. Mr. Ackerman has long been a trustworthy help to this school and has escorted many of our young ladies. There are several others who come to our aid when needed, and you will be introduced to them by and by."

Abrianna counted the students in the room. They were back to having a full dozen. Last summer had seen the marriage of six young ladies, so their numbers had been halved until shortly before Christmas, when two women from southern states joined them. The last had been Tabitha, who came to them just after Christmas from New York. With Abrianna, her aunts, and Liang, the total came to seventeen women under the roof of the Madison Bridal School.

"Everyone here will help with all of the chores. We do not have servants," Aunt Miriam said, emphasizing the last word. "We do have Liang, a young Oriental girl who helps in the kitchen and elsewhere when needed, however, she answers to me, my sister, and Mrs. Gibson. No one else.

"Each of you will be responsible for your own laundry, mending, and personal needs. You will help each other dress and attend to your hair. Each girl will share a room, and both will be responsible to clean that room from top to bottom once a week while maintaining daily cleanliness."

That reminded Abrianna that she hadn't made her bed that morning, and while she had a room to herself, Aunt Miriam was just as insistent that she follow the rules. She hoped the new students had kept her aunts too busy to inspect her room and she'd have the chance to run upstairs and see to the matter when they concluded these introductions.

"You will also be given a schedule of chores that involve cleaning other areas of the house, as well as tending to the yard and gardens. We do have a man who cuts the grass in the summer months, but you will learn to plant the vegetable garden and keep the flowers and shrubs. It's important to know these things as a potential wife, for you never know what level you will marry into and exactly what your responsibilities will be. We have added additional duties this year, although those will not begin until spring. In March we will receive several animals. This will allow us to raise our own chickens for eggs and meat. We will also have two milk cows to tend."

Abrianna was actually excited about this prospect. She could see it benefiting her food house for the poor. Of course, her aunts might have other thoughts on the matter. She shifted uncomfortably, wishing she could slip out of the room. That would never be allowed, however. Aunt Miriam would make a scene and call her forward if she even dared. No, there was nothing to do but endure.

Goodness, why do these things always have to happen when I'm at my busiest?

"You should also know that we will conduct a variety of classes, including etiquette, elocution, music, and foreign languages. These are important for ladies of society to know. Some of you may never hold a dinner party or host a ball, but you will know how to if the need should arise." This caused many of the girls to giggle, but Aunt Miriam quickly put a stop to that.

"I will not brook silly girls in my school. We will be pleasant and enjoy our studies and each other's company, but there is no tolerance of nonsense." The clock sounded the hour of one, and Aunt Miriam gave a slight nod. "We will now conclude and conduct ourselves upstairs, where Miss Poisie Holmes, my sister, will instruct you in the art of ladylike comportment. You are dismissed."

Abrianna had participated in more comportment classes than she liked to remember. She had walked with more books balanced on her head than were shelved at the university's library. Of course, not all at once, but in such a succession of volumes that it was a wonder she had reached a sizable height at all.

Liang appeared as the other girls were making their way upstairs. She pushed through the crowd and made her way to where Aunt

Miriam and Aunt Selma were deep in discussion.

No doubt they are discussing my tardiness. Abrianna closed her eyes and uttered a quick prayer that they might overlook her actions just this once.

Liang reached the older women and spoke in a hushed tone. At once, Abrianna's aunts headed for the door, motioning her to come. Abrianna joined them none too quickly. Aunt Miriam frowned. "I will speak to you about your lateness after we address another matter. It would seem some of the elders are awaiting us in the receiving parlor. I want you to go there and make them comfortable while I freshen up." She turned to Aunt Selma. "Go get Poisie. Tell her to have one of the older girls read to the girls from the etiquette book until she can return."

Abrianna thought it marvelous that she was being included in the meeting. No doubt the men had come to discuss calling a new pastor. This was something quite important to consider.

"Good afternoon, gentlemen." She entered the room and smiled at the three men. "My aunts will join us shortly. In the meantime, please make yourselves comfortable." She took a chair near the window, knowing they would not sit until she did.

"Good afternoon, Miss Cunningham," Brother Mitchell said, nodding. "We are sorry to arrive unannounced, but the matter is of the utmost importance."

"Filling the pulpit?" She posed the question, hoping they would jump right into the details.

"Yes." Brother Mitchell said nothing more, but took a seat with the other men.

In a matter of minutes the three hostesses of the Madison Bridal School entered the room, one after the other. They crossed the room to greet the three elders as they rose.

"Brother Mitchell," Aunt Miriam said, extending her hand. "To what do we owe the pleasure of your visit?" She nodded toward Brother Adams and Brother Williams. "It is good to see all of you but most unexpected."

The two trios finished with their greetings and everyone took their seat before Brother Mitchell began. "It seemed imperative that we begin an immediate search for someone to fill the pulpit. We met with the elders, and it was determined that because you ladies have been some of the most faithful and generous supporters, we should seek your wisdom on this, as well."

Abrianna's aunts nodded, as if this were completely expected. She still wasn't sure why Aunt Miriam had decided to include her. Perhaps it was simply to keep her from escaping again. However, if given a chance, Abrianna intended to share her thoughts on the type of man they should bring to the church.

"Of course no one can replace Pastor Klingle," Brother Mitchell started.

"God rest his soul," Aunt Poisie said.

"Amen," Abrianna's aunts chimed in.

The gentlemen also added their murmured amens before Brother Mitchell spoke again. "However, a church without proper leadership is bound to lack accountability, which could lead to many issues that might well destroy our congregation. Already there has been talk of disbanding."

"Oh, that mustn't happen," Aunt Selma said, shaking her head in a most vehement manner. "I will not allow for that thinking at all. Mr. Gibson, God rest his soul—" she paused to look at Aunt Poisie as if in apology for overstepping her bounds—"always said that proper leadership cannot be underestimated. Of course he wasn't speaking in terms of the pulpit, poor man, but truth is truth."

"I believe that, as well." Aunt Miriam looked rather like a queen on her throne. She sat perched on the edge of a walnut side chair with an intricately carved back that betrayed a combination of Gothic and rococo designs.

The burgundy seat cushion only added to the richness, and all that was missing was a crown.

Abrianna smiled to herself at that image. Aunt Miriam would have made a perfectly elegant monarch. Perhaps if the girls performed a play dealing with Queen Elizabeth they could persuade Aunt Miriam to act the part. That reminded her. She and Militine still needed to figure out the staging of the play they were working on. But at this rate, it wouldn't even be ready for next month's reception.

"I have heard about some of these newer pastors," Aunt Selma said with an expression that suggested such men were out of line in their teachings. She lowered her voice to a hush. "Some of them are speaking of strange subjects indeed, and I, for one, will not allow that in my church." She straightened and looked to Poisie. "Isn't that right?"

"Oh yes." Poisie bobbed her head. "Some of them even excuse the theories of . . . Mr. Darwin."

Aunt Selma shuddered. "There is no place for scientific fairy tales within the walls of the church."

Brother Mitchell nodded with great enthusiasm. "We certainly agree with that, Sister Gibson."

Impatient to join the conversation, Abrianna

cleared her throat, but no one looked to her to offer her a chance to speak.

"We have drafted several letters to send out to a variety of respectable seminaries," Brother Mitchell said. He produced a list and handed it over to Aunt Miriam. "As you will see, all of the most notable schools have been included."

Aunt Selma moved closer to Aunt Miriam, prompting Poisie to do likewise. Together the three studied the list. "It looks most conclusive, Sister." Poisie leaned back. "However, I have my misgivings about younger men. I realize that the apostle Paul said we should not look down on anyone because of their youth, and truly I am not of a mind to condemn. Even so, we should seek a mature man, not someone just out of school."

"I agree," Aunt Selma quickly added. "I will not have an inexperienced man of youth in the pulpit. They are too easily swayed by life's troubles. Their lack of years often precludes them from having had a chance to build a strong faith."

"I quite agree," Aunt Miriam replied as she handed back the list. "I would also assert that he be a family man."

"I agree," Abrianna declared, unable to keep silent any longer. "Married men with families seem much more settled and reliable.

Goodness, if a man were to take on our church without a wife, he might well become discouraged and feel tempted to seek a mate for support. That would only serve to divide his mission."

Having pulled in everyone's attention, Abrianna continued. "It's good to have a knowledgeable and scholarly man, but Pastor Klingle was not one who boasted a lengthy education from seminary. Instead, he took it upon himself to study God's Word and live the example of Christ. I only say this because I don't believe we should fault a man for not having a seminary certificate."

"And if he works outside of the church," Aunt Selma added, "then it should be a position of respectability, such as a teacher or professor at the college."

"However, it should not be someone who dapples in the sciences." On this Aunt Poisie was adamant. "We cannot have his mind distracted by the nonsense found there." She grew thoughtful. "I suppose we could have a pastor who is also a fisherman." She looked to her sister. "It's not ever been done in our congregation, but even the Lord called fishermen."

Selma shook her head. "Oh, but Poisie, He called a tax collector, as well, and we cannot allow for that. I believe people would be too uncomfortable with a government man in the pulpit."

"I quite agree," Aunt Miriam said. "God alone knows exactly who He would have come to our congregation, but I would prefer the man's thinking be solely based upon the Word of God. I suggest we hold a prayer meeting and spend some time petitioning the Lord for direction."

"That is an excellent idea, Sister Madison." Brother Mitchell looked to his companions. "We could arrange that for Sunday evening."

"I believe that would be quite acceptable. We will be there." Aunt Miriam spoke for the group.

"I think we need to avoid a Democrat, as well," Abrianna threw out without thinking. "We shouldn't put politics in our churches, but somehow it always manages to slip in, and I fear a Democrat might send us in the wrong direction. I mean, look at what has happened just in the last few years."

The three men seemed taken aback by this sudden declaration. Abrianna wasn't in the least bit intimidated by their confusion. "Our congregation needs to safeguard itself against political blinding. During this last election there were many underhanded dealings, and some were promoted from the church pulpits. Not ours, of course, but there were churches where votes were bought and sold."

"Our president-elect, Harrison, was once a Presbyterian church leader," Aunt Selma threw out. "I believe he will guide us in a godly and reliable manner."

"I pray it might be so." Abrianna smiled at the men, who appeared to be stunned by this kind of talk coming from women. "However, he didn't win the popular vote, and we must remember that. There, but for the hand of God, we might have had another four years of President Cleveland and his taxes."

"Well, that said, we should be on our way." Brother Mitchell got to his feet and the other two followed suit.

"Will you not stay for refreshments?" Aunt Miriam asked as she rose.

"No. We must be going. We have another stop or two to make." He glanced at his companions. "We will keep in mind everything that you shared today."

Abrianna beamed the men a smile. "It is just as you should. Godly counsel is of the utmost importance when addressing such deep spiritual matters. We will look forward to the prayer meeting on Sunday."

The men grunted their acknowledgment while Aunt Miriam turned to Poisie. "Sister, please show the gentlemen out."

Aunt Poisie got to her feet and pressed her hands down the front of her woolen skirt. "Certainly."

She led the men from the room, and Abrianna decided that would be a good time for her to exit, as well. With Aunt Miriam's thoughts otherwise occupied by church matters, perhaps she would be less inclined to berate Abrianna for her disregard of the rules.

"And where do you think you're going?" Aunt Miriam's severe tone stopped Abrianna's escape.

Abrianna cringed. It wasn't to be. Aunt Miriam would have her moment, and there was nothing to do but take her punishment. Turning with a smile, Abrianna awaited her aunt's lecture. Pity the elders couldn't have stayed for refreshment.

5

"And I want to put a large work table along the back wall by the stove," Abrianna instructed.

For all intents and purposes, she sounded as though she were planning an affair for the governor rather than the friendless. But Militine knew better than to comment. Once her friend got a bee in her bonnet, she was hard-pressed to be convinced that anything else might need attention.

"Oh, and, Wade, I'll need you to vent the stove and get it working right away. I want to serve our first luncheon on Monday." The instructions continued from their fearless leader.

Militine worked hard not to laugh or offer

a salute as she pictured Abrianna in a captain's uniform with a ruler in hand.

Thane threw Militine a smile. It was almost as if he could read her mind, and while she found their growing friendship a comfort at times, Militine knew better than to believe it could last. Friendships were for people without pasts.

"Thane, I looked over the drawings you made for positioning the cabinets. I think they'll work perfectly. Can we get them up today?"

He straightened from where he'd been nailing together one of those very cabinets. "I'm not sure I can have all of them built today as well as get 'em nailed in place."

"Well, it's only Friday." She turned her attention to her list. "I figure if we work into the evening, we can have the entire place painted and the new floor laid tonight. Tomorrow we can finish building and painting the tables and benches. Militine and I have convinced Aunt Miriam to let us have six of the old tablecloths we used to use at the school, as well as two very nice gingham curtain sets."

"Honestly, Abrianna, we could hold off opening this place for another week. I do have work to do at the shop, as well." Wade's exasperation was clear in his tone.

Abrianna stopped and looked at him. "I

am sorry. I know I've been pressing each of you to give above and beyond all reason." She lowered her paper. "If you need to leave and tend your other duties, I'm certain Militine and I can figure this out."

Wade shook his head. "You know I won't leave you here alone. I suppose the sooner we complete your instructions, the sooner we can get back to our own responsibilities."

Abrianna reached out and took hold of his arm. "It is for the poor, Wade. They haven't anything, and another week might well see the death of many a soul. I know I haven't the right to ask this of you, but it's more important to me than anything. I've prayed and prayed about it. I know that the Lord has this ministry for me, and I would be a terrible steward if I were to ignore it for my own comfort."

Wade was no match for her. Militine had seen this time and again. He was like clay in her hands, molded and formed to Abrianna's will. Thane had seen it, too. They had even discussed it. Thane believed Wade to be in love with Abrianna, but Militine wasn't convinced. He definitely was devoted to seeing her stay out of trouble, but Militine couldn't say that it was love.

But what did she know of love? Her life had been void of that since the death of her mother.

Her father's bitterness and dependence on the bottle gave him no time for such insignificant matters, and there was no one else.

"You look troubled," Thane whispered against her ear.

Militine jumped back, her arms extended as if to ward off blows. Thane looked at her in confusion. Thankfully Abrianna had pulled Wade off to the far side of the room to show him yet another project.

"I'm sorry." Militine looked to the ground. How could she explain her actions without sharing the nightmares of her childhood?

"I'm the one who's sorry." He offered her a smile. "I didn't mean to startle you, and I know it's not proper to whisper."

"I shouldn't be daydreaming." She turned back to stir a can of white paint. "I guess I'm ready to get this up on the walls." She picked up one of the paintbrushes. "You're welcome to join me if you tire of building cabinets."

He chuckled. "Abrianna would skin me if I ignored her orders. I swear that gal could do wonders in organizing the city council. If she were in charge, few problems would go unresolved."

From somewhere outside bells began to clang in a metallic cacophony. Thane pulled off his apron. "Got to go, Abrianna. There's a fire. I'll be back as soon as I can." He dashed for the door before any of the remaining trio could respond.

Abrianna shook her head. "I suppose when the department calls, one must respond. Bother it all, anyway." She put her hands on her hips. "I suppose I should have hired more workers."

"Are we getting paid?" Wade asked from where he'd started working to cut a hole in the wall for the stove flue.

"Of course you're getting paid," Abrianna replied. "The worker is worth his due. I wouldn't call you here to work without seeing you compensated."

Militine's eyes widened as Abrianna pulled a wad of money from her skirt pocket. "This is for you and Thane to share." She plopped it on the makeshift worktable. "I have additional money for you, Militine. I left it back at the house."

"You should have left it all back at the house." Wade came to the table and shook his head. "Abrianna, do you mean to tell me you've had this on your person all this time? Don't you know how dangerous it is to walk around town with that kind of money?"

"Well, I don't have it on me any longer. Now it's your responsibility. Yours and Thane's. There's enough there to encourage you both to work all night and tomorrow. But if you like, I could probably get a couple of the old sailors to help."

Wade put out his hand to stop her. "We will manage without their help and without your pay. I'll hang on to this until I can talk to Thane, but I'm pretty sure he'll feel the same. You should use this money to buy food. For now, however, please promise me you won't walk around with this kind of cash on hand. You never know what danger lurks just outside the door."

Militine jumped nearly a foot when a man's voice rang out as Priam Welby entered the shack.

"My, my. What have we here?"

Militine moved further toward the back of the building. She'd never liked Priam Welby. There was something about the local businessman that served to remind her of the degenerates who regularly visited her father's trading post. Welby had purchased Mrs. Madison's downtown building and was responsible for the beautiful estate that now housed the school. Even so, the man disturbed her. He might be well dressed and groomed, but there was something almost vulgar about the man.

"I had heard there was a pretty little redhead leading the rebuilding of this shack, and I could only imagine one woman." He doffed his hat. "I see I was right."

"We are opening a food house for the poor," Abrianna said, crossing the room. "Perhaps you would like to contribute to the financial needs. We have food to buy, as well as additional plates and mugs. We also need dish towels and soap."

He laughed, and to Militine's surprise reached into his coat pocket and pulled out his wallet. "Of course I'll contribute. I'm known for my generosity around the city." He handed Abrianna two dollars.

She took the money. "I'd heard you were far more generous than this."

Welby met her gaze, and his leering smile made Militine shudder. She wanted to warn Abrianna to take nothing from the man. He looked like a wolf about to consume his victim. Abrianna, however, didn't seem to notice. She waited instead without blinking until Welby peeled off several larger bills and pressed them into her hand. He allowed his hand to linger on hers as he spoke.

"You are a determined and intelligent young woman, Miss Cunningham. I suppose that's why I've always found myself drawn to you. When I'm near you, I seem to find myself weak in the knees and light-headed. Reason quite escapes me."

Abrianna pulled her hand away from his and stuffed the money into her pocket.

"Perhaps it's the grippe," she said, turning away. "Aunt Miriam said there's a lot of it going around."

Wade smiled but said nothing. Militine, however, continued to stare unabashed. She worried for Abrianna. The girl seemed to have no sense or understanding where men were concerned. There was something evil about Mr. Welby. A cold and calculating evil that she'd seen only once before . . . in her father.

Saturday night Thane took a seat beside one of his fellow volunteers. The man he knew only as Gabs offered Thane a nod before turning his attention back to the front of the room. Thane was exhausted from Abrianna's round-the-clock endeavors to put the food house in order before the Sabbath but knew his attention here was expected. He only hoped he wouldn't doze off.

Fire Chief Josiah Collins took to the podium and brought the meeting to order. "We have a great deal to address during our meeting, so if everyone would take a seat, we can proceed." The men who'd been conversing at the back of the room found their places, and the room quieted.

"As you know, when I came into this position last May, fire stations around the town were sorely under-equipped. The city council was good to listen to my recommendation for new horses and hydrants, as well as a new hose carriage for the Belltown area and additional hose for several of our carriages elsewhere.

"I also petitioned them for a new fire alarm system, and while some of the money has been approved, we have not yet managed to obtain what is needed. That is one of our biggest needs, and we will address this in detail in a few minutes." He took a drink of water and cleared his throat before continuing.

"For now I wish to address morale in the ranks. You will remember we were put to the test last May and failed when fire completely destroyed the home of Edward Reynolds at Fifth and Bell. The newspaper claimed we lacked organization. There were also trouble-makers among our own people who suggested our volunteers were uninterested in attending to their duties due to a lack of paid positions. I do not believe you men are so petty that you would see families put out on the street because money had not exchanged hands on your behalf.

"Instead, I believe our problems lie with other issues. Perhaps organization can be made better. However, until our water mains are improved, we will continue to suffer. It is absolute nonsense to talk about fire protection until we have water available all over the city."

Murmurs of approval rose from the volunteer firemen in the audience, as well as others who had joined to keep apprised of the city's plans. A newspaper reporter from the *Post-Intelligencer* stood to one side of the audience quietly taking notes. Perhaps he'd been the one who'd written the harsh article about the fire department the previous summer.

Fire Chief Collins continued. "The present resources of the Spring Hill Water Company are overtaxed for all the areas requiring its water. I believe the remedy is for the city to own and control its own water supply and construct a system of new water mains and hydrants with fire protection in mind."

The audience erupted in applause, but the fire chief waved his hands to quiet them once again. "Our volunteer numbers have fallen dramatically, due to the negative articles written by the press. I am hopeful that this demoralization will cease. Otherwise I fear for our city. We are reliant upon our volunteer firemen to pull our fire engines, since we have only six horses in our possession. We rely upon them to answer every fire call, which is quite tiresome, given there is no way of knowing for sure where the fire is or whether other stations have already responded to the alarm. If we could pay the volunteers what they were worth, there would not be enough gold in all of the continent."

Again applause broke out, but this time Collins didn't attempt to stop it. He smiled and nodded his approval. When the audience once again settled down, he addressed the matter of the fire alarm system.

"Our system is barely a system at all. The bells from the various fire stations are indistinguishable from one another. The steam whistles that most generally join in offer no indication of location or intensity. None of the alarms currently used can offer the fireman any idea of whether it's his station's responsibility or another's. Men come running at breakneck speed and gather their equipment to face what they hope and pray will not be a major conflagration. Often this is to the detriment of all involved, as various engines converge on one area for perhaps nothing more than a trash fire that got out of control, while across town a house burns to the ground for lack of an available crew.

"A new notification system would eliminate this problem. A fire alarm telegraph is available, which would allow for each stationhouse to know the location of the fire and its intensity. There are all manner of helps out there to assist us in our endeavors, and I assure you that I am pressing the city council to see that these things are accessible." He paused to fix his gaze on the young man from the *Post-Intelligencer.* "I hope our reporter from the newspaper will note this meeting accurately and without prejudice."

Thane looked to the young man, who now stopped taking notes and raised his head. He appeared embarrassed by what seemed to be the suggestion he would do anything else.

"I hope they end this soon," Gabs whispered. "I promised the missus I'd be home by seven-thirty."

Thane nodded and silently wished there might have been someone waiting at home for him. The loneliness that had followed him for over fourteen years left a burning hole in his heart. He thought of the life he'd known back in Missouri. His youth had been fraught with episodes of violence, given his father's short-fused temper. Usually it was other men who riled Samuel Patton, and generally it was over insignificant things like drink or cards. Too often, young Thane had witnessed the bloody altercations that more than once had ended in death. Death that came at the hands of his father.

Thane never breathed a word of this to anyone with the exception of Wade. Wade was a godly man who always seemed to accept Thane, in spite of his flaws. He was faithful to share a prayer or word of wisdom from the Good Book, but when Thane wearied of discussing the matter, Wade was also good to let it drop.

When the meeting concluded and the men separated to go their own ways, Thane tried not to think about the places they would go—the people who would be there for them. He had often imagined how comforting it might be to have a home with a hot meal waiting and children squealing in delight at his return.

But I could end up being just as bad a father as mine was to me.

Perhaps that was the reason that when these longings came upon him, he forced them into mental boxes and buried them deep in the graveyard of forgotten dreams. Memories were dangerous. He didn't need the Bible to tell him that, although Wade had read him more than one Scripture that mentioned not dwelling on the past.

With the room nearly empty, Thane finally got to his feet and headed for the door. Outside, a cold blast of wind hit him and staggered him back a step. He thought of his tiny apartment and tried to maintain a positive outlook. At least he had a place to stay—a warm bed—and a stove in which to build a fire. And best of all, no one in Seattle knew he was the son of a murderer.

6

If everyone will make an orderly line, we can begin serving." Abrianna looked at the growing group of raggedy men and silently prayed there would be enough food for everyone. On Sunday she'd put many of the street urchins to work spreading the word that there would be a free lunch served precisely at noon on Monday. Apparently they'd done a good job.

Militine stood behind a long table where Wade and Thane were just now depositing a large kettle of soup. This was the last thing to be done, as Abrianna had already seen to putting out bread. She glanced over her shoulder to make certain that all was ready and then turned back to the hungry men just as one of the harbor whistles blew the noon hour.

"All right, gentlemen, remember what I said. There is one piece of bread and one bowl of soup for each man. There is also coffee. Mr. Patton will be handling that at the far table. Please be careful with the cups and bowls. We must make them last for a good while. You will find spoons and napkins at each chair. Please use these. I know many of you are given to drinking from the bowl, but this is a civilized eating facility, and we will comport ourselves as such. Agreed?"

She knew they would agree to most anything if it meant being fed. "And before our meal, Mr. Ackerman will offer a prayer." She looked back to Wade and waited until he came forward.

Those who had caps on their heads pulled them off in quick fashion as Wade bowed his head. "Father, we thank you for this day and for the provision you have given. We ask a blessing on each man here. May the food they receive nourish their bodies and the company encourage their souls. Amen."

With the line neatly formed, Abrianna ushered them into the building. She took her place behind the soup table and helped Militine ladle soup. The men, most of whom she knew, were old sailors and loggers who'd lost their jobs because of injury or age. They shuffled along in an orderly manner, tipping their caps to Abrianna and Militine as they passed by.

"Yar an angel from heaven, Miss Abrianna."

"Now get on with you, Jeb, you know that people aren't angels. I'm just a Christian woman extending the love of God to those in need."

"Well, yar one of the only Christians, male or female, what cares about us old salts."

What he said was true. It seemed there was a sad lacking of offering even the basic comforts to those who had so little.

"She's a saint," Captain Jack said, coming to take his bowl of soup. "A perfect saint."

She couldn't help but smile at this. If only they knew the trial she was to Aunt Miriam and the others. Her aunts would never consider her to be anything but vexing. *Saint* wasn't a word Aunt Miriam would ever choose to describe her ward. More likely her aunts would call her *Trouble*.

Convincing her aunts to allow her duties at the food house hadn't come easily. Only when Wade assured them that he would watch over her did they acquiesce and allow Abrianna and Militine to spend each day from midmorning until two o'clock to manage the affairs of helping the hungry. Even so, it did not come without fussing and fretting, and there would no doubt be more to come.

Seeing the men settled at the linen-covered tables, Abrianna smiled. Tablecloths and napkins always helped to make a meal seem special. She wanted these men to know at least one place and one meal where they were treated like human beings rather than the scum of the earth.

"Hi, Abrianna," several young boys greeted as they approached the serving table.

She smiled at them. "I hoped you would make it on time."

Their self-appointed leader gave her a toothy grin. "Wouldn't miss a hot meal. What's on the menu?"

Abrianna handed him a bowl of soup. "It's beef and vegetable soup, Toby. You each get one bowl and one piece of bread. I expect good manners."

He turned to his companions. "You hear that? Miss Abrianna says we gotta act right. Now get your bread and soup and follow me."

"There gonna be food tomorrow, too?" another orphan asked.

"Every day but Sunday, if the Lord wills it."

"How come not on Sunday? Folks get hungry then, too," the boy replied.

"I quite agree, and it seems to me that folks should be particularly generous on Sunday, given that it's the Lord's Day." Abrianna handed the boy a bowl of soup. "However, the

Bible speaks of it being a day of rest, and there are those who expect me to dedicate it to the Lord. Although, God knows I dedicate this work and every day to Him.

"It seems to me that people sometimes use the Sabbath as an excuse to just lie about and sip tea. I don't think the Lord had that in mind when He told us to keep the Sabbath holy, but who am I to say?" She shrugged her shoulders. "All I know is that folks are hungry on Sunday as well as Monday."

"Come on, you lot," Toby declared. "Don't be holdin' up the line. There's gonna be other hungry folks comin'." He looked at Abrianna and smiled. "Thanks again, Miss Abrianna. You aren't like some of those Christian folks who just talk about helping the poor."

A few more men entered the building and made their way to the table. They seemed stunned that the news of a free meal was true but wasted no time in accepting the gift and heading to the few empty chairs left. Wade and Thane stood to one side eating, while Abrianna and Militine circulated around the room to see that everyone had what they needed.

"You make this soup, Miss Abrianna?" one of the men asked.

"I did. Of course I had help." She leaned in to whisper. "I'm not all that good at cooking, but I figure this will give me a chance to practice. Hopefully you men won't mind making this journey with me. If it tastes horrible, I'll expect you to tell me."

"Seems perfect to me, miss. I ain't had anything so good in a long while." This came from a scruffy-looking man Abrianna hadn't yet met. "Last hot food I had was some watered-down oatmeal."

"Well, I'm glad you are enjoying it. I'm just happy to offer it. You know, there are some very kind people in the city who were worried about you the same as I was. They gave me money to set this place up, so when you say your prayers tonight, you might want to thank God for their generosity."

"To be sure," he replied, and some of the others looked up from their bowls just long enough to nod.

Within an hour everyone was fed, and Abrianna knew she would have to ask them to leave the warmth of the building so that she and the others could clean and close up for the day. If she didn't return home at the appointed time, Aunt Miriam might well put an end to her venture.

"Now, please take your bowls and spoons to the table up front for washing. Just leave the napkins on the tables. We'll gather those after a while." She wished she could allow them to stay, but time was already getting away from her. "I'm sorry to say that I will need everyone to leave for now, but be assured we will return tomorrow. Lunch will be served at noon, just as it was today. If you know others who are hungry, please let them know about this place."

She wasn't sure how the men would respond to being kicked out, but to her relief they all began to get up and do as she had asked. Making her way back behind the table, she and Wade received the bowls and silverware. Thane and Militine had readied the washtubs and already managed to clean the soup kettle and serving ladles. For their first day, Abrianna found the entire arrangement to be more than satisfactory.

"I hope it goes this well every day," she told Wade.

"With you in charge, it wouldn't dare go otherwise."

She laughed. "You do sometimes say the silliest things, Wade Ackerman. I cannot control how the day might play out. That is solely in the hands of the Almighty."

"Maybe so," Wade said with a grin, "but sometimes I wonder if He doesn't consult you first."

"Wade Ackerman! That's a blasphemous thing to say. I know you cannot possibly mean it, but it grieves me that you would even offer it in jest." By now the building was empty, with the exception of her friends. "And here I thought the day would go by without you causing me difficulty."

He laughed. "I'm not being difficult, just honest. I know He doesn't get your approval on things, but I also know He has to make provision for you on a regular basis because you're headstrong and determined to do whatever comes into that pretty little head of yours—good or bad."

"You are . . ." She paused, trying to think of something to call him. Words didn't usually escape her, but this time she found herself tongue-tied. She'd never really meant to give the impression that she was headstrong or unwilling to receive counsel. With a sigh she gave Wade a nod. "You are probably right. I'm sure God does make additional provision for me."

She left his side to gather the napkins and check the condition of the tablecloths. Those that were clean enough she left in place, and gathered the others for laundering.

Wade followed her to the table. "I didn't mean to hurt your feelings."

"You didn't. As I said, you are most likely right. People who answer God's call on their life often find that the world does not understand it. Especially when a woman is involved.

Hence, I believe God does make additional provision, not only to protect me from the harm of those less-than-honorable folk, but also from those good Christians who judge me to be crazy."

"I never said you were crazy, Abrianna. Just a little headstrong in a way that often puts you in danger. Your stubbornness might cost you your life, even if you are acting in the name of God. I just don't want you to be foolish."

She picked up a napkin, then looked him in the eye. "I read the other day from *The Miscellaneous Works of the Rev. Matthew Henry* about his father, Philip Henry. He told of his father's loving generosity and kindness. Reverend Henry said that his father was known to speak this bit of wisdom: 'He is no fool who parts with that which he cannot keep, when he is sure to be recompensed with that which he cannot lose.' Wade, even if I lose my life in serving God, I will be at peace and hope you will be, as well.

"I know that I'm often foolish in my choices. I act more quickly than others and often don't think through my actions. But my heart is fixed on doing what I believe God wants me to do. If that costs me everything, then it is a price I am willing to pay to obey Him."

He looked at her as if finally understanding her heart. "You amaze me sometimes. I'm sorry if I've acted as a stumbling block."

She smiled. "You are a good man who cares about your friends. I cannot fault you for that."

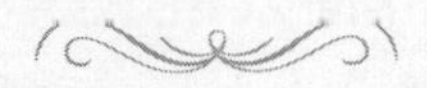

The first Saturday of February the ladies of the Madison Bridal School held their monthly reception. After a successful but tiring week of feeding the poor, Militine dreaded having to dress up and pretend to be interested in hosting would-be suitors.

"Honestly, Abrianna, I appreciate your help, but I detest having to play dress-up for a party I'd rather not attend." She looked at the gown Abrianna had forced her into. "I feel like a cow in lace."

Abrianna laughed and tied the sash. "How would you know what a cow in lace feels?"

"Well, if a cow were forced to don an elegant gown, she would no doubt feel just as out of place. She would also no doubt resent being forced to perform like a trained . . . trained . . ."

"Cow?" Abrianna asked, moving to inspect her work. "You look perfect, so stop fretting. Honestly, Militine, you are quite lovely. And while I know you do not seek a husband any more than I do, you might as well enjoy Lenore's cast-off gowns. Goodness knows, I can't wear them all. Now come along, or we'll be late, and that will only bring Aunt Miriam's rebuke."

The monthly receptions were always a trial for Militine. The men would come and pay a fee to Mrs. Madison and then spend the afternoon listening to recitations, songs, and piano music, all while eyeing the ladies with a point of getting to know them better. It was all very respectable and well chaperoned, but Militine didn't want anyone to know her better.

Several young ladies performed prior to Militine, but it didn't relieve her stress any better when Mrs. Gibson announced her.

"And now Miss Militine Scott will recite 'The Lamplighter' by Robert Louis Stevenson."

Militine fought down the bile that threatened to rise. At least she didn't have to worry about that silly play Abrianna had wanted to perform. She had finally given up on the entire idea, with her new focus on the soup kitchen.

She smoothed the lavender skirt of the gown and then drew her hands together. Often, like today, the poem she quoted left her feeling strangely displaced. She had no idea why, but it seemed very sad to her. She couldn't help but wonder who the people were of whom the poet spoke. She wondered if the child from whose view the story came was sickly, because of the reference to one day being stronger. All in all, she felt herself strangely connected to that child.

"'The Lamplighter,'" she said, as if to remind them all of what had just been announced. Her heart pounded furiously as she began.

"My tea is nearly ready and the sun
has left the sky.
It's time to take the window to see
Leerie going by;
For every night at teatime and before
you take your seat,
With lantern and with ladder he
comes posting up the street.

"Now Tom would be a driver and
Maria go to sea,
And my papa's a banker and as rich
as he can be;
But I, when I am stronger and can
choose what I'm to do,
O Leerie, I'll go round at night and
light the lamps with you!

"For we are very lucky, with a lamp
before the door,
And Leerie stops to light it as he
lights so many more;
And oh! before you hurry by with
ladder and with light;
O Leerie, see a little child and nod to
him to-night!"

The audience applauded, and Militine made a little curtsy before hurrying to the back of the room. She breathed in slowly to steady her nerves and closed her eyes as Clara, one of the new girls, was announced. Militine made a quick glance around the room then slipped into the hallway, nearly running over Thane.

"Whoa," he whispered, reaching out to steady her.

She shrank back from his hold. She hated herself for cowering, but years of abuse had made it reflexive. "Sorry. I was determined to get to the kitchen." Before she could leave, however, Miss Poisie stopped her.

"Sister says we are in need of more refreshments. Would you ask Liang to bring the trays?"

"Yes, ma'am." Militine swallowed hard. Beyond Miss Poisie's fragile frame, Thane continued to watch her. His expression warned her that most likely questions would follow, but she ignored her fears and hurried to the kitchen.

"Liang?" Militine glanced around the kitchen.

"I here, in the pantry. Mr. Wade, he help me get the flour." She popped out with a smile. "You need something?"

"Mrs. Madison wants more refreshments brought to the hall."

Wade stepped out from the pantry, his arms wrapped around a fifty-pound bag of flour. He carried it to a large crock and deposited it inside. “Seems like someone always has something for me to do,” he said as he straightened. “I missed your poem.”

“That’s quite all right. I wish I had.” Militine crossed the room to get a glass of water.

“It was a great poem,” Thane declared, startling her. “She didn’t forget a single word. At least I’m guessing she didn’t. I was a little confused. Who’s Leerie?”

She put down the glass. “I have no idea. Who are Tom and Maria? Goodness, when people write poetry they don’t concern themselves with explanations, and I give it no further thought.” It was a lie, but she hoped it might close the subject.

Wade laughed. “Leerie is the lamplighter. Abrianna told me all about that poem. I guess she helped you memorize it.”

“She did.” Militine wanted to forget about the recitation and the awaiting time of visitation with the men.

“Mr. Wade, you help me?” Liang asked, hoisting a big tray.

“Of course I will.” Wade strolled across the kitchen as if he had nothing else in the world to do. “I will, however, take a few of these lovely little cakes for my pay.”

Liang giggled. "I save you plenty."

They disappeared from the room, leaving Militine to face Thane on her own. His expression sobered. "What happened back there?"

"What do you mean?" She knew very well what he meant. She had cowered away from him on more than one occasion. He no doubt thought her behavior warranted an explanation.

"You act like a whipped pup every time I reach out to you." He came closer but stopped when he was still a good two feet away. "Did I do something wrong?"

Heaving a sigh, Militine tried to reason what she would say. She didn't want to share the past with him. She feared speaking the words would somehow conjure it to life. "You did nothing wrong. I had . . . I had a very stern father. When I was clumsy . . . well . . . he wasn't very tolerant."

Thane nodded. "My pa used to beat me for spilling my milk. I think I understand." He smiled. "But I'd like us to be friends."

She saw something in his eyes that went through to her heart. Here was a fellow journeyman, someone who understood the pain that could be inflicted upon a child. The tenderness he offered her was almost her undoing. None of the men in her life had ever been kind. "I need to get back, I suppose. It sounds as though Clara has finished her piece. She was the last to perform."

"Just think about what I said," Thane replied.

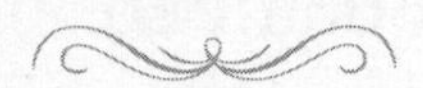

That night the horrors of the past came to life for Militine. Her dream started out simple enough. There was a peaceful stream by which she lingered. The air held the scent of mountain ash, and the sky was a brilliant blue. For a wonderful moment in time she felt safe and happy. But as was always the case, the scene changed and the skies grew dark with heavy storm clouds. She rushed to find shelter before the rain came, running until the ache in her legs and the stitch in her side nearly caused her to cry out. But that pain was minimal compared to what awaited.

She found no solace as the trading post came into sight. She knew there was no safety, no refuge to be found in that place. As quiet as a mouse, Militine worked the latch and tried to enter unseen.

It was not to be.

The belt came down on her back over and over. Her father's enraged bellowing filled her ears even as thunder rumbled outside.

"You ran off again, and you knew I expected you to be here. You're no better at obeying than your mother was." White hot pain ripped her back as he continued his attack.

"No!" she shouted over and over. "No! No! No!"

She felt someone take hold of her arms. Then shaking. The voice of her father faded as another took its place.

"Militine. Militine, wake up."

She opened her eyes to find her roommate, Virginia, patting her face. "Wake up. You've had another nightmare."

A knock sounded on the door, and Abrianna peeked inside. "Are you all right, Militine? I heard your screams."

Militine sat up. The nightmare was too fresh to find any comfort in the present. "I'm sorry. I suppose I've awakened the entire house."

Abrianna crossed the room. Sitting beside her on the bed, she picked up Militine's hand and squeezed it. "It doesn't matter. We all have our bad dreams from time to time. I'm sure the others will go back to sleep. Besides, I'm not sure anyone heard you besides us. My room is right next door, and the bath is on the other side of your room, so I'm sure it acted as a barrier."

"I appreciate your saying so, but we both know I've disturbed the others before." She closed her eyes, wishing she could escape the memories. Why couldn't a person simply erase the past from their mind?

"I'll stay with you as long as you'd like," Abrianna said. "I can even read to you if it doesn't bother Virginia." She looked to the other young lady, who had already crawled back into bed.

"It won't bother me. Maybe it will settle my nerves, as well."

Abrianna smiled. "Then that is what I shall do." She pulled a Bible from her robe pocket. "I thought this might help."

At that point Militine didn't care what was read or said. Anything that would help to bury her nightmare was worth enduring.

7

Priam Welby looked over the new shipment of imports and nodded in approval. "These will do nicely. I have a collector in Kansas City who will take them."

One statue in particular captivated his attention. It was crafted during the Jin Dynasty nearly seven hundred years earlier. Made of heavily painted wood, the statue was titled *Guanshiyin*. Supposedly she was some sea goddess, but otherwise he knew very little about the piece. Nevertheless, he liked what he saw.

"I think I'll keep this piece for my own collection." He motioned to his man. "Take this to the Madison Building with the other cargo. Put this in my office."

"Sure thing, Mr. Welby." Carl Neely picked up the piece as he might a sack of potatoes.

"Be careful with that," Priam chided. "It's ancient and priceless."

The man looked at the piece for a moment, then nodded. "You want me to check on the girls?" He gave Priam a leering smile. "There are a couple in there that speak a little broken English. Not much, but—"

"Never mind that. Leave the girls alone. You know full well I can't get my price for them if you go damaging them."

"Didn't wanna damage them." He turned to go. "Just wanted a little sport."

"Well, find it elsewhere. Those girls are not to be touched."

Welby knew Carl would do as he was told. It was the reason he'd hired the man in the first place. He was willing to work hard and do all manner of illegal tasks, and he could keep his mouth shut. The latter made him most valuable of all.

Looking at his inventory list, Priam felt confident he'd have little trouble selling the lot. Times were good and the rich were willing to pay for any number of foreign oddities. Despite the negative attitude—especially in the western states—toward the Chinese, their artifacts continued to be of great interest to museums and private collectors. That, coupled with the strong number of opium clients on his files and those seeking exotic young women, would soon leave Welby with a small fortune. Not too shoddy for a man who came from nothing.

He tucked the list into his coat pocket and pulled out a cigar. He was nearing his fortieth birthday, and the future was looking better and better. Of course there were those who still opposed him—those who recognized him for what he was. Mostly because they, too, were of that same cut of cloth. With enough money, however, Priam found that he could win almost anyone over to his side. He'd even managed to get the Madison Building away from that teched old lady, Miriam Madison.

She and her cronies were a bunch of loons, as far as he was concerned. Running a school for would-be brides seemed ridiculous in this day and age. Some marriages were still arranged for the benefit of business and family connections. Some were relationships made out of loneliness, but none, as far as he was concerned, needed the help of three ancient women.

Still, it had benefited him to make their acquaintance. The Madison Building was located in perfect proximity to the docks and his warehouse. It provided him with an office from which he could do his business and a wonderful basement hold where he could keep his human cargo. And all it had cost him was a mansion in Lower Queen Anne that he had won in a high stake game of cards. Of course, in order to spare the councilman he'd won it off of from public shame, Priam had announced that it was being purchased. But the lie served him as well as it served the owner. The councilman would save face and keep his gambling problem quiet, and Welby would have yet another asset with which he could barter.

The only thing he hadn't gotten out of the arrangement had been Abrianna Cunningham.

She hadn't been something he'd really wanted in the beginning. She was feisty and obnoxiously honest about her feelings. But over the course of dealing with the old ladies and considering how he might finagle the building away from them, the idea of marrying their ward had presented itself as a possibility. At first it was just a lark. He had no real interest in marriage. But upon getting to know Abrianna Cunningham better, Priam found her to be a most curious challenge.

She didn't like him, and that was something Priam wasn't used to—at least not with the fairer sex. Women had found him appealing ever since he'd been young, at least prior to his father's disinheriting him for unacceptable behavior. Had it not been for his mother, Priam would have left Philadelphia with nothing. Thankfully, she had slipped him several expensive pieces of jewelry, telling him these would allow him to start fresh. She'd died only a year later, a sorrow that followed Priam even now.

During his youth, his mother had seen that he was introduced to all of her wealthy friends. Especially those with daughters. Priam had been quite the catch. Son of a wealthy and highly respected Philadelphia investor, Priam was being groomed to one day take over the family fortune and businesses. But his life didn't work out that way. When his father discovered his penchant for cheating people at cards and on college exams, the comforts were quickly and without ceremony stripped away. Disgraced by his son's actions, Vernon Welby cut his son off without a second thought, and despite his mother's pleadings, Priam was put from the house with no thought of forgiveness.

"Vindictive old man. One day you'll pay for everything, and I'll see you ruined."

Welby smiled. That was what made all of his successes that much sweeter. One day he would be in a position of such power and wealth that he would crush his father's empire and leave him in ruins, just as he'd done to Priam nearly twenty years earlier.

"You just wait, Father. The gears are already turning, and little by little I'm tearing down your kingdom. By the time you even realize what has happened, you'll have nothing."

"I'm so encouraged by the help we're getting from local merchants," Abrianna said as she continued to study the ledger before her. They were seated at one of the tables where they would soon be serving lunch. "The grocers have donated some food, as did three bakeries. Several of the mercantiles and grocers donated sacks of flour, sugar, and salt, and one even gave us a bolt of cloth from which we can make additional tablecloths. And others have promised support to come."

"Sounds like Seattle approves of your helping the poor and needy." Wade handed her a receipt. "This is for the chickens you had me get."

She took the paper. "Good. I like to keep everything in the ledger so I can show Lenore and Kolbein. Speaking of them, they plan to stop by today and see how we've set up everything. I told them to join us before lunch and perhaps stay to see how we operate.

"I'm sure there are other places that handle things differently. I'm not one to be saying our way is perfect, but I think it's gone rather well. We've had enough food each day without anything left, so there's no waste. Each day last week we fed a few more than the day before, but I'm sure the numbers will remain right around the fifty or so we've had." She frowned. "But if we get a great many more, this place will not house them all. That is a big concern, and I'm not at all certain how we would handle it."

"We could have them eat in shifts. One group at eleven and another at noon. You're here by ten in the morning cooking and usually have at least part of the food ready."

"Wade Ackerman, you are a profound genius." She jumped up from the table and gave him a quick kiss on the cheek. "God surely gave you extra provision when it came to brains and patience."

His face reddened slightly, but he laughed nevertheless. "Why do you say patience?"

"So you know that you're a brilliant man," she teased. "Your intelligence is obvious for everyone. I say patience because you constantly endure me."

"I don't really endure you, Abrianna." He sobered and fixed her with a piercing gaze. "I care about you. I hope you know that by now."

"Of course, silly, and I care about you. No man is dearer to me. If not for you, I might have given up on the entire male gender. Well, Pastor Klingle was a wonderful man."

"God rest his soul," Wade murmured.

Abrianna giggled. "Amen. And I suppose I must admit that Kolbein and Thane are of a decent nature, but I honestly don't know about the rest."

"What about your old sea dogs?"

Abrianna considered that for a moment. "While many are gentle and kind, I do not trust in their nature. Most are heavy drinkers and smokers. They swear regularly and tell bawdy stories—even to me—which necessitated making new rules for our establishment here. None of that is to be allowed. And they aren't given to proper bathing and often smell worse than the fish market.

"I suppose that the latter issues might have more to do with their poor housing situation, but honestly, a good bath would go a long way to help most of them. Aunt Miriam says that bathing is healthy for one's soul as well as one's body. She says there are those who believe bathing to be necessary only once or twice a year, and some doctors actually state that bathing too often is unnatural and unhealthy. Did you know that?"

She didn't wait for his answer. "I can't see the harm in it myself. Nothing gives me greater pleasure that to soak in a tub of hot water." She shook her head. "No. I'm given to exaggeration, and here I promised you I would try to be reformed in all my ways. There are a great many things that give me more pleasure, but that is definitely right up at the top."

Wade surprised her by taking hold of her hand. "Abrianna, you make me sound like a vigorous taskmaster. I don't believe all your ways need to be reformed. You are a woman of deep consideration. Your love of mankind shames me. In fact, what you told me the other day really got me thinking."

"Something I said?"

"Don't act so surprised. You actually do speak with great wisdom at times. When you talked about being willing to give of yourself—to lose everything in order to gain something greater—well, it really spoke to my heart. It made me realize there is so much more I should be doing for the Lord. So I thought I'd ask you if you would mind if I held a Bible study for the men here at night. Maybe one night a week."

Abrianna had never been prouder of him. Wade had always been a strong man of faith, and to see him willing to share his love of God with those friendless folk who even the churches often turned away in disgust touched her deeply.

"You are a wonderful man. Of course you may use this place for such a worthy commitment. In fact, I don't know why it didn't dawn on me to ask it of you. I think, however, it's all the more precious that you came up with it on your own."

The look in his eyes suggested his delight in her praise. Abrianna thought he'd never looked so handsome, with his brown hair tousled and his sleeves rolled up to accommodate his work. One day he would make some woman a wonderful husband. His spirit was gentle and his heart tender. He didn't fear making a fool of himself, and he walked with God. All in all, he was a remarkable man.

"Why, one day you might even become a preacher or a missionary to a foreign land."

"Whoa," he said, holding up his arms as if in surrender. "Let's see how the Bible study goes first."

"Hello, you two," Lenore called as she opened the door while knocking on it. Kolbein escorted her into the dressed-up shack, and they paused to take it all in.

"I love what you've accomplished here," Lenore said. "After the description you gave, I feared it would never be accommodating."

"It longed only for loving care, which we provided." Abrianna paused and shook her head. "No, that wasn't all it needed. I'm trying so hard to be careful with my words. Your provision of money was very much necessary to see it brought up to a proper standard."

"I can't believe I heard you say you're

worried about being careful with words. You, who have always been given to saying whatever popped into your head at whatever given moment in time," Kolbein said. "When did this awakening of conscience come about?"

She tried not to feel insulted by his comment. After all, it was true. She was given to talking much and listening little. Aunt Miriam was always chiding her for it. All of her aunts corrected her loquaciousness on a daily basis.

"I suppose the fact that so many people have told me I should refrain from talking so much has given me pause." She picked up the ledger and took it to Kolbein. "Therefore, I will let the figures speak for me, and I will get back to work."

Kolbein took the book and reviewed her work. "You've kept very good records here, Abrianna."

"I pride myself on being accountable."

Wade laughed out loud. "Since when? You, who sneak about after everyone else is in bed. You, who put herself at risk and tell no one about it unless caught in the act."

"Why, Wade Ackerman, just moments ago you talked about my great wisdom." She put her hands on her hips. "Now, which is it to be?"

"It's both." He threw her a wink. "Sometimes you are quite well behaved, and I think there is nothing to worry about. Then you sneak out to confront would-be murderers—"

Protest rose up and she couldn't keep quiet. "That's hardly fair."

"Maybe not, but it is true. Deny it if you can."

He was speaking of one night in particular. One she remembered well. A number of murders had taken place near the school when they were still downtown. One night she'd spied a man in the dark alleyway behind the building. She feared he might be the murderer and wanted only to frighten him away or convince him to turn himself in. As it turned out, he wasn't a murderer but rather a man hired by Kolbein to guard the building.

"Simple and neatly done." Kolbein handed the ledger back to her. "But Wade's got a point, Abrianna."

Lenore raised a brow, which seemed to dare Abrianna to deny the truth. Instead, she sighed. "Honestly, I don't know why any of you continue to be my friend, since I'm of such obvious faults. What an arduous task it must be."

Wade patted her on the back. "It is, but we are pledged to do the job. Aren't we?" He looked to Lenore and Kolbein.

They laughed and she ignored them. Squaring her shoulders, Abrianna shook her head. "I am so . . . fortunate."

Just then the men started showing up at the door for the noontime meal. "Oh goodness, look at the time." Abrianna went quickly to retrieve her apron. "You shall all have to wait to rebuke me another day. The friendless have come to eat, and I don't imagine they mind at all that I am given to daring feats."

8

"Why, Brother Mitchell, we weren't expecting you." Aunt Poisie handed Abrianna a basket of mending. "Take this, dear, and tell Sister that the elder has come to call."

Abrianna did as she was instructed, wondering if the deacons and elders had finally found a new pastor for the church. It was nearly the end of February, and already some in the congregation were talking of leaving.

Finding her aunt in the kitchen instructing a group of girls on the fine art of rendering lard, Abrianna announced the elder's arrival. She put the basket aside as Aunt Miriam turned the lessons over to Liang.

"Ladies, I want you to give Liang your utmost attention. She will continue the lesson, and I expect each of you to be able to perform your own rendering, so be diligent in your learning. Remember, this is a task that requires your constant attention. You could suffer a terrible burn from the popping lard, and we wouldn't want anyone to get marred for life."

The girls nodded and murmured among themselves as the petite Chinese girl took charge. Abrianna fell into step behind her aunt.

"Honestly," Aunt Miriam declared, "I shall never get used to people just dropping in to call without waiting for the appropriate time. These newfangled ways of doing things seem completely foreign to me."

"Do you suppose the elders found a minister?"

"I do hope so. God knows we have prayed very hard for it, and it would be completely to His glory."

"I agree. I only hope they've done a thorough job regarding his experience and theology. It would be a pity to have a man in the pulpit who did not hold with all the teachings of the Bible."

"I hardly believe the elders would overlook that matter, dear."

They entered the parlor and the man rose, as did Aunt Poisie. "Brother Mitchell has wonderful news. The deacons and elders have found a new man for our pulpit."

"I will withhold judgment on the wonder of such news until I hear more," Aunt Miriam said. "Where is Selma?"

"Oh, Sister, don't you remember, she accompanied Miss Lenore and her mother on a shopping trip?"

Abrianna remembered well enough, because she had been upset that Aunt Miriam wouldn't let her accompany them. Instead, she had chided Abrianna about neglecting her household chores for those of the food house and demanded she remain at home. Now, Abrianna wasn't quite as disappointed.

Aunt Miriam nodded and took her seat. "Of course. I quite forgot. Now tell me, Brother Mitchell, about this new pastor."

"He comes with strong recommendations from his seminary as well as from the church he recently pastored. He had already given them notice, saying he knew God was calling him elsewhere, and this was before our inquiry as to his consideration of our church."

"It certainly seems as though the Lord was making provision, where he was concerned," Aunt Miriam declared. "How old of a man is he?"

"Thirty. But before you concern yourself with his youth," Brother Mitchell said, "I will say that he has been preaching since he was twenty. He attended seminary at a young age and excelled in all of his courses. Former teachers declared him to be their most brilliant student."

"That is all well and fine," Abrianna interjected, "but what does his congregation say about him?"

Brother Mitchell pulled a letter from his pocket. "I will read to you a portion of what the men of his church wrote to me." He scanned the first page of the letter and began to read. "'Pastor Walker is a most astute young man. He makes serious study of the Bible and has proven to preach in a direct manner that goes straight to the point. He is good to visit the sick and offer encouragement to the dying. In these last ten years we have known him to make many converts for the Lord and to baptize over forty people.'"

"That's four people a year." Everyone stopped at Abrianna's comment. She shrugged. "Seems to me that is a fairly low number when you consider the overall amount of time."

"She makes a good point," Aunt Miriam said. "I cannot say I'm overly impressed."

Abrianna gave her aunt a nod. It felt good to point out something and have her elders esteem it. So often they considered her troublesome and difficult, and it did her heart good to receive their approval.

If only I could better fit their idea of what I should be. But that would surely take a miracle.

"Where is he from, Brother Mitchell?" Aunt Poisie asked.

"Texas. He was born and raised there and attended seminary there, as well."

"Oh dear." She looked most vexed. "How are we ever to understand him? Sister, do you recall that Texan who came here several years ago looking for a bride?" She looked back to Brother Mitchell. "We could scarce understand a word out of his mouth." She leaned closer and lowered her voice. "Those Southerners speak in a most peculiar manner. I fear I would never be able to follow the sermon."

"Sister makes another good point," Aunt Miriam said, fixing Brother Mitchell with an inquisitive look. "Do you know if his speech will be understandable to the common man?"

"I do. He arrived in town two days ago, and I have been privileged to have many conversations with him. While he does have something of a drawl, he is quite distinct in his speech, and I believe you will find him to be rather charming."

"Is he married? Does he have a family?" Abrianna pressed. It was possible her questions might cause Aunt Miriam to dismiss her, but for now she would dare to ask. It was important to know the man's personal background as well as his current situation.

"He is single. He has devoted himself completely, at least to this time, to God. He told us that he had not yet felt God release him to marry."

"My beloved captain Jonathan, God rest his soul, once told me the same thing," Aunt Poisie said in a most thoughtful manner. She pulled out an ever-ready hankie and dabbed her eyes. "He said that he was so long married to the sea that he could not marry me until he gave her up. He was to have sold his ship and married me, but on his final journey he was lost at sea."

"Tragic," Brother Mitchell said.

"So very sad," Aunt Miriam agreed. "However, we must not dwell long on the past, Sister. Especially now when Brother Mitchell has so much to tell us about Pastor Walker."

Poisie's brows knit together. "I knew a young man named Walker once. Of course, he wasn't from Texas, but perhaps they are related." She looked to Abrianna, as if for her agreement, but already Aunt Miriam was taking the floor.

"I believe we as a congregation should give the man a set time to be tested. After all, we need to know for ourselves if the man is of sound character and motivation. Many a man may say he is a man of God and even get others to write on his behalf, yet be nothing more than a wolf in sheep's clothing."

"We, too, had considered this." Brother Mitchell put the letter back into his pocket. "The elders and deacons agreed that we would call him for a six-month period. At the end of that time we would let him know if we wished to retain him as our permanent pastor."

This was great news to Abrianna. She had hoped there would be thorough consideration to the man's character and methods, along with his theology and general interaction with the congregation. She clapped her hands together.

"That is a wonderful plan. I think too often people rush into decisions without giving them to God in their entirety. The very nature of man is to deceive, and I would be remiss if I didn't stress the importance of being completely thorough. You might not remember it, but only two years ago there was that scandal in Tacoma, where a man who claimed to be a man of God bilked a large number of people out of their savings. I don't believe he was ever caught, and we could perhaps find ourselves in the same position. I don't recall, but that man might have been a Texan, as well."

"Oh my!" Poisie waved her handkerchief under her nose. "That would be too tragic to bear."

"Ladies, that's quite enough." Aunt Miriam smiled. "We have good men of God in our church, and I'm certain they will investigate everything wisely. We will leave it in their hands."

Brother Mitchell seemed to puff up a bit, but such a declaration didn't impress Abrianna. There were far too many examples of men duping others. Why, the Bible was full of such reminders.

"All I know," Abrianna couldn't help but add, "is that even David—a man after God's own heart—sinned and deceived. He was also responsible for the murder of another. Wouldn't it be awful if we were to bring in a pastor who was a murderer?"

"Goodness, Abrianna, you do let your imagination run wild." Aunt Miriam gave her a look of reproof, and Aunt Poisie gave a small gasp.

"Sister, she is correct. The Bible tells us not to put our trust in man. Even our dear elders and deacons fall into that category. Our trust must be in God alone."

Aunt Miriam heaved a sigh and rolled her eyes. "I believe we are all in agreement about that. Furthermore I believe Brother Mitchell would dismiss any man who turned out to be a murderer."

"I would hope so." Abrianna crossed her

arms in exasperation. "Preferably before he murdered again. I would hate for us to be known as the church where a murderer held the pulpit."

Aunt Poisie bobbed her head. "Oh, indeed!"

Everyone else much anticipated the Sunday service, but Militine was indifferent. One pastor was pretty much the same as another, and she had little love for anyone who declared her to be a terrible sinner bound for hell. Although, what if they were right? She stole a glance at Abrianna. She was always completely absorbed in church. *Could I ever be so devoted? Could I ever believe like she does?* A sigh escaped her, and for a moment she feared someone might have overheard, but no one seemed concerned and she shrank back a bit more into the pew.

They sang the regular hymns and offered the usual prayers before Brother Mitchell took to the pulpit to introduce Ralston Walker. The young pastor was a tall, very pleasant-looking man, but otherwise Militine judged him to be no different from any of the other men in her life. Worthless.

Well, there was Thane, who continued to be increasingly kind. There was no way of knowing his purpose in being so, but her guard was up, and she wouldn't be fooled. It was better to distrust all of them than to trust a few good ones only to have a bad one slip through.

Pastor Walker spoke of his background, telling the congregation about growing up the son of a cotton planter who was now deceased. His mother too, had gone to glory, leaving behind four sons and a daughter and numerous grandchildren.

Militine tried her best to appear interested. The last thing she wanted was for someone to notice her boredom and bring it to Mrs. Madison's attention, so she did her best to mimic those around her. If the old ladies nodded, she did the same. If Abrianna appeared thoughtful, Militine gave her head a little cock to one side, as if truly considering the words. Of course where Abrianna was concerned, she was probably assessing the situation for purposes that went beyond Militine's interest. No doubt she would barrage the new pastor with questions later.

There was to be a celebratory dinner after the service, which would give the congregation an opportunity to get to know the new pastor better. Militine almost felt sorry for the man, knowing that Abrianna would not be satisfied until she queried him about everything but his shoe size. Then again, knowing Abrianna, one's shoe size might well have some unknown indication of spiritual well-being.

Wouldn't that be a wonderful gift? To be able to understand and recognize someone's spiritual qualities and know the truth of it. Militine smiled. *If I understood things like that, I might not feel so misplaced or vulnerable.* She immediately sobered at that thought. Vulnerable. All of her life she had lived in fear of one thing or another. To protect herself she had hidden her feelings deep, causing most people to think her hostile or intolerant, when, in fact, she was just plain afraid.

The service came to a conclusion, and everyone stood as Brother Mitchell offered the benediction. Militine earnestly wondered if God was really listening.

"Did you make something for the feast?" Thane's question startled her out of her thoughts.

Apparently the amen had been said, for people were moving to the fellowship hall. "I'm sorry. I was rather deep in thought."

"Not in prayer?" he asked. His blue eyes sought her face for the truth.

"No. Not in prayer, but I'd rather you keep that between you and me."

He smiled. "I'm happy to keep your secrets. Anytime."

While his statement was kind, Militine

knew he had no way of knowing what an ugly job that could be. If she were to tell him all of her secrets, she had no doubt he would have nothing more to do with her. Not only that, but Mrs. Madison would probably remove her from the school.

"Some secrets are best never shared," she whispered, thankful that Thane didn't seem to hear. She put it behind her. "But as for your question, I did make a pie. It turned out looking rather nice, but the inside could be absolutely abominable."

"Like some people," he said with a questioning look. "When it comes to pie, I tend to be quite adept. Point me in the right direction."

She laughed, and when he extended his arm, she took hold of it. To do otherwise would only cause a scene, and that was the last thing she wanted.

"I've been thinking." They followed the others toward where the dinner would be held. "I wonder if you might agree to accompany me to the fireman's dance."

"What?" Her knees went weak.

Thane was undaunted. "There's a fireman's dance coming up, and I need someone to accompany me. I figure you and I are quite comfortable together, and perhaps it would be fun for us to share an evening."

"I . . . uh . . . I've never thought about such

a thing." That wasn't entirely true. Many had been the time she'd longed to just be a normal young lady courting a respectable young man.

"Well, think about it. I'll need to get Mrs. Madison's permission, and the dance is this Friday."

She didn't know what to say. He was looking at her with such innocent hopefulness that she hated to say no. "Mrs. Madison would require I have a chaperone."

"I don't mind," he replied, looking even more enthusiastic. "Perhaps Abrianna could come with us. I know the boys would love to have another female to dance with, and she can talk the ear off anyone who doesn't want to dance. The way I see it, everyone wins."

There didn't seem to be any way out of the invitation without hurting his feelings, and Militine had no desire to do that. Thane had been kind to her—a good friend. "Very well. If Mrs. Madison agrees to let me go, I will attend the dance with you, but be warned of two things. I'm not very good at dancing, and Mrs. Madison will most likely insist it be her sister who accompanies us."

"I saw you from the pulpit." Ralston Walker stopped the young redheaded woman who'd watched him so intently throughout the service.

"I'm certain you did," she declared, putting her hand out. "It's hard to miss me with all this red hair, and we always sit very close to the front. I'm Abrianna Cunningham."

He frowned at her openness. "Have you long attended this church, Miss Cunningham?"

"All of my life. I held great love for Pastor Klingle."

"It sounds as though he was a fine man of God." He was ready to move on and speak to someone else. It was never good to give too much time to any woman. They always wanted to talk about the silliest things.

Abrianna Cunningham seemed to study him with a critical eye, however, causing Ralston to linger. What was it she was about?

"Pastor Klingle was a very good man, a godly man who lived by the words he spoke. It won't be easy for you to win over the hearts of the people, given their deep respect and love for him."

Her directness offended him, but he knew it would never do to offer a harsh rebuke on his first day. "You are certainly a woman who speaks her mind. Are your parents here with you today?"

She shook her head. "My parents are dead. I was adopted by Mrs. Madison. She and her sister and Mrs. Gibson have acted as my aunts for all my life. I have no other family."

"So you're a part of the Madison School for Brides? I heard about that from Brother Mitchell."

"It's the Madison Bridal School, and yes, that is my home. As I recall, your parents are also deceased."

"Indeed. I see you were listening." He saw her reach into a small reticule and pull out a piece of paper.

"I was listening and hoping you would answer most of the questions I'd compiled."

What a meddlesome young woman. "You have a list?" He forced a smile.

"Indeed. I didn't want to forget anything. It's very important to me that you be scrupulously investigated."

He raised his eyebrows and had no trouble wiping the smile off his face. Her words took him by surprise. "You are but a woman. Do you not trust that your deacons and elders would be complete in seeking a pastor for this congregation?"

"I don't put my trust in men, Pastor Walker. That is reserved for God alone."

She wasn't in the least bit cowered by his rebuke. Ralston wasn't used to females stepping into the roles he believed belonged solely to men. Perhaps it was because she was brought up in a houseful of women without a male authority to guide her.

"I must say, I'm not used to such an outspoken woman. In my family and indeed my church, women were to remain silent."

"You're the one who approached me and started this conversation," Miss Cunningham countered. "However, if you feel intimidated by women, perhaps it would be best to put this discussion aside." She eyed him with a look of disapproval. "I doubt, however, that it will bode well for you. There are a great many women in this congregation, and I'm certain I won't be the only one with questions."

She left him at that, and he was thankful. He wasn't at all sure what he would have said had the conversation continued. Miss Cunningham would be a challenge. The thinking of strong-willed women these days had caused problems to creep up throughout the country with issues of property ownership, voting rights, and demands of education. Ralston wasn't about to stand for that kind of thing in his church. As their leader, he would make it clear that women had a place, and it wasn't in a position of authority.

9

Abrianna offered a bowl of soup to a man she didn't recognize. "Are you new to us?"

The old man lifted his head and smiled. "That I am. Name's Jay Bowes. I heard about this place and thought it something I should look into. It's a nice thing you're doing here." He seemed to linger, looking behind him as if to make sure no one else was coming.

"And where are you from, Mr. Bowes?"

"Nowhere important." He sniffed the soup. "How about you? You live here all your life?"

"I have." She spied several men entering the building. "I would love to talk more, but I must move you along. We have other hungry folks arriving."

He smiled. "I'll be around. We can talk anytime you want."

The regulars knew the routine well. They took up their bread and bowls of soup without comment until the very last man came through. He winked at Abrianna. "I see yar havin' me favorite today."

"Oh, Captain Jack, I thought of you this morning when I was making the fish chowder. I knew you'd be pleased." Abrianna couldn't help but feel great affection for the old sea dog. She had known him for over ten years, and he often brought her something he'd carved.

"Gonna have ya a trinket afore long," he said with another wink. "I know how ya enjoy 'em."

"I do." She laughed. "I'm the only girl in all of Seattle who has her own little wooden menagerie. Honestly, I don't know where you've had opportunity to see all of those animals, but the carvings are wonderful."

"I ain't seen most of 'em face-to-face," he admitted. "But I found me a book, and it shows 'em all proper like."

"That's wonderful. I shall look forward to the next masterpiece."

The man nodded and headed off to join the others. Abrianna let a sense of accomplishment settle over her. She loved what God had done in this place.

"You look exhausted," Militine said, coming alongside Abrianna. "Why don't you let Wade take you back early? Thane and I can clean this up, and then he can bring me back to the house."

Abrianna sighed. "That does sound good. Pastor Walker sent a card saying he plans to call this afternoon. I would like to be there when he arrives."

"Do I detect some interest in our new pastor?"

"Of course I'm interested. I intend to figure the man out and know what he's thinking. I don't want to see our people lulled into a false sense of peace, only to learn the man is deviously taking the offering to line his own pockets."

"Surely you don't think he would do that. I mean, he's just arrived."

It was never wrong to be watchful, and had that church in Tacoma been of the same mind, they might not have known such a disaster. Still, she didn't expect Militine to understand. The girl didn't even like going to church, so why should she care what happened to its people?

"I'll see if Wade agrees to take me back. If he thinks that would be acceptable, then I will go. Otherwise, I'm committed to remaining until we have everything cleaned up."

Half an hour later, as the clock chimed two, Ralston Walker stood at the door to the Madison Bridal School. He thought the large estate house to be quite grand and could only imagine that it had cost a small fortune. Pity they hadn't thought of what good that money might have done the church. Their little church needed so much work. Perhaps he would need to convince the elders that it would be smarter to rebuild elsewhere.

"Hello," Miss Cunningham greeted him. "Won't you come in, Pastor Walker?"

"Thank you." He handed her his outer coat. "It's a rather blustery day."

She hung the piece on a coat-tree by the door. "Why don't you come into the parlor and get warm. I'll let my aunts know you're here."

"I thought we were to speak alone."

She turned back. "I would be happy to do that, but my aunts will consider it bad manners if we do not include them at least for a time. Bad manners are something we do not allow at Madison Bridal School. Surely you are familiar with etiquette, aren't you?"

"To a degree," he said with a smile. "I don't find etiquette lessons written in the Bible."

She paused with a look of disagreement. "But of course there are. The greatest of them is written there for all to read and hopefully follow. John 13:34, 'A new commandment I give unto you, That ye love one another; as I have loved you, that ye also love one another.'"

"That's hardly an etiquette lesson, Miss Cunningham. That is a command of the Lord."

"Exactly. It tells us how we are to treat one another. Etiquette does likewise. The Bible is full of such references for treating others as better than ourselves, treating others with kindness and forbearance. Just as I am with you right now. If I were to be rude to you, I wouldn't bother to help you understand. I'd merely tell you that you're wrong, and quite foolish for believing otherwise." She smiled. "Now, if you'll excuse me, I'll fetch my aunts."

He looked after her in dumbfounded silence. He'd never had anyone take him to task in such a manner. Especially where the Scriptures were involved. That this mere slip of a girl, hardly old enough to be a woman, should chide him for his behavior caused him no end of grief. He would wait his time, however, and find a way to put her in her place.

The older ladies came bringing refreshments on a tea cart. They were a funny lot whom he'd gotten to know a little at the church dinner. Mrs. Madison was of medium height and slender weight. She had her gray hair in a fashionable bun atop her head, but it was her piercing blue eyes that held his attention. She didn't miss much. This was one woman who studied the details around her and weighed each one carefully. It was clear that she led this group of addlepated females.

Mrs. Gibson, a well-rounded widow, seemed only slightly more reserved than Mrs. Madison. Neither lady was what he would call obnoxiously bold, but they were opinionated, something he did not think respectable in women. At church they had both found it necessary to quiz him about his prior education and ministerial duties.

The last of the trio, Miss Poisie Holmes was a funny little thing. From what he'd observed at church, she appeared completely subservient to her sister. Short and petite, Miss Poisie had a penchant for bobbing her head and blessing the dead. She seemed harmless enough.

"We are glad you could join us today," Mrs. Madison said, bringing him a cup of tea. "When Abrianna told us you had made an appointment to visit, we were quite surprised."

"And why was that, Mrs. Madison? You are one of my parishioners." He took the cup and saucer and offered her a warm smile. "Thank you."

She nodded and Miss Holmes followed behind with a dish of shortbread. "I'll just put this here on the table beside you."

"Thank you, Miss Holmes."

She bobbed her head several times and took her seat.

It was apparent that Miss Cunningham was watching him, studying his actions and words. Funny young woman, but if she thought to best him, she had another think coming.

"The elders tell me that you have been most faithful to support the church all these years. I commend you for your good stewardship. I'm certain it has blessed many and the Lord is pleased with your faithfulness."

When no one uttered a word in comment, he continued. "I feel as though I've found a home." He smiled and turned on the charm that he'd found worked so well with weak-minded women. "Of course with such lovely ladies and women of faith who not only sing like choirs of angels in the service but also cook dishes that taste as if they came from heaven itself, who could not feel at home?"

"How do you know what food from heaven tastes like?" Miss Cunningham asked.

He swallowed hard, determined to hold back the snide retort that came to mind. "I apologize. It is the quality and taste of which I would expect heaven capable. Of course, we cannot know for certain that such things will even matter."

"Pastor Walker, we understand that you

have studied the Scriptures for most of your life," Mrs. Madison began. "Perhaps you might tell us what you have found personally most rewarding in such study."

Her question caught him off guard. Usually people asked why he'd become a minister or whether or not he had ever considered other vocations. Some even asked if he intended to take a wife, but few ever asked about his Scripture study. He could see they were all awaiting his answer, however, and knew he would have to think fast. Hoping to appear humble, he bowed his head for a moment and then looked up with his best look of serenity. At least that was his goal.

"I find that few people care about such deep thinking. I'm pleased to know that you value this matter. It speaks highly of your spiritual maturity, something I often find missing in women."

He hadn't meant to take the conversation in that direction and quickly worked to interject some additional thoughts. "Perhaps in my experience the women were not nearly so desirous to know God as you three . . . four obviously are. However, since you asked about my reward in such study, I must say that God's Word has opened my eyes to the truth of how He wishes His church to be. God has gifts for the body of believers, and in those gifts we see His completion of what the church is to do and be."

"And what would that be?" Mrs. Madison stared at him while she sipped her tea.

"Theologically speaking, the church or body of believers has been created to do God's work, to share the gospel and extend the love of God to all mankind. I am certain you are familiar with the diversities of gifts—faith, healing, wisdom, prophecy, and such. The body is a compilation of all those gifts, and with those gifts we see the church made whole. Some of the elders and deacons will teach or will administer. Still others will be prophets and discerners of spirits, both good and evil.

"God, of course, assigns one such as me to head the church. It is my job to be in authority over the rest of the body."

Miss Cunningham cleared her throat. "Excuse me, but I thought Christ was the head of the church."

He pushed aside his irritation. "God the Father is head overall, and Christ is head of the entire church. I merely meant that as pastor of a church, I have certain authority."

This was clearly not going the way he'd hoped. Abrianna Cunningham fixed him with a look that made him begin to perspire. How was it this mere slip of a girl could make him feel so compromised? He'd faced off with lifelong theologians who prided themselves on having memorized the entire Bible and had never felt this way.

"I believe accountability is critical for each of us." Miss Cunningham looked away after another testing moment and turned her attention to one of the cookies on her plate.

"I suppose we all have our various views," Mrs. Madison interjected, "however, I am of a mind to agree with Abrianna. The Bible speaks of how we must all give of ourselves to the Lord, to take up our cross daily and follow Him. I believe that we should be not only accountable in our actions but hold others accountable, as well. Particularly those in positions of leadership. After all, the Bible does declare that such people will be held to a higher degree of accounting."

"Ladies"—he rose from his chair and looked down on them—"I see you are quite knowledgeable." Never mind that they were also very annoying. He would deal with them in time. "I find your knowledge of the Bible refreshing." It was a lie, but it would no doubt soothe their womanly pride. "I understand that you have long been without a man in your home. For that I am very sorry. As your pastor, I do worry about your safety and protection. And because of that, I am happy to offer myself as your protector and adviser."

Miss Cunningham snorted, and Mrs. Gibson gasped. Miss Holmes was the only one who didn't seem upset by his declaration. Mrs. Madison most systematically took one last sip of tea and set her cup aside. Getting to her feet, she gave him a look that reminded him of a chastising mother.

"Pastor Walker, I am touched by your consideration, but we have many years of experience, and God himself has provided His Spirit as our counselor." She moved to the tea cart. "Would you care for more tea? My sister and Mrs. Gibson must get back to their work, but you may stay on and speak with Abrianna, if you desire."

Was she dismissing him? He didn't want to leave them on a negative note. "Thank you, but no more tea. I had hoped for a few minutes to speak with Miss Cunningham. I do hope that I haven't offended any of you." He chose his words carefully. After all, these women were some of the church's best financial supporters. It was a pity, especially given they didn't understand their place, but he would find a way to soothe their riled souls. "I have found our discussion to be quite enlightening and hope to again one day visit you."

"We would happily receive you," Mrs. Madison offered without a hint of a smile. "It is our desire to know you better."

He nodded. "I wish each of you a good day."

One by one the ladies left him to the company of Miss Cunningham. Ralston turned to her and smiled. "Thank you for receiving me today. I wanted very much to answer that list of questions you had for me." And put her in her place at the same time.

"Well, please do take your seat. I don't wish to strain my neck staring up at you." She set aside her now empty plate. She produced her list from her pocket. "I suppose a lot of people wouldn't consider such matters important, but I feel that in order to decide if you are an acceptable leader for our church, we should be clear on your theology."

He frowned, unwilling to take directions from her. "Do you not trust your deacons and elders to learn that?"

"Of course, but I feel it's also my responsibility to test the spirits. After all, that is what the Word says. We are to be wise as serpents." She cocked her head. "I do wish you would sit. I'm getting a pinch in my neck looking up."

He decided it would be best to humor her. He'd learned early on to assess the people in his congregation and divide them into two groups: those he could easily manipulate and those he could not. She was clearly in the latter group. "I find you quite interesting, Miss

Cunningham. You have a boldness about you that might shock a lesser man. I can say confidently that I like you and hope you feel likewise about me."

"I don't know about that." She gave a shrug. "I cannot say whether I like you or don't. We haven't known each other long enough. I've heard you speak only the one time, and while it was interesting to hear of your life and calling, I found the shortness of your testimony did little to give me true insight.

"I suppose it is possible that you had been instructed by the elders to be brief. Was that it? I know sometimes men tend to limit such things, lest the speaker bore their listeners. Maybe they felt you needed to speak briefly and with minimal theology." She looked at him as if it was finally his turn to answer.

Ralston held his temper in check. She was obviously headstrong and had too long been allowed to speak her mind unchecked. Even so, her aunts were wealthy women whose money was needed. He forced a smile. "I shall endeavor to answer each of your questions, Miss Cunningham."

Abrianna joined the other ladies for the evening meal. It seemed that Pastor Walker was the subject of much discussion, although she would just as soon forget about the pompous man.

"Well, I thought he had lovely diction," Aunt Poisie finally said, "for a Texan."

"He acted in a rather secretive manner at times," Aunt Selma said, shaking her head. "His temperament reminds me much too much of Mr. Gibson." She put her hand to her throat. "You don't suppose he read Darwin, do you?"

Abrianna didn't much care what he read. She'd been completely put off by his belittling attitude. His answers to her questions suggested that he felt women in general were of very little value to the church. He hadn't come right out and said as much, but the implication was there.

"I suggest we spend time in prayer for our new pastor and for the church," Aunt Miriam suggested. The table of young ladies nodded. "We will soon enough see what his beliefs are, not only in his teachings, but even more so in his daily actions."

10

Thane nervously paced and awaited Militine's arrival. March second had not come soon enough as far as he was concerned. This was the first time he'd anticipated the fireman's ball and was most anxious.

"Here we are," Miss Poisie announced. She would, of course, accompany them this evening. Militine walked in behind her, and Thane felt the breath catch in his throat.

"You look beautiful." She was a vision in blue silk and lace. Her hair had been swept atop her head with all sorts of curls.

"Abrianna provided the gown and accessories. They were given to her by Lenore." She smoothed down the folds of the voluminous skirt with her gloved hands. "I feel out of place," she said, her voice low, "but

Abrianna assured me that I will be happier dressed according to what's expected."

He chuckled. "I think every woman at the dance will wish she were you."

"Only because she will be on your arm," Miss Poisie said, smiling. She was wearing a simple navy blue gown with a lovely piece of lace draped around her shoulders. "Shall we go?"

Thane held out his arms. "I shall escort you both with great pleasure. Miss Poisie, do promise that you'll give me at least one dance."

Miss Poisie giggled like a schoolgirl and Militine smiled. For Thane it was shaping up to be a wonderful night.

The short drive by carriage to the Frey Opera House, where the dance was to be held, gave Thane little time to converse. The traffic was quite heavy as carriage after carriage vied for close parking. Thane paid a young man to watch his borrowed carriage. The boy looked familiar, and he couldn't help but wonder if he was one of Abrianna's orphans. He had no time to ask, however, as Miss Poisie started to alight from the carriage.

"Let me help you, Miss Poisie." He took firm hold of her arm and helped her to the ground. Next he reached up to help Militine. She hesitated only a moment, then smiled and took his arm.

"Just look at all the beautiful people," Miss Poisie whispered in awe. "It's been a long time since I've gone to a public dance. The ladies are all dressed so regally."

"They also dress beautifully for the school's annual ball."

"Of course they do, Mr. Patton," she replied, "but I always see those young ladies ahead of time. Even in the planning stage while they are still attempting to figure out what they will make for themselves to wear. This is almost like Christmas morning and unwrapping new gifts. One is never certain what will next appear."

She was such a dear old woman. They all were. They had treated him like family since he first became friends with Wade. Escorting the ladies into the building, Thane paused to give over his top hat to an awaiting steward. The orchestra had begun to play as they made their way to the dance room.

"Now, you two don't mind me," Miss Poisie said, moving to take a chair by the wall. "I will visit with some of the other chaperones while you dance and enjoy the evening. Do mind your manners, Mr. Patton. I am expecting you to be a perfect gentleman."

He nodded and led Militine to the edge of the dance floor. "I doubt very much she'll get perfection, but I shall endeavor to do my best."

"I don't expect you to be perfect," Militine replied. "I certainly am not."

"You seem nearly so to me." He smiled, hoping his casual nature would put her at ease. "Would you care to dance?"

"I suppose we should. After all, that is why we've come." She flashed him a smile and added, "Although I'm just as content to stand here and watch the others."

"No, no. That will not do. You are clearly the most beautiful of all the women here and must be shown off." He swept her amidst the other waltzing couples, and they began to dance.

"You told me you weren't any good at this," he teased as they made their way around the room. "You dance quite well."

"It isn't my favorite thing to do." She met his gaze, and her dark brown eyes seemed to look right through him.

"What is your favorite thing to do, Miss Scott?"

"Please, don't call me that. I'm just plain Militine."

"There is nothing plain about you, Militine. I know you think yourself so, but you are an amazingly beautiful woman. I have always found your dark hair and eyes to lend themselves to something of the exotic."

"Unlike red hair?"

He laughed. "Red hair has never bothered me one way or the other. I know there are those like Abrianna who find it something of a curse but not me. It's just hair. Onc day it will most likely turn white."

"Did your father's hair do that?"

The question was innocent enough, but Thane was caught off guard. "I don't know. He didn't live long enough to see that."

"I'm sorry. I shouldn't have asked that." She looked away.

"It's all right. I'm the one who's sorry. This evening is meant for light-hearted fun." The waltz concluded and a polka began. Instead of dancing, Thane led the way to the refreshment table. "I'm parched after just one dance. How about you?"

Militine glanced at the punch. "Yes. I'd like a cup, please."

Thane handed her one and then took one for himself. "Would you like some cookies, as well?"

"No. This is quite enough. I'm afraid if I eat anything, I won't be able to breathe. Abrianna . . . well . . . she snugged me in this dress pretty tight."

"I can't imagine that you needed all that much snugging. You're not that big. In fact, I was going to say that you seem much thinner than when you first arrived at the school."

"I am that," she agreed. Turning to watch the dancers, she shrugged. "I think it's all the hard work. Not that I didn't work hard at home, but . . ." Her words trailed off.

"Militine. That's a really unusual name. How did you come by it?"

For a moment she said nothing, and Thane worried he'd made a mistake by getting so personal.

"I'm a compromise." She looked up and smiled. "My mother wanted to name me Millicent, and my father insisted on Christine after his mother. So they came up with Militine, and that makes me a compromise."

"I would never think of you as a compromise."

She frowned and once again looked away. "I'm . . . I'd rather we talk about something else."

Thane couldn't help but want her to continue. She rarely spoke about her childhood or home prior to coming to Seattle. He had tried on more than one occasion to speak to her about it, about the fact that they obviously shared tyrannical fathers, but that would mean he'd have to talk about his past, as well.

We're quite the pair. She won't talk about her past, and I won't talk about mine. Seems there's very little we trust each other enough to share.

But surely there was a way to get beyond that obstacle.

"So what do you think of Abrianna's food house?"

Militine still refused to look at him. "I think anything Abrianna wants to accomplish, she will. She has amazed me since we first met."

"I've never known anybody who could talk more than she can. Wade and I used to count the words she could say without drawing a breath. It got to be pretty high, so we stopped." He put down his empty punch cup and reached for hers. "Would you like more?"

"No. I'm fine. Thank you."

He placed her cup beside his, then extended his arm. "I believe a quadrille is next. Would you like to join them?"

She shook her head. "I'd rather wait. Do you mind?"

He looked across the room at the couples gathering in groups of eight. "Not particularly. I'm not much of a dancer."

"You dance perfectly well. I'm afraid . . . well . . ." She heaved a sigh and finally looked him in the eye. "You probably already know that I'm not comfortable in large crowds, especially around . . . around . . . other men." She paled a bit. "I'm sorry. If you'd rather take me home, I'll understand."

Thane led her away from the dance floor

not far from where Miss Poisie sat completely engrossed in a conversation with another matron. "You don't have to apologize, and I don't want to take you home. I don't care if we dance or not. I'm just happy you agreed to come with me. I hope you'll feel up to dancing the fireman's waltz with me. They reserve one especially for the men who are volunteers." He gave her hand a light pat as she continued to hold on to his arm.

"I'd be honored."

She trembled under his touch. "Are you cold?"

Militine shook her head and pulled away. "No. I'm just rather anxious."

He reached out and took one of her gloved hands in his. "Don't be. I won't let anyone hurt you." He paused for a moment. Had she heard him? "Militine?"

She looked into his eyes. "Yes?"

"I mean it. I won't let anyone hurt you. I don't know what has hurt you in the past, but I won't allow it to happen again."

Her expression softened, and for a moment Thane thought surely she would open up and tell him some troublesome secret. But she didn't.

They spoke very little throughout the evening, and when the fireman's waltz was called, Militine looked to Thane and smiled. He led her into the sea of dancers and proudly claimed her as his partner. The music began and Thane joined his hand to hers. He pulled her close enough to put his gloved hand on her waist.

For a time they were lost in the music and motion. Thane had never known a greater pleasure. Militine, too, seemed pleased. She never missed a step or came down on his toes. For all her supposed discomfort, she was quite accomplished.

"You know you are very good at this." He enjoyed teasing her.

"I have a good partner. Mrs. Madison says that any young woman might dance well in the arms of a man who knows well what he is doing."

Thane couldn't help but laugh. "I don't know about that, but at least I haven't made a fool of myself . . . at least not yet."

The music ended, and once again the call went out for a quadrille. Thane didn't bother to ask Militine about dancing. He knew what her answer would be, and it seemed only right to spare her the embarrassment. They weren't quite off the dance floor, however, when a tall stranger approached them. The man was at least a head taller than Thane, and his shoulders seemed twice as wide.

"Pardon me, but don't I know you?"

Thane shook his head. "I don't think so."

"No. I meant the young lady."

Thane felt Militine stiffen. She glanced to her right, as if looking for an exit. Thane tightened his grip on her arm.

"I'm sure we've met somewhere before," the stranger declared. "I don't forget eyes like yours, so dark and beautiful."

"Excuse me, but you are annoying the lady. If she knew you, I'm sure she'd say so." Thane pulled her a tad closer. "Now, if you'll excuse us."

"I didn't mean any disrespect. I thought to pay the lady a compliment and figure out where we'd met." It was clear he remained puzzled. Thane could also see that he wasn't trying to be a threat to either of them.

"I understand. However, we are expected elsewhere." Thane drew Militine along with him. She walked as if frozen stiff. He didn't know what the problem was. She didn't like to deal with men in general, and especially not strangers. How Abrianna had ever convinced her to help at the food house was a mystery, but perhaps with her trio of friends at her side, Militine felt safe.

"Please take me home," she whispered as soon as they were away from the man. The pleading look on her face left him no choice. "Of course I will. Let's get Miss Poisie, and we can leave."

But before they could even reach the older woman, Militine began to sway on her feet. Thane steadied her and got her to the door just before she collapsed, sinking against him in a dead faint.

"And then she just passed out in my arms," Thane told Wade hours later in Wade's cozy quarters.

"Was she ill?"

"I think she was terrified. I've never seen anyone look like that, as if she'd seen a ghost or something. She was trembling and all white. Miss Poisie saw what was happening and came with her smelling salts. Luckily, we didn't draw a lot of notice and were able to slip out of the opera house without making a scene. Poor Militine. She was mortified."

"She probably just got too hot. It can happen in a room with a lot of people." Wade leaned back in his chair and pushed aside his Bible. "Still, you got her to go to the dance with you. That had to be special."

Thane rested his elbows on the table and then his chin in his hands. Wade could tell by the look on his face there was more troubling his friend. Otherwise his friend wouldn't have stormed into his apartment to disrupt Wade's Bible reading. Waiting for Thane to speak,

Wade went to stoke up the fire in the stove and then sat back down. After what seemed an eternity, Thane finally lifted his head.

"You know my past. You know all the sordid details. Things I've never told anyone else."

"I do."

"I never wanted to tell anyone. I only wanted to run from the past and all that it represented. I wanted to forget who I was and who others thought I'd become. I might be crazy, but I think Militine feels the same way. I mean, she never wants to discuss the past, and I think it's because there's violence and ugliness there that she can't bear to remember."

Wade toyed with the edge of his Bible. "A lot of folks have bad things in their past that they'd just as soon forget. What makes you think she's got it worse than most?"

"She mentioned once that her father was strict and intolerant. I'm pretty sure he beat her. A couple of times when I reached out toward her, she cowered like I might hit her."

Wade could only imagine that a great many young women were mistreated in just such a manner. He'd often seen men bullying and belittling the women in their company. Just watching the way they interacted, it wasn't hard to imagine the men becoming physical in their anger.

"I know that she's been hurt, Wade. What I don't know is how to make her forget about it. Or at least how to get her to talk about it. Sometimes talking helps. I need her to know she's safe with me."

"Did it help you? I thought you told me not so long ago that you wished you'd kept it to yourself."

"Only because of the burden it put on you to remain silent. I hate that you have to think on all that just as I have had to do. My life back in Missouri was hell on earth, and no one should have to relive it or even imagine it."

Wade opened the Bible and thumbed through the pages. "It's funny you say that. Tonight, when I was preparing for the Bible study, I did think of you and your past. Leaving home and all you knew at the age of thirteen. Facing the unknown and working your way to the next meal."

"What made you think of that?" Thane seemed almost confused. "Don't tell me there's a similar story in the Bible."

"Well, similar enough." Wade opened to the book of Daniel. "See, I was reading here about a young man who was separated from his people when he was young. An enemy came and took over his country and Daniel, being one of the best youths—good looking, intelligent, and in pretty good shape—was taken to be trained."

"Trained for what?"

"The king thought he might be useful in his court, so he educated Daniel and some friends of his. Fed him and clothed him. He offered the best wines and foods to Daniel."

"How could that possibly remind you of me? I've never been offered the best of anything. I was lucky if folks didn't show me the door."

"Well, here's where the story takes a turn. Daniel and his friends had been trained to put their trust in God. They were Hebrews and believed in the God of Abraham. Their folks had obviously been good about teaching them what was right and wrong. Daniel and his friends didn't want the best foods and wines, because it was against their law, against their faith. Instead, they just wanted vegetables and water. They were sure it would be better for them in the long run to be obedient, and it was."

"Wade, I don't see how that relates to me at all." Thane shook his head. "I don't have faith in God, and frankly, I'm not real fond of vegetables."

Wade laughed. "Both you and Daniel were young men who had a choice. You could lie down and die or survive as best you could.

In both cases, there had to be a willingness to endure changes. But there also needed to be a firm foundation of strength from deep inside to see you through. Daniel's foundation was fixed on God. He knew God, because his folks had seen to that. Daniel trusted God. He had great confidence in what God could do for him and with him."

"But I don't feel that way. I didn't know anything but pain and misery, lies and death. I don't have that kind of hope. My hope or strength always had to come from myself, and that proved to be a disaster."

"I know, Thane. But you could have the kind of hope Daniel had." Wade eased back again. "You were taken out of what you knew and set into a place that you didn't. You had to find the will to go on. I saw that in Daniel, too. It couldn't have been easy remembering the past, even a good past. But I don't know that Daniel's past was good. After all, the enemy took over his people. Maybe his folks were murdered in front of him. I don't know. What I do know is that God made all the difference for him."

"And you believe He'll make all the difference for me? Is that it?"

"You know it is. I know that the past still haunts you. Just as you suspect it does with Militine. I know you both have your hearts set against God for one reason or another." Wade yawned and gave a stretch. "I also have a feeling that the time is soon coming when you're going to have to make a choice to go on being chained to the past or to find liberty in a new life with God's help."

"I don't know if that's possible." Thane again put his head in his hands.

Wade smiled, knowing Thane wouldn't see it. "Well, I do."

11

Priam waited for his new client, Anthony Jessup, to make up his mind. The man seemed insistent upon scrutinizing every detail of the contract Welby had drawn up.

Weeks of profitable trade had made Priam Welby wealthier than he could have imagined. Seeing his money accumulate pleased him more than anything else in the world, but waiting for this man to conclude their business only served to irritate him.

He had better things to do with his time, and time was money. With every new goal he met, Priam moved one step closer to stripping his father of all comfort and financial well-being. His latest venture had gained him the majority control of stocks in one of his father's largest companies. Things were going along just as he had hoped and planned for so many years.

The human commodities he'd supplied to various clients had netted him considerable money; however, shipping people proved more difficult than shipping items of ceramic, glass, or powder. Drugs and artifacts brought him a good price and required no upkeep along the way. And drugs and artifacts couldn't die. Much to his frustration, Priam became all too aware that sickness could easily claim his fleshly cargo. Four young women had contracted smallpox on the trip to America and died within sight of the coast. The financial loss was great and caused Priam to reevaluate his business. With that in mind, he decided he would put aside that part of his industry after a few more shipments.

Five young Chinese girls, barely women, stood trembling before the men, awaiting their fatc. Welby had instructed Carl to tie them together earlier to avoid any escaping while Jessup made up his mind. Carl was standing near the enclosure where the girls were kept, looking just as annoyed at the length of time the transaction was taking.

"I believe things are in order," Anthony Jessup finally declared. "How long will you have . . . stock available ? I assure you Kansas City has never seen anything like this."

"I don't plan to be at this for much longer. Perhaps into the summer. After that I'm getting out," Priam told the man who stood at his side.

"That's a pity. I've heard wonderful things about your . . . inventory."

"I think you'll have to admit my girls are some of the loveliest." He looked to the man and smiled. "Do they suit your needs?"

"They are definitely a good start. The place I plan to open is going to be filled with exotic women from all around the world. Can you supply me with others?"

Welby motioned for Carl to take the women back to their locked room. "I believe I can. As I mentioned, I intend to receive a few more shipments." He motioned to Jessup. "Let's go upstairs to my office and discuss this. I'd like to know what you have in mind."

Jessup kept abreast as they walked toward the stairs. "I am opening an exclusive club in Kansas City. I want to have some of the most beautiful and yet unusual women in the world. I've seen women from India who were quite lovely. From the Scandinavian countries, too. Oh, and from Africa. I'm not talking about those blacks who have been slaves here in America. No, I've met some of the African women abroad. They are more subdued and obedient. Not to mention there are some truly beautiful women to choose from. Especially in Egypt."

"I understand." Priam led the man up the stairs and down the hall to his office. "Let's discuss the numbers."

Jessup nodded and took a seat opposite Priam's massive mahogany desk.

"Would you care for a cigar?" Welby opened a humidor, and Jessup reached inside.

"Nothing like a good cigar to smoke over business."

Priam took his seat and nodded. "I agree."

"Is that piece original?" Jessup asked, pointing to the Chinese statue Priam had kept for himself.

"Yes, it's from the Jin Dynasty. They call it *Guanshiyin.*"

Jessup nodded. "I'm familiar. I have quite a collection of pieces from around the world." The older man studied the piece a bit longer. "It isn't for sale, is it?"

"No, I'm afraid not. However, I have a great variety of pieces that are. After we conclude our business here, I'll take you to my warehouse. I think you'll find enough to interest you there."

"Sounds good to me." The man clipped his cigar. "As for the girls, I want the five you showed me downstairs. I'm also going to want at least another ten."

"That shouldn't be a problem. I'm expecting a new load of girls any day now. And I have made arrangements to bring in a few from India, so that should please you, as well. How long will you be in town?"

"I can stay as long as needed." The man lit his cigar. "Perhaps I can mix my business with pleasure while I wait. I have a room over at the Arlington Hotel. Maybe you could send some diversion my way?"

Priam chuckled. "For the right price, my good sir, I can send an entire harem your way."

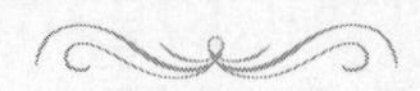

As April approached, the women at the Madison Bridal School had plans well underway for the June bridal ball. It had been decided some months earlier that this year the theme would be patriotic. The country hadn't added a new state to the union since Colorado in 1876, and in February, Congress passed an enabling act allowing for Montana, North and South Dakota, and Washington to seek statehood. The prospect excited Abrianna.

"I knew that once we got rid of that preposterous Mr. Cleveland," Aunt Selma declared, "God would once again bless this country."

"So true, Selma." Aunt Miriam nodded her agreement. "It would seem God has trouble with Democrats, just as we do."

Abrianna placed the eggs she'd just gathered on the counter. "The political party might not be so offensive to Him as is the nonsense each man brings along to clog up the works."

Aunt Poisie bobbed her head in agreement. "I was just reading the other day that President Harrison's wife has asked for a large amount of money to renovate the White House. She wants to put in more bathrooms. I fail to understand why two people need more bathrooms. The article stated there were already several bathrooms available in that grand building." She paused, looking quite confused. "You surely can't use more than one at a time."

"It's true," Aunt Selma agreed. "It would seem a waste to me."

"But it is 'the People's House,' as they call it. They have a great many people visiting the White House each year." Abrianna offered this, although she, too, felt that additional bathrooms were foolish.

Poisie gave a *tsk*ing sound. "I say save the money and put up an outhouse for extra visitors."

"Oh, I can hardly believe an outhouse would be acceptable for the president's yard," Aunt Miriam replied. She began to inspect the eggs. "I can't say that I see any purpose in renovation, however."

Abrianna shrugged. "I read that there is a terrible rodent infestation."

"A good cat or two would alleviate that problem," Aunt Poisie offered. "Do you suppose no one has thought to tell them that? I could write a letter."

The other two older women looked at her for a moment. Finally Aunt Miriam nodded. "That might be wise, Sister. Write and let them know that there are a great many economical ways to eliminate pests. Perhaps they've lived so long in the city that they've forgotten the simple things."

"And cats are so very nice to have on your lap in the winter," Aunt Selma added. "I do believe we should take up a few ourselves. After all, it would help with our own situation. I haven't seen the return of that mouse since earlier in the year, but that doesn't mean he isn't still around."

"Oh yes, Aunt Miriam. I would love to have a cat." Abrianna had always begged for pets while they lived downtown, but her aunts refused. It was far too dangerous, according to her aunts, for the animal might well escape the building and rush out into oncoming traffic.

"Then it seems we are all in agreement." Poisie clapped her hands. "I shall immediately look into it. We should have at least two. Perhaps I can find some for the president, as well." She grew thoughtful. "Do you suppose they would prefer tiger-striped?"

The delightful thought of getting a pet stayed with Abrianna throughout lunch at the food house. She stood humming and handing out bowls of soup and smiling on all who passed by. Even Wade noted her pleasant mood.

"Usually when a young lady acts this cheery, she has a secret. Do you have one to tell?" he whispered in her ear.

"If I did, it wouldn't be a secret once I told it." She chuckled. "But if I had a secret, you would be the first to know."

"Well, while you are never one for gloom, you seem far happier than usual, Abrianna."

"I am. My aunts have decided we are to get two cats. I've long wanted some pets, and this will suit me just fine. I had thought to seek solace with the cows and chickens, but they simply do not make good pets. I suppose if one had raised a cow from birth it might make an acceptable outdoor pet, but we certainly couldn't have a cow in the house."

"No, I don't think that would work under any circumstances. Although I do recall hearing about an old lady who kept chickens in her house."

"That would never bode well with Aunt Miriam. First, they would create quite a mess.

And then, once we had cats? I do suppose they might worry the chickens. Don't you think?"

"I do indeed. I'm certain that chickens and cats would not make for lasting friendships. Now tell me, how did this come about?"

She turned her attention to the man who'd come for soup. "Here you are, Captain Johnson. It's chicken and dumplings, just like you requested." Brianna pressed the bowl into the gnarled hands. Most of the seamen were missing fingers, sometimes two, but Captain Johnson was missing two on each hand and that, coupled with his age, made it difficult for him to grip. However, Abrianna wasn't about to shame him by offering to carry the bowl to the table. She'd made that mistake once before with another old sailor. It was best to let them handle the situation for themselves. She knew the men at the table would help him in a manner that wouldn't make him feel bad.

Turning back to Wade, she tried to remember what it was he'd asked. "Oh yes. You wanted to know about the cats. Well, we were having a discussion and one thing led to another. Aunt Poisie had read about renovations to take place at the White House. Apparently they need extra bathrooms. Although none of us could really imagine why.

"Then I mentioned that there was supposedly a rodent infestation, and we all decided a cat or two would surely handle the problem easily enough."

He looked confused. "But how does that account for Mrs. Madison getting cats for the school?"

Another group of men straggled up to the table. As they formed a line, each man picked up a piece of bread and waited for Abrianna to serve the soup. "We decided we could probably use a cat or two to ward off mice, and Aunt Poisie volunteered to find us some."

Ladling the thick soup into a bowl, Abrianna was pleased that she'd mastered the art of talking and serving at the same time. But oh, what would Aunt Miriam say about her pride? Goodness, she always had more lessons to learn. A thick dumpling plopped onto the tablecloth, as if to punctuate the point. A quick glance at Wade and the twinkle in his eye pushed Abrianna to continue her story and cover her embarrassment, lest they both break out into laughter. "Aunt Poisie also said she would see about securing the White House a couple."

"Did she now?" Wade stifled a laugh. "I'm sure Mrs. Harrison will appreciate that."

"You can never tell." She shrugged. "Many of those folks in the Capitol often seem not to have any idea of how to make the simplest decision."

Jay Bowes approached Abrianna with a smile. "You're lookin' like sunshine today, Miss Abrianna."

She noted her yellow gown, now protected by a large white apron. "I felt like wearing something bright and cheery to go along with our wonderful weather." She handed him a bowl. "I hope you like chicken and dumplings, but if you don't, I'm not sure what to tell you. We haven't yet seen the need to serve more than one kind of soup. I have considered it, though." She grew thoughtful. Serving more than one kind of soup each day would cause more problems than she cared to think about. They had no way to keep remaining food from going bad. Even if they managed to purchase a large icebox, the papers had made clear there was a shortage of ice in the city.

"Did you hear me?"

She startled. "What?"

Mr. Bowes laughed. "I said the kind of soup doesn't matter nearly as much as the company. I'm pleased to be here just for the honor of sharing a few words with you."

"You are very kind, Mr. Bowes. But I did notice you've been absent for several weeks. Might I inquire as to the reason? You weren't ill, were you?"

He scowled. "No, not ill. Just wrongly accused."

"Oh dear. What happened?"

Mr. Bowes shook his head. "The details aren't worth hearing for one so innocent as yourself. I was in the wrong place with the wrong people and got hauled off to the jail. I tried to explain that I had nothing to do with the dealings of the others, but the police wouldn't listen to me. It wasn't the first time this has happened to me."

"The company we keep is often our downfall." Abrianna had heard this from her aunts on more than one occasion. "We must be mindful of those people around us, lest we earn their reputation instead of being allowed to prove our own."

"That's the truth of it, Miss Abrianna. But a poor man like me doesn't get a lot of choices. I sleep where I can, and others do the same. Weren't my desire to sleep with thieves. One day I'll tell you a story about just such a mishap that kept me locked up for a very long time."

"I will look forward to it—if a person can look forward to such a tale of woe." She shook her head, wishing she could offer him more than a cup of soup. Goodness, but there were so many needs to be met. Maybe she could ask Kolbein and Lenore for additional money to open some sort of sleeping house. Then again, perhaps she could allow men to stay in the food house if they promised to leave come first light. She would have to discuss the idea with the others.

"Please do be careful, Mr. Bowes," she admonished. "I, that is we, won't hold against you the wrongful arrest, but as I said, we are known for the company we keep. You should try to find another place to sleep."

"And what does that say about you, Miss Abrianna? Are you known for the company of all these raggedy sailors and loggers? Men who haven't got a nickel to their name and have been down on their luck so long they don't remember what luck is?"

"Oh goodness, I hope so." She beamed him a smile. "What better company could I hope to be associated with? These men are God's children, and they are honorable and kind. I know they have issues and problems that cause sinful natures to rear up. Some of them fight and some speak in abominable ways, but they refrain when around me. I believe I am a good influence."

"I believe you are, too." He winked. "I know you are for me. You do this old heart of mine more good than you know. Just be careful who you go trustin'."

"I needn't be careful. My trust is in God alone. He has never let me down, and He never will."

The food house closed at one o'clock for cleaning. Thane decided the best thing for him to do was to dry dishes, since Militine had settled herself at the great sudsy pot of water. As they worked at washing and drying the food-house dishes, it was obvious she was troubled by something. Thane determined he would put her at ease by sharing something about his past. Something harmless. Something perhaps lighthearted. But nothing came to mind. His past was not exactly laden with lighthearted moments.

Wade and Abrianna were arguing at the front of the building over something to do with turning the food house into a hotel.

"I don't know why Wade argues with her," Thane began, hoping he could coerce Militine into a conversation. "Abrianna never listens to him, and she always gets her own way."

"I suppose he keeps hoping that one of these days things will change."

"I suppose you're right. I heard Abrianna mention getting some cats at the school. Do you like cats?"

Militine nodded and handed him a large platter. "I do. I had several when I was young. They were really rather wild little things, but they seemed to like me well enough to visit from time to time."

"I had two dogs. They were big and obnoxious. Their names were Rusty and Roper, and they were given to us when they were just pups. No one had any idea they would grow to be the size of ponies." He paused to note if she was listening.

A small laugh gave him all the encouragement he needed.

"I wasn't all that big. In fact, I was rather small for my age. When I'd come outside, they used to come running at me and would knock me on my backside every time. If I tried to run from them, that just made it all the worse."

"I suppose when you got older, they didn't do that."

He frowned. "I don't know. I left home when I was pretty young."

"Truly?" She passed a glass bowl and actually made eye contact. "How young?"

Should he tell her the truth? What if that just led to more questions? Thane squared his shoulders and dried the bowl. If he opened up to her, at least in part, perhaps Militine would know it was safe to tell her tale, as well.

"I was thirteen."

For several minutes neither one said anything. Militine passed additional bowls, and Thane dried them, but all the while he hoped he'd not ruined his only chance to draw her out. Finally she paused in her task.

"Thirteen is awfully young. You must have been scared."

"I was," he admitted. He wanted to shout for joy that she hadn't been afraid to share his secret. "I don't tell many people, but I feel like you and I are good enough friends that we can trust each other."

To his surprise Militine nodded. "I feel that way, too. I know you care and won't betray my trust. That's something I can't say about any other man."

"Just men?"

"Well, my experience with women has been quite different. My mother was a gentle woman I could trust with my deepest secrets. But she's gone now."

"My mother died just a few weeks after my thirteenth birthday," he told her.

"Was she ill?"

Once again he was on the horns of a dilemma. Did he tell her the truth and risk her rejection? Something inside him suggested that only by baring his soul could their relationship grow. Was that God's prodding? Wade was always saying that God's Spirit would nudge him on all sorts of matters. Was God's Spirit nudging him to be honest with Militine?"

"She wasn't ill," he finally said. He nearly dropped the slippery bowl she handed him. "She was murdered."

"What are you two whispering about back here?" Wade's voice made Militine jump. He came to stand beside her, shaking his head all the while. "I've been listening to Abrianna ranting and raving about finding beds for those without, and you two seem to be all private and cozy." He paused. "Should I come back at a better time?"

Militine cast Thane a sidewise glance and shook her head. "No. I was just thinking on the fact that the April reception at the school is next Saturday. I hate them, you know."

Wade laughed. "No. I hadn't heard."

"Well, I do." She turned back to the pot and began washing the silverware. "I have been desperate to figure some way out of having to attend."

"And I have come up with the perfect solution." Thane put the wet dish towel aside to dry and took up a fresh one. "I plan to ask Mrs. Madison if I might escort Militine to Denny Park. There's to be picnicking and a concert. It's to start late in the afternoon and run into the evening."

"I had heard there was to be a band concert, if it doesn't rain, of course. Sounds like fun."

"Well, perhaps you can come along, Wade. Abrianna too. We can catch the streetcar and take a picnic lunch. That is, if Militine will pack us one." He winked.

Wade nodded. "That does sound good. I'm almost sure Abrianna would like to go. Mrs. Madison wouldn't object to the four of us acting as chaperones for each other. I'll ask her about it." He walked off in the direction of where Abrianna was still wiping down tables.

For several long moments Thane said nothing. He wasn't at all sure what to say. He didn't want to refocus the conversation on the death of his mother, but he wanted Militine to know his gratitude. "Thank you for saying nothing to Wade."

She smiled. "Thank you for getting me out of the reception. At least I hope you meant what you said."

He returned the smile. "I did. I kind of like the idea of asking Mrs. Madison for an afternoon and evening in your company." He could look at her smile for the rest of his life. If only she'd let him in.

"So long as she doesn't try to force you into a formal courtship."

"And what would be wrong with that?"

Her eyes widened and her jaw dropped at his comment.

Thane laughed. "Don't look so surprised. You have to know I enjoy your company. I like the idea of courting you."

12

Whatever happened to that old trunk of costumes we used for the patriot celebration we had in 1885?" Mrs. Madison asked her niece. "It's already April, and we need to gather everything we'll need for the ball's decorations."

Militine looked to Abrianna, who appeared to be considering the matter in her diligent manner. If anyone knew where that trunk was, it would be Abrianna.

"I believe . . . yes, I'm almost certain we stored those costumes in the basement at the Madison Building. You don't suppose we forgot to bring them in the move?"

"Oh dear," Miss Poisie declared. "I would hate to think of our belongings lying to waste in Mr. Welby's care. I'm sure he couldn't possibly be bothered by such things." She stroked a long-haired calico she'd named Miss Muffy. The cat seemed most content on the older woman's lap.

Militine waited for someone to suggest the trunk could be retrieved. It was only a moment before Abrianna offered to do just that. The girl was always willing to brave the unknown for whatever she wanted.

But I've done likewise. I left the known for the unknown by coming here. And look at me now. I'm safe and relatively happy. She frowned. She hadn't thought of herself being happy before this moment.

"I believe we could make a side trip there on the way home from the food house." Abrianna reached down to pick up a gray cat whose black mustache had prompted Miss Poisie to name him Mr. Masterson. Militine thought it very interesting that Miss Poisie did so based on memories of a newspaper article about Bat Masterson. Miss Poisie told her that since Mr. Masterson too sported a black mustache and had killed several men, perhaps such a name would lend itself to encourage the tomcat to do likewise with mice.

"Militine?" Hearing her name pulled Militine out of her reverie.

"Oh yes. I'm sure a side trip would be possible."

Abrianna stroked the happy cat. "I'll just ask Wade to drive us there. He has his own wagon now. I think he tired of having to borrow one to take us and our food stock to the wharf. It's not all that big, but it should suffice for the trunk."

"If he agrees to go with you and Militine, I won't object," Mrs. Madison replied. "I would very much like to have those costumes returned. After all, with our bridal ball theme to be patriotic, it would be a waste of money to create new ones if the old will suffice."

Delight shone on Abrianna's face. Militine couldn't help but wonder if they were getting themselves into yet another of Abrianna's messes.

"Wade will be here to pick us up in fifteen minutes. I'll let him know of our need on the way to the food house."

"I have heard good things about your work there, Abrianna." Mrs. Madison rose from her chair. Her action startled Mr. Masterson, and he leapt to the ground and scurried from the room. In his place, the final of three cats Miss Poisie had secured sauntered into the room and rubbed up against Mrs. Madison's skirts. "Go on now, Buddy, I must work." The cat seemed unconcerned and continued to show her affection until Mrs. Madison bent down to scratch him behind the ears. Buddy had received his name from Mrs. Gibson, who, upon inspecting the gray tiger-striped cat, decided he would make a most congenial buddy.

With the cat satisfied by Mrs. Madison's attention, the old woman straightened. "As I was saying, I've heard good things about your work at the food house." She moved to a pile of mending that awaited attention. She chose a piece and returned to her seat. "Mrs. Bryant told me that her ladies' aid group was quite pleased by what you had accomplished. I believe they plan to send some small donation your way."

"That would be wonderful. I've had talks with several of the nearby businesses and have managed to get pledges for monthly help in the form of goods. I've been trying to talk the merchants out of blankets, as well. It would seem that so many of those penniless men have no decent place to rest, much less a blanket.

"In fact, I was hoping perhaps we might consider donating some of our older blankets to the cause," Abrianna said, looking at Mrs. Madison with an expression of innocent hope. "If only you knew how they suffer, Aunt Miriam. Those poor men are left exposed to the elements. Some even sleep on the ground, in the alleyways, or wherever they can go unnoticed. I told Wade I thought we should consider setting up cots at the food house. It's dry, at least, and they could stay there at night and leave come first light."

"So now you're to run a hotel?" Mrs. Madison shook her head. "Honestly, Abrianna, it's a wonder I'm not given to the vapors. You put me through such ordeals. Imagine what would be said if you were to open that place to bedding down rowdy sailors. No, I think it's already a huge compromise that I allow you and Militine to do what you do with the feeding."

Militine couldn't voice her opinion without offending Abrianna, but she wholeheartedly agreed with Mrs. Madison. There were times when she felt quite exposed to disparaging reminders of her childhood days at the trading post. Gruff, free-speaking men who drank more than their share of liquor were constant visitors. She preferred to have less to do with Abrianna's homeless men.

"But didn't Jesus himself say that whatever we do unto the least of these, we do unto Him?" Abrianna stood and clasped her hands to her breast. "Would you have our Lord sleep without a blanket? Sleep in the cold, snow-laden streets?"

Mrs. Madison rolled her eyes. "Honestly, Abrianna, you do make quite a scene. And furthermore, there is no snow for anyone to sleep in at this time of year."

Militine couldn't help but smile. She quickly looked away, lest anyone notice. Miss Poisie, however, let go a little snort of amusement that did not bode well with her sister.

"Do not encourage her, Sister. I will not have further bad said about our Abrianna."

At this Militine looked up. Abrianna's brow furrowed. "Bad? You just said that my efforts were praised. Did someone else say something bad about me?"

"I didn't want to make a fuss about it," Mrs. Madison declared. She turned her attention to the mending. "I'm afraid Pastor Walker was not complimentary about your involvement in such a project. He has spoken several times to me about how troubling it is."

Militine braced herself for Abrianna's ire. There was no way she would let this matter go without comment.

"Well, he ought to spend time studying for his sermons instead." Abrianna began to rant like a fire had been lit beneath her. "That man speaks week after week about one thing or another, and yet he seldom ever uses Scripture to back up what he says. Honestly, I'm not sure he even opens his Bible." She started to pace.

"How dare he say such unpleasant things about me? I'm answering a calling from God. I'm serving the poor. Wade is even leading a Bible study there, and the men are finally starting to attend in decent numbers. Pastor Walker—and I do use the term *pastor* with great reservation, for I've not seen or experienced anything that suggests the man can pastor—speaks for less than half an hour. I know this because I've timed him each Sunday. Pastor Klingle used to speak from the Bible for over an hour."

"God rest his soul." She looked to Miss Poisie, who was nodding.

"Amen," Abrianna said in unison with Mrs. Madison. "See, even Aunt Poisie knows it's true."

"I do not give Pastor Walker's concerns that much attention. You surely realize that if I did, I would have done something to stop you." Abrianna opened her mouth to speak, but Mrs. Madison raised her hand. "There is no need to offer further defense. I have already spoken to Wade, and he assures me that everything is as it should be."

"You spoke to Wade but not to me?"

Militine lowered her gaze to the floor. She knew Abrianna well enough to know that this was a most grievous offense.

"Goodness, Aunt Miriam, am I such a child that you cannot trust me to give you an honest answer?" Abrianna plopped into her chair as if the very thought of her aunt's action had taken the wind from her sails. "I am deeply and profoundly wounded."

"Well, I'm sure you will recover." Mrs. Madison gave her a smile. "However, for now you must collect your things. I believe I hear the wagon coming up the drive."

"Oh, my stars and garters!" Abrianna jumped up again, indeed appearing fully recovered.

"Abrianna, that is a most vulgar expression, and I will not allow it. I suppose this is the kind of thing you're learning from those sailors."

At this Abrianna laughed out loud. "Goodness, Aunt Miriam, the very thought threatens to send me into hysteria. I cannot see old Captain Johnson or Hairless Mike ever saying such a thing."

"Hairless Mike?" Miss Poisie said in a questioning manner. "Is he truly without hair? My, but that must be difficult in the winter months. Does he wear a cap?"

"He does," Abrianna replied. "But I'm sure he wouldn't have one if Pastor Walker had his way."

Militine followed Abrianna from the room. There was no sense even trying to comment on the conversation. Abrianna would no doubt go on and on about it throughout the day and have little need of anyone's response. Sometimes having a conversation with Abrianna was more like listening to one of Mrs. Madison's lectures. Abrianna didn't so much want anyone to interact as much as she wanted to make certain they knew her opinion.

As if to prove her right, Abrianna met Wade at the wagon and began to interrogate him. "Why didn't you tell me that Pastor Walker was speaking ill against me? For all our years as friends, I thought I could trust you to tell me when people were maligning my good character."

"Hello, Abrianna. I'm fine, thanks." Wade helped her into the wagon.

"Thank you. And I'm glad you're fine. Now, are you going to answer me?" She pointed to a basket of cabbage. "Don't forget that."

Wade came to assist Militine and afterward loaded the basket and crate that were to accompany them. He leisurely climbed into the wagon and picked up the reins. Without a word to Abrianna, he urged the horse to walk.

"Are you feeling deep guilt? Is that why you say nothing?" Abrianna pushed. "I do not hold any ill feelings against you for Pastor Walker's interference, but do tell me that you defended my honor."

"Oh, Abrianna, no one needs to defend you. You do quite enough on that count. However, if it makes you feel any better, I did tell

Pastor Walker that you were well supervised and protected from any harm."

"Supervised? Protected? That's all you told him?" She gave a heavy sigh. "It is truly a burden beyond measure to be me. As if having red hair isn't enough of a curse, I cannot even count on the defense of my friends in times of trouble."

Wade chuckled, which did not sit well with Abrianna. With a huff she crossed her arms and looked away from him. Militine could tell he was only amused at her pretense to give him the cold shoulder. However, after a few minutes of silence, Wade spoke.

"I am sorry that I didn't defend you in the way you believe I should have. I did do my best to point out to Pastor Walker that you were serving God by serving the poor. He doesn't have to understand your actions for them to be right. I don't know why you worry about what he thinks, anyway."

"Because he worries Aunt Miriam and the others with his constant complaints against me." She whirled back around. "Don't you see, Wade? He doesn't like me, so he figures to put a stop to my ministry."

Wade gave her a stern look. "Your ministry? I thought it was God's."

Abrianna closed her eyes. "Yes. You are right. I am wholly out of line. Goodness, but the man so upset my senses that I have been given to wrong thinking. Forgive me." She straightened and looked toward the sky. "God, please forgive me. Of course it is your ministry. It might be my calling, but it has always and ever been your ministry."

To hear her friend so quickly humble herself impressed Militine. Abrianna might be the first to head into trouble, but she was always good to yield to correction. Well, at least when she could see that she was in error. Militine admired her for that. The very idea of admitting to such a thing was yet another area that left Militine feeling vulnerable. In time, she hoped she might be able to be as willing to give in to such a point as was her friend.

Of course, maybe such humbling required a better relationship with God. It bore some consideration.

Hours later, Abrianna was still fuming over the pastor's unkind remarks. Her frustration was such that she hadn't even bothered to get Wade's help in accompanying her and Militine to the Madison Building. Now they had to deal with Mr. Welby's man without Wade's protection, and for once she questioned her decision.

"Mr. Welby ain't here," a tall man with

brown hair and a scar on his forehead told Abrianna and Militine. He leered. "I'm sure I could help ya."

Abrianna looked past him to the closed office that Lenore's father had once occupied when the bridal school had resided upstairs. "Do you know when he'll return?"

"No. Why don't you tell me what you need." He let his gaze travel the length of her body.

"There is a trunk of costumes that my aunt believes was left behind in the basement. If you would allow us, we can just make a quick search and be gone. However, I suppose if the trunk is found, we might need you to carry it upstairs for us."

"I can't allow you in the basement." He scowled and his lewd nature faded. "Ain't no one allowed down there. Got some repairs going on."

"I suppose we can return another time. We do need that trunk, and it would certainly put Mrs. Madison in your debt if you were to at least look for the trunk."

"I tell you what. Once you go, I'll be happy to go downstairs and take a look. I've been down there many a time and can't say I've ever seen any sign of a trunk, but I'll search it out."

With nothing else to be done, Abrianna nodded. "Thank you. Please tell Mr. Welby we were here."

"He ain't often here, but I'll tell him if I see him," he called after them.

Once they were outside Abrianna was surprised when Militine touched her arm. "We should go back to Wade's and get him to take us home."

"Nonsense. He would only question me as to what I've been doing. We can catch a streetcar. I have the coins."

They hurried up the street and across the intersection to wait for the streetcar. Abrianna once again allowed her thoughts to go to what the pastor had said. His remarks were uncalled for, and she felt new determination to make certain he knew exactly what she thought on the matter.

"Thane wants to court me."

A bustle of people momentarily separated them. Abrianna looked at Militine and shook her head. "I'm not sure I heard you right."

"Thane wants to court me."

Two men tipped their bowler hats and hurried past the girls, giving Abrianna a moment to consider the comment. "I do not know whether to be happy for you or alarmed. You've told me on more than one occasion that you do not intend to marry. It was our secret."

"I know. I'm not suggesting that I would marry, but I rather like the idea of courtship."

"But courtship is set aside for the ultimate

goal of marriage. Courting without marriage in mind would be like planting potatoes with no thought of eating them."

"But courtship doesn't always work out." Militine pointed down the street. "The street-car's coming."

They boarded and Abrianna paid the toll before they took seats toward the back. Uncertain how she should respond, Abrianna reached out to pat Militine's arm. "Whatever you decide, you know I am a faithful friend. I will neither condemn you for your choice nor advise you toward it. I will simply support you either way. I know from experience that I am given to doing things in an unconventional way, and I cannot fault you for desiring to do the same."

"Thank you, Abrianna. No one has ever been so accepting of me or my choices."

On Sunday, Abrianna could hardly contain herself as Brother Mitchell rose to give the benediction. It hadn't been easy to sit for the short sermon Pastor Walker had given, nor to sing every verse of the final hymn with the rest of the congregation. Pastor Walker finally left the pulpit and moved down the aisle to the back of the church. It was his habit to greet the parishioners as they exited the building, and today was no different.

Abrianna slipped out while the pastor was occupied with one of the elders who seemed to have quite a bit to say. The day outside was fair, and most of the congregants seemed happy to mingle on the church lawn and catch up on news with their friends. Abrianna was determined to have a word with Pastor Walker, but first she needed to assess the situation and determine if there was enough time. She knew that Aunt Miriam was off in search of Aunt Poisie, who had told her of some problem in the children's Sunday school. Abrianna overheard Aunt Miriam instruct Aunt Selma to gather the others to wait for their return, so they could all walk home together. This gave Abrianna the perfect, if not God-appointed, time to berate Pastor Walker for his maligning comments. But she would have to wait until he was alone. There was no sense in humiliating him publicly. Even if he was given to speaking ill of her to others.

When the last man bid the minister good day, Walker started back inside the church. Abrianna approached him with what she hoped was a look of confidence. "Pastor Walker."

He turned back, looking reluctant. "Good day, Miss Cunningham."

"No, it is not a good day, and you are the reason." He appeared shocked by her outburst, but she didn't allow that to deter her. "You have been given to the sin of gossip and dissension."

"I beg your pardon?"

"You should. How dare you approach my family with your so-called concerns about my work with the poor? You have no right to condemn me. I am answering a call upon my life and will continue to do so whether you understand such a thing or not. It's no different from what Deborah did in the Bible. That's found in Judges, just in case you are confused." His eyes widened and mouth fell open.

"Apparently you aren't used to seeing people follow the Scriptures. I think in all the weeks I've listened to you preach, you've only quoted the Bible on three occasions. Instead, we've been forced to hear stories of a personal nature that seldom correlate to Scripture and often upset old ladies' sleep."

"Now just a minute, Miss Cunningham. You are at fault to speak to a man of God in such a manner. I spoke to your aunts out of concern for your well-being. Not only that, but as far as the Bible is concerned, you should not be in a position of leading men."

"I'm not leading them. I'm feeding them, something the church should be doing. Perhaps it is foolish to speak to you about this. It might be better for me to take it up with the deacons and elders. After all, they know me and my heart. You have been here for only a couple of months and apparently have decided to judge my actions with no regard to the fruit being produced."

"I have to say, Miss Cunningham, I did consider the matter, and that is why I spoke with Mrs. Madison. It is not appropriate for a young unmarried woman to display herself in such a manner. You put yourself in grave peril, and risk not only your reputation but your life."

She couldn't help but smile. A calm came over her that Abrianna hadn't expected. "Such things are only of this world, Pastor Walker. The Bible makes it clear that we needn't worry about those who can take our lives but not our souls. I am not afraid to die. However, I would be afraid to face my God and not have done all that He gave me to do."

"You are an arrogant woman, Miss Cunningham. Furthermore, I know very well what the Bible makes clear. I know more about what is in this book," he said, holding up the Bible, "than you could ever know."

"I didn't realize it was a contest. Seems to me your job is to teach the Word so that all in your congregation might know. If you believe there is a deficit, perhaps you should search your own soul for the reason."

His mouth dropped open, and it seemed words were stuck in his throat.

Abrianna knew she had no need to further chide this man. It was obvious he felt the impact of her statement. She walked from the church with a peace she hadn't thought possible. Perhaps the confrontation was uncalled for. For certain her actions done out of anger had been wrong. She prayed God would forgive her for allowing her temper to get the best of her. However, now instead of anger, she just felt sorry for Pastor Walker. There was something of a void in his spirit. She could sense it but not truly understand it. Perhaps God would show her in time. If not, it didn't matter. Only the truth did. Of course, the truth might include her aunts learning about what had just transpired, and then she would have to smooth those troubled waters.

"It simply isn't easy being me," she murmured to herself.

13

Why is he here?" Abrianna asked Lenore. She cast a side glance across Lenore's parlor to where Kolbein Booth and Wade were entertaining Pastor Walker.

"Kolbein wanted to invite him to dinner, since we hadn't yet hosted him in our home. I thought having you and Wade here would round the number out nicely and give us a time to chat. Honestly, Abrianna, what have you against the man?"

"He is a thorn in my flesh." Abrianna smoothed out the elegant satin of her gown's skirt and sighed. "I do not wish to say anything more."

"Now, that is a surprise. I don't think I've ever known those words to come from your lips."

"It wouldn't do any good to speak on the matter. Suffice it to say, we have our differences. I'm praying fervently for the man. He seems to need it."

"I honestly know very little about the him. I can't say that I enjoy his preaching as much as I did Pastor Klingle's, but I suppose every minister has his own style."

"And agenda."

The butler came to announce supper, and Lenore and Abrianna rose. Lenore moved to stand beside her husband. "Might you offer a prayer of thanksgiving?" she asked Pastor Walker.

Abrianna grimaced but bowed her head. Pastor Walker gave a short blessing, much to her relief. She wanted most fervently to hold her tongue for Lenore's sake, if for no one else's.

When he concluded, Lenore took hold of his arm. "I would be honored to have you escort me in to dinner."

Abrianna stiffened at the sight of her dear friend on the arm of the pastor. She had to give her feelings of frustration over to the Lord. To do otherwise would only prompt sin in her heart. *Please, Lord, help me to see the good in this man.*

"You've been awfully quiet, Abrianna. Are you ill?" Kolbein asked as he offered his arm.

She took hold. "I'm quite fine, just deep in thought. There are a great many things on my mind these days."

"I wouldn't expect it to be otherwise." Kolbein led her to the dining room. He assisted her into a beautifully carved mahogany chair before leaning down to whisper, "Try to behave yourself."

She looked at him and caught a wink. "I will endeavor to do nothing that will shame you or Lenore." She looked across to Wade, who was now seated. He smiled but said nothing. He looked quite handsome in his black suit. Unlike Pastor Walker, who was wearing the same boring gray suit that he preached in every Sunday. Goodness, but couldn't the man dress in black like most respectable ministers? And that mustache of his was abominable. He should preach with a clean-shaven face, lest others think he had something to hide.

She shook her head. She was again allowing thoughts of the man's shortcomings to occupy her thoughts. *God, help me to move beyond such thinking.*

"I do want to thank you and Mrs. Booth for having me to your home for dinner. I am eager to know you better," Pastor Walker said as a servant placed the first course in front of him. "My, what beautiful china and silver."

"Thank you," Lenore replied. "They were wedding gifts from my parents."

"You come from a wealthy family?"

Everyone around the table looked surprised except for the man who'd posed the question. It was appalling bad manners to speak of finances in public, but apparently he didn't realize this.

Kolbein took charge of the matter. "Her father is now retired, but in his younger years he was a prosperous businessman. Now, I understand that you are new to the Northwest. What prompted you to leave such a warm climate as Texas?"

Abrianna sampled her soup and tried not to act as though she cared in the least what Walker had to say. The delicate flavors of the leek soup were soothing to her stomach, which had been in knots since arriving to find the pastor in attendance.

"The climate is of no concern," Pastor Walker replied. "When God calls you to a place, you must obey." He tasted his soup and then picked up a piece of bread on the dish to his left. With no concern for table manners, he tore the piece up and plopped it into the bowl to soak up the liquid.

No one said a word, and while the silence was most uncomfortable, Abrianna knew better than to promote a topic of conversation.

For several awkward minutes they did nothing but eat. Finally the servants arrived with the next course, a buttery fish served atop steamed asparagus. There was no telling what the Texan would do with this.

"I have to say your cook does a wonderful job," Pastor Walker praised. "However, I am accustomed to much simpler fare. I'm afraid the wages earned by a man of God are often quite inadequate."

Kolbein cut into his fish and, without looking to meet the man's gaze, said, "I find the meal to be perfect." He gave Lenore a smile. "You have outdone yourself in the planning, my dear."

"Of course such finery as you have here could go a long way to benefiting the church and spreading the gospel. The setting on the table is a thing of beauty, but providing adequate funding to do God's work is perhaps more honorable. Your church has a great many needs, and the proper funds could benefit the congregation and make my living arrangements much better. For example, the silver you have here. There is quite a bit of it, and I assume the value of such is high."

Lenore coughed into her napkin, and Abrianna shook her head in protest. "Sir, you offend with this constant discussion of money."

"I would think you might be on my side

where this subject is concerned," Pastor Walker declared. "After all, you seek support for that food house you have. Think of the money that could be offered on behalf of the poor should wealthy people live more simply. If more money were provided the church, we might not have need for our fairer sex to be doing business on the wharfs."

Wade looked to Abrianna and shook his head. She knew it was his unspoken warning to say nothing more, but she couldn't help it. Pastor Walker made her ministry sound like she was instead running a brothel.

"I trust in God to provide for the needs of His ministries. I answered the call prior to there even being financial support. I find that when we obey God, He always provides. Not only that, but you did agree to a particular salary and provision when you took on the pulpit of our church."

"While that is true, Miss Cunningham, I did so on the assurance of God that the small wages would soon be increased to better support my needs."

"I'm sorry, Pastor Walker," Kolbein interjected, "but I do not approve of such a discussion over dinner. You and I can speak more at length about these things afterward. As a deacon of the church, I feel confident that we can look into any concern you might have."

Walker speared a stalk of asparagus and drew it to his lips. He was completely undaunted. "I must say, asparagus has never been a favorite of mine. I would think a good potato might serve better."

"Potatoes are not served with fish, Pastor Walker. However, if you would rather, I can have your asparagus removed," Lenore offered.

"I cannot bear this," Abrianna declared as she sprang to her feet. "Such rudeness shouldn't be tolerated. This man is a guest in your house, and yet he acts with far less manners than the men I serve on the docks."

Kolbein rose. "Abrianna, please don't let this ruin your time with us. It is apparent that Pastor Walker isn't used to formal dinners. Let us be considerate and advance him some grace for his indiscretions." He helped her retake her seat. Turning to Walker, he added, "Perhaps we might speak on a lighter subject."

Something was mentioned about the uncommonly nice weather, and then someone else brought up the beautiful abundance of flowers blooming in the parks and neighboring lawns. Abrianna began to relax a bit. The last thing she wanted to do was make things difficult for Lenore and Kolbein. Aunt Miriam had always said that if a person couldn't say something nice about or to someone, then perhaps it was best to say nothing at all. It was a most difficult proposition for Abrianna, so she kept her mouth full of food in order to stave off words.

By the time the servants cleared the table for dessert, it appeared that Pastor Walker finally understood appropriate dinner conversation. He complimented Kolbein and Lenore on their home without any reference to money and then shared some of his insights about the city of Seattle. Everyone seemed less guarded as the desserts were set on the table. But the peace was not to last. Once the chocolate-rose pound cake had been topped with a warm cream sauce and served to each person, the conversation once again plunged headlong into dangerous waters.

"Wade, how are things going with your Bible study on Daniel?" Lenore asked.

"Very well. We have nearly twenty men who attend each Thursday evening. I must say at first I wasn't at all certain it would be something the men would want to attend. Most are hardened, grizzled men, whose lives have been lived around superstition and self-determination. At first, I think they came to get out of the cold and damp, but now they seem to be genuinely interested. We had a rousing conversation about King Nebuchadnezzar last week."

"Am I to understand that you, a common layman, are teaching the Word of God?" Pastor Walker looked quite disapproving.

"I am," Wade replied.

"Wade is an elder at the church, so he's hardly just a layman," Kolbein offered.

"I'm sorry, but I disagree about your doing such a thing. You come under my authority, and I have given no such permission to teach, nor would I. You have no formal training and cannot possibly understand the Bible. That is why you have a minister to interpret it for you."

Abrianna nearly spit chocolate cake from her mouth. She forced the bite down and quickly took up the water goblet to keep from choking.

"I didn't see any reason to seek your approval." Wade's expression suggested that he was more than willing to take the pastor's objections head on. "As I helped Abrianna with the food house, it came to me that perhaps some of these men—men I might add who've been rejected as acceptable by many of the churches—would find encouragement in the Word of God. I prayed on the matter and felt God wanted me to offer teaching in our casual setting, where the men might feel comfortable and welcome."

The pastor shook his head. "No. That is not acceptable. You are not ordained to teach the Word. You have no background or education."

"I beg to differ with you, Pastor Walker." Wade very slowly put his fork down. "I have studied God's Word since I was a boy. I learned Greek and Latin in my studies and from time to time have even sought out guidance in Hebrew from a local rabbi. I've not only read the Bible but have also studied a variety of commentaries and listened well to the sermons given over the years by Pastor Klingle. It was he who first convinced me that we needed no formal education in order to share God's love and the gospel message. After all, Jesus said to go into all the world and preach the gospel, and my little part of the world has a need that I am seeking to fill."

"That was spoken to the eleven disciples who were with Jesus after His resurrection," the pastor countered. "That was not given to you."

"I believe it was given to all of us who call ourselves children of God," Wade countered. "Otherwise, how do you explain Paul and others who taught?"

"They were given direct teaching from the disciples and then those taught and trained others in the truth. It was a specific gift given first to the disciples by Jesus and then by the disciples to additional disciples and so forth.

It is the lineage of the priesthood. You are not of that lineage, Mr. Ackerman, and therefore you must cease what you are doing."

"You're wrong!" Abrianna could no longer refrain. "We are all disciples of Jesus and gifted by the Holy Ghost to serve the body and others. How dare you!"

Lenore burst into tears and fled the room, prompting Abrianna to go after her. As much as she wanted to stay and give Pastor Walker a further piece of her mind, she wanted more to offer comfort to her friend.

"Lenore, stop." Abrianna hurried down the hall to catch up with the tearful woman. "I apologize if my outburst caused you pain, but that man had ruffled my last feather."

"It's not you. My dinner is ruined," she sobbed, falling into Abrianna's arms. "Utterly ruined. How can that man say such contrary things? I do not pretend to know the Bible as well as he, but it would seem to me that his attitude is not very loving."

Abrianna hugged Lenore and then pulled back a bit in order to see her face. "He's wrong. Jesus asks all of us to be living witnesses of God's love. We are all ambassadors called to share the truth. Pastor Walker is wrong to believe he alone has that calling." She glanced back down the hall. "I feel confident your husband and Wade will make certain Pastor

Walker hears the truth. I pray also that Kolbein will escort him from the house and tell him never to return, but that's just my own personal desire."

"It's mine, as well," Lenore said, pulling a lacy handkerchief from her sleeve. "Oh, Abrianna, I do apologize. You told me how argumentative he could be. I thought perhaps it was just because . . . well . . . because you are outspoken . . . for a woman."

Abrianna nodded. "That I am, but I assure you that is not where my misgivings regarding that man were borne. He has done nothing but offer false teaching and unsound doctrine, and I believe it is time the deacons and elders are apprised the situation. I hope Kolbein and Wade will approach them. I'm certain that their opinion would hold more weight than ours."

Lenore dried her eyes and dabbed the cloth to her nose. "He seems to be such a vulgar man. I do not understand all his focus on money."

"Perhaps he is like that man who stole offerings from the church in Tacoma," Abrianna said, then immediately regretted it. "I apologize. I am angry and should not make false judgments. If Pastor Walker is doing anything underhanded, it will be realized in time. Until then, my hope is that when his six-month trial period is up, the elders will dismiss him and find someone else to lead our church."

Kolbein came down the hall just then, and Lenore made her way to him immediately. "Did you ask him to leave?"

"Yes. What a pompous man. I am so sorry I encouraged you to host him here. I've had better behavior out of my sister's theatre friends." He looked to Abrianna. "Wade is waiting to take you home. I told him I thought it best we conclude the evening."

"I understand. I would expect no less." She came to Lenore and gave her a kiss on the cheek. "I love you most dearly, Lenore. Please do not give that man another thought."

"I shan't," she promised, then paled. "Oh dear, we will have to see him again on Sunday."

"No we won't," Kolbein declared. "I do not intend to sit under his teaching anymore. I had found very little positive in my experience of churches until meeting Pastor Klingle, and now I find myself back to the same opinion."

"But no one leaves the church of their youth." Lenore shook her head.

"It is not the church of my youth, and that man's attitude leaves a bad taste in my mouth."

"Oh, Kolbein, do not say you'll never attend church again," Abrianna said, touching his arm. "Not every man who claims himself to be a preacher is like Pastor Walker. Don't despair and turn away from God."

"I have no intention of turning away from God, Abrianna. Just from Pastor Walker."

She shook her head in sorrow. "But if we do not fight for our church, who will?"

Wade held his silence as he walked Abrianna back to her home. The damp evening air further dampened his mood. He wanted to talk over the events of the night, but he had no desire to get Abrianna worked up by speaking about his anger. Thankfully, she seemed to understand.

"I was sorry that the rain last week kept us from our picnic. I would very much have enjoyed missing out on the monthly reception, but I'm also intrigued by Thane and Militine's courtship. Do you suppose anything can come of it? Militine has never had a true interest in marriage. Of course you mustn't say anything, or Aunt Miriam might send her from the school."

"I won't," he promised.

"And then there's the matter of the June seventh bridal ball. A patriotic theme will require a great deal of red, white, and blue. Aunt Miriam has taken advantage of the situation to teach the young ladies how to dye cloth without staining their hands in the process." She paused and shook her head. "It has not been completely successful."

He halted at the bottom of the steps that led up the long walkway to the house. "I'm sorry for being so out of sorts."

She shook her head. "You did nothing wrong. God will bless you for your desire to share the Word, and I, for one, am very proud of you." She stretched up on tiptoe and kissed his cheek. "You are a good and faithful man, Wade, and I'm proud to call you my friend."

He smiled against his will. Abrianna could always bring a smile from him, whether due to her zany antics or her long-winded soliloquys. He loved her company. Loved the way she trusted God. Loved her. But where would that love lead him? She seemed completely oblivious to his heart. It hadn't been easy to accept that he had gone from loving her as a zany little sister to a potential mate for life.

"Do you ever think about what you will do with the rest of your life?" The question left his lips before he had time to consider how it might sound.

"Of course. I hope to continue doing whatever it is God has for me to do. I certainly don't want to run the bridal school, as Aunt Miriam wishes."

"What about marriage and a family of your own?"

She shrugged. "I don't know. I haven't seen that God has called me to that as of yet. Paul did say to the unmarried and widows that it was good for them to abide even as he had."

He also said it was better to marry than to burn. Wade pushed the thought aside. "But wouldn't you like to have children of your own, a husband to care for?"

"What a strange conversation for us to have." She shook her head. "I try not to long for anything. God knows I longed for many years to have my mother and father returned to me. Instead, He taught me the value of love through my aunts. Their kindness and generous charity has been richer for me than many ever know. I am content to trust that if God has a husband and children for me, He will bring them to me." She drew a deep breath. "Now I must go inside and explain the evening to my aunts. Goodness, but I do not look forward to Sunday."

"I think I might go to the Lutheran church. What with Pastor Swanson being a close friend of Pastor Klingle, I thought I'd ask him some questions and seek his counsel. I don't intend to just hand over our church to a man like Walker. Even so, I want to approach this in a manner that is biblical."

"That seems very wise of you, Wade. I will pray for you to have peace about this." She kissed his cheek once again. "Good night."

"Good night, Abrianna."

He watched her make her way up the stairs and across the lawn. Once she was in the house, he let out a heavy sigh. How was he supposed to share his feelings with her, knowing that she wanted to serve God rather than a husband? Could there ever be room in her life for both? After all, he wanted to serve God, as well.

14

May had warmed the area with unusually high temperatures and little rain. Unfortunately, both contributed to an increased number of fires. Thane helped gather the long fire hose with his fellow firemen. His arm muscles ached from the process of hand pumping water, and his eyes and throat still burned from the thick smoke. The blaze they'd been called to hours ago was caused by an improperly vented stove. The fire had spread so fast and the water supply was so insufficient that there had been little they could do but watch the house disintegrate before their eyes. Nothing had ever been quite so discouraging. After all, they were there to save, yet they could do nothing.

All he wanted now was a hot bath and a

cold drink. After a long day of work to repair the hull of a small fishing boat, the firefight had left him with barely enough energy to make the walk home.

Despite his weariness, Thane's mind churned with burdensome thoughts. For some time they'd nagged and troubled him. Militine had agreed to court him, and while they had enjoyed a couple of rather awkward outings with Miss Poisie, he knew he would have to come clean and tell Militine about his past. That was, if they were to turn this courtship into something more permanent.

He turned down Front Street, but instead of making his way home, Thane found himself heading for Wade's. He knew his friend would probably be working late. With the four hours of each day taken to help Abrianna feed the poor, Wade generally needed the evening hours to complete his work. The only exception was his Thursday night Bible study.

Seeing the light in the shop and hearing rhythmic hammering, Thane knew a sense of peace. Wade always seemed to have the answer to his problems, and now more than ever, he needed those answers. There was so little in his life that made sense.

He let himself into the shop, and the hammering stopped. "It's just me, Wade. Got a minute?"

His friend popped out from the back. “Sure. I was going to work another hour or two, but you give me a good excuse to stop early.” He wiped his hand against the leather apron and then untied it. “Looks like you’ve been to a fire.”

“Yeah. It wasn’t worth the trouble, though. The house was a total loss. We just didn’t have the water we needed to fight the blaze. I know the city council understands the problem, but no one seems inclined to do anything about it.”

“Give ’em time. Eventually one of their houses will catch fire, and then they’ll move faster.”

“I hope it doesn’t come to that. It’s a terrible thing to watch a man’s whole life go up in flames. The family got out, but with just the clothes on their backs. There wasn’t anything else left to them. We took up a collection amongst ourselves and gave them enough money to get a room for the night. Hopefully, there will be others who lend them some aid.” He shook his head. “But I didn’t come here to commiserate over that.”

“Then what?” Wade hung his apron on a peg and motioned to the door of his living quarters. “Coffee?”

“I’d rather have a good old glass of water, the colder the better. I’m parched.”

"Hey, you're in luck. I actually have a little ice. I'll chip some off for you."

"That would be great." Thane followed Wade to the back of the shop. He drew the handkerchief from around his neck and wiped his face and hands. Seeing the amount of soot left behind on the cloth made him all the more determined to seek out a bath.

"So what did you want to talk about?"

Thane took a seat while Wade went to get an ice pick. "You know I asked Militine if I could court her."

"Sure. And she said yes."

"She did, but she also knows that I have a bad past. I haven't told her everything, but I think I need to in order for us to have any chance at a future."

"So tell her." Wade went to work on the ice. "I don't see a problem. It's not like you did anything to cause what happened."

Thane eased back against the wooden chair. "I know, but maybe if I'd said something about my father to the authorities, my mother would still be alive. When I start thinking about all the mistakes I made, well, then I think I'm crazy to consider courting anyone. What if I turn out to be just like my pa? That's what most people figured."

Wade gathered the ice in a glass and poured in water from a pitcher. He brought the glass to

Thane and then returned to put the ice back in the icebox. "I think it's a dangerous thing to try to second-guess what might have been or what might be." He went to the stove and tapped the coffeepot. "It's cold." He shrugged and went to work to build a fire. "I meant to keep a closer check on this."

Thane gulped down the water. The cold liquid eased the burning in this throat and helped to cut the taste of ash. He set the glass on the table only to have Wade pick it up and refill it with water. Smiling, he put it down in front of Thane again.

"You want something to eat?"

"No. I just need to talk."

Wade nodded and pulled up a chair. "So talk."

"Some of the things you've said to me in the past—about God—have really been making me think. I guess I want to ask how you can be so sure that God really is who you think He is."

Wade shrugged. "Since I was old enough to remember, I heard stories about God and how good He was and how He loved me. I heard folks say it was important to trust Him and to repent from wrongdoing. When I was old enough to read for myself, I could see a lot of me in the lives of some of those people who did wrong. I didn't like it much.

"Pastor Klingle told me that we were all pretty much the same in the eyes of God—sinners who need a Savior. He told me that to God sin was sin and He hated it. Man was sinful and God hated that man chose to go on doing wrong, even though He'd sent Jesus so that we could be reconciled to Him. The older I got, the more I saw evidence of God, not only in the Bible but in real life. When my ma got sick and pa prayed about what to do, he felt certain God was telling him to move away from Seattle, but he didn't know where to go, so he prayed some more. Then one day when he was talking to the doctor the answer came. The doc said Ma needed a drier climate and suggested a place in California. Pa took her there, and she immediately got better."

"But that was the doctor telling him where to go."

"But who told the doctor?" Wade smiled. "I think it was all in God's hands, and He directed Pa's steps and the doctor's advice. There's been a lot of times in my life like that."

Thane couldn't discount Wade's beliefs. After all, it was Wade's confidence in God that drew Thane there in the first place. "But you've never had to deal with anger like mine. I swear it threatens to eat me alive some days. It makes me afraid that I'll turn out to be a killer like my father."

"God can deal with that anger, Thane. You don't have to wrestle it by yourself. Anger is a spiritual battle. Only Satan benefits from such rage and violence. It's not what God wants for you. Besides, you aren't your father, and you don't need to fear his actions will be yours. You saw a lot of violence growing up, but you don't have to be violent because of it."

"How do I explain this to Militine without scaring her away? She had to live with an angry father. I can tell. She said he was strict and harsh. I'm afraid when I tell her about my father and all the things he did—the things I saw and said nothing about—well, I'm afraid she'll worry that I'm just like him, or will be."

Wade shrugged. "I can't tell you what to do, but I've known you for a long time, Thane. I've seen how you treat folks, even when you are upset by their actions. You aren't a violent man like your pa. Fact is, I don't think you're nearly so angry as you are afraid."

The words slammed into Thane like a freight train. He *was* afraid. Afraid the past would catch up with him. Afraid of being like his father. Afraid that no one could ever love him.

"I saw my father kill men over stupid games of cards. I saw him kill, and I said nothing when the sheriff came and demanded answers."

"You were a child, and you didn't have a lot

of options. Besides, there's no way of knowing if they would've listened to you. And if they didn't, then you would have had your father to contend with. We both know he wouldn't have let that go unpunished. I can't say that I blame you for saying nothing. You had to protect yourself."

Thane took a long drink. He turned the glass in his hands, as if there might be something there to see. "Pastor Klingle once said that even a child was known by his doings. I should have done something more. If I had, my mother might be alive today."

"Maybe." Wade released a long sigh. "We all have our regrets, Thane. But even those can be given over to the Lord. God knows I've given Him plenty."

For several minutes those words echoed in Thane's ears. If only he could believe. If only all those things were true—the Bible, God's love, forgiveness. Was it possible? Could he really find a way to be rid of the pain of the past? Could he be redeemed? "I really want to believe," Thane finally said. "I'm so tired. I've been carrying this burden since I was thirteen, and it gets heavier with each passing year."

Wade smiled, his intense eyes meeting Thane's. "Then maybe it's time to give it over to God."

The last person in the world Abrianna expected to see at their weekly baked goods sale was Priam Welby. Yet there he was, waltzing across the park lawn like a man with a purpose. He spoke with several of the young ladies and purchased a variety of baked goods, but all the while he continued looking around. It was clear he was looking for someone. Abrianna had the dreaded feeling she was that someone. When Welby caught sight of her and his smile broadened, Abrianna knew her assumption was right.

Instead of going to him, however, Abrianna moved away. No matter what he had come to say to her, she was almost certain she didn't need to hear it. She worked her way through the bridal students and then backtracked. With any luck at all, she could hide behind a tree until he gave up looking for her. She positioned herself behind a maple and waited.

"Why, Miss Cunningham, you look quite lovely."

He'd found her. Abrianna turned and met his amused expression. "Thank you."

"I have always thought that this particular shade of material looked remarkable in contrast to your lovely hair." He took off his hat and swept a bow in greeting.

Abrianna glanced down at the peach-colored gown overlaid with a fine white muslin.

"To which shade are you referring—the peach or the white?"

He chuckled and replaced his hat. "Both combine to accentuate your beauty."

"Goodness, but you're full of flowery words today. I know better, however, than to believe you. I learned a long time ago that when men start saying things to tickle your fancy, they're up to something. I suppose you've come with some purpose?"

"Indeed I have. First, to commend you for your work on the docks. I have to admit I thought perhaps it would be folly. After all, those men are generally lacking in manners and are often given to brawling. They have such a fondness for drink that I found it hard to believe they would remain sober long enough to come for a hot meal. I'm glad to have been proven wrong."

"Some of them do show up a bit into their cups, but we just see to it that they have plenty of hot coffee. I don't understand how a man can drink, anyway, but how he can do it so early in the day is beyond me completely. Aunt Miriam once gave me a hot toddy when I was sick and the taste was abominable."

He chuckled. "I do not believe liquor was created with the fairer sex in mind. That aside, you can be proud of what you've accomplished, Miss Cunningham."

His voice was smooth like Aunt Miriam's prized caramel when it was first poured from the pan. And probably just as dangerous. In the case of the caramel just off the fire, it was extremely hot and burned the tongue. Abrianna knew this firsthand. And with Priam Welby—well, who could be certain of anything where that man was concerned?

Even so, she wasn't a fool to be puffed up by his words of praise. Priam Welby was a man of purpose. She'd seen him in action too many times to suppose he'd come here with the sole purpose of complimenting her.

"So what else brought you here today? Surely not your sweet tooth."

He eyed her momentarily then gave her a look that caused Abrianna to flush. He was such a cad and didn't care at all what anyone observing him might think. She took a step back and felt the trunk of the tree press against her. Unfortunately, Priam Welby took that opportunity to move closer, very nearly pinning her in place.

"I think you probably know that I am attracted to you, Miss Cunningham. I have asked before to court you, and I find that I cannot help but ask again. You see, I am quite besot. I find myself thinking about you at the most . . . interesting times. Sometimes I can't even get to sleep at night."

His suggestive smirk made her shiver. "I am sorry that I am such a bother. Perhaps Aunt Miriam can teach you how to make a hot toddy. Apparently the entire purpose is to help you sleep. I wouldn't want to be the cause of your not getting your rest."

This caused him to laugh. "You are so very charming. I love that you speak your mind. I'd love even more if you were the cause of me not getting enough rest every night. It's no wonder I think about you all the time."

She tried to hide her shock. No man had ever spoken like that to her. "Then you shouldn't be surprised to know that I rarely ever think about you." She lowered her gaze momentarily, almost afraid to look away lest he make some move upon her person. "I don't say that to offend but rather to be completely honest. I've done nothing—at least knowingly—to encourage your thoughts of me."

"Maybe that's why they are so intense. You are a challenge to me, Miss Cunningham, and I am convinced that if you would but give me a chance, I could make you fall passionately in love with me."

Goodness, how did one respond to such a statement? The man was positively not discouraged no matter what Abrianna dreamed up to say. She had hoped her blunt honesty would dissuade him, but apparently it was not to be.

"I have a proposition for you."

She put up her hand. "Wait. Please don't take offense, but I've already told you that I have no interest in courtship. I want to serve God as best I can, and I realize that is not your present goal." She hoped he wouldn't be offended by her comment but pushed on in a hurry just in case. "You have your plans and goals in life, and I in turn have mine. I know that my interests have very little to do with yours, so I do not see a future in courtship with you."

He was undaunted. "Miss Cunningham, Abrianna." He paused and said her name again. "Such a beautiful name. It just rolls off the tongue. Anyway, as I started to say, I have a proposition. I realize you have no interest in me at the present. However, I believe I can change that. To entice you to give me the chance to do so, I am willing to make it worthwhile to you."

"In what way?" She had to admit he had her attention.

"You have a great desire to see the poor degenerates and needy of our city helped. I remember from one of our first conversations that you said it was your calling from God. And you might recall that I applauded your efforts even then. The other day I heard you say that you were now concerned with finding them appropriate sleeping quarters before the cold weather once again sets in. I believe you said you were praying about it. Well, that statement stuck with me. It humbled me to think that you cared so much for those people that you would spend time in prayer over it. I suppose it deepened my spiritual insight somewhat."

His statement took her completely off guard. "I'm . . . well . . . if my words or actions caused you to grow in your faith, then God be praised."

"Indeed." He smiled and cocked his head slightly to one side. "Because of overhearing that desire, I wondered how I might help to answer your prayers. After all, God certainly uses people to work His plans. With that in mind, I propose to provide you with such a place and all its furnishings. A large place where you could move your dinner service and be completely contained under one roof. I would even go so far as to provide a couple of trustworthy men to act as guards to the facility. I only ask that you in return give me a chance to win your heart."

She was stunned into silence. The very thing she had been praying God would provide was laid out before her like a Christmas gift. Just the other day Wade asked her if she didn't want to marry and have a family of her own. Was this also a nudge by God to consider such a plan for her life?

"I can see I've intrigued you." He crossed his arms casually against his chest. He smiled as if pleased with himself and certain of her answer.

Abrianna wished she knew what that answer should be. Had he suggested anything else, she would have given him her regrets and refusal. "I don't know what to say."

"Why not say yes?"

"Because I . . . because I don't want you to court me."

"You don't know what you want, Abrianna. You've so long had old ladies directing your steps and everyone else dominating your thoughts that you've had no time to know what you want out of life. I'm here to tell you that I believe we could be a good team. I'm not nearly so terrible as you think."

"I did not say I thought you terrible, Mr. Welby. Goodness, but you needn't put words in my mouth. As you well know, I have plenty of my own. I can say that your actions have at times seemed most unreasonable. Your rudeness on occasion has been most intolerable and your aggressive nature gives one pause to wonder if you are a man of compromise."

"Compromise?" He chuckled. "I can't say that I relish compromise, but only because

I generally feel quite passionate about my desires. Just as I do now. However, I am willing to compromise when it is called for. Is that what you are suggesting now?"

She felt trapped by her own word. "Mr. Welby, I truly do not know what to say. You have taken me by surprise. However, you need to know my heart."

"I'd like very much to know it," he said in a low husky voice.

"At this time I do not intend to marry anyone, and courtship is done for the purpose of such an outcome." Only then did she remember Militine's thoughts on the matter. To her friend, courtship could also be for the sole purpose of having fun with another. There needn't be any intention of marriage. But what Welby was dangling in front of her was too serious to pass up without further thought. She had prayed about this and begged God to provide for the men on the docks. Recently, women had also started coming for food, bringing their children, as well. It would be wonderful to offer a separate place for them to dine, and in a big enough facility Abrianna could do just that.

"So you won't even give me a chance to prove myself? That's rather unfair, don't you think? Not only that, but you would be denying those you claim to care so much about.

Can you in good conscience leave them without for fear of falling in love with me?"

"I'm not afraid of falling in love with you, Mr. Welby." That actually was the least of her concerns.

"Then what? What could possibly stand in the way of your agreement?"

She tried to think rationally. He made a very good argument. A thought came to mind. "Let's say that I agreed to your arrangement." She held up her hand at his broad grin. "Just for the purpose of further understanding. You would provide this facility and all that is needed to house and feed the poor. But for how long? What if you could not accomplish what you believe and make me fall in love with you? After all, such feelings are rather precarious things to place wagers upon. I'm certain my aunts would say it was impossible. However, for the sake of this argument, let's say we courted, and I didn't fall in love with you. Would you then strip away the provision offered those needy souls?"

"Absolutely not. That would be cruel."

"Yes, it would be, but how could I be assured that you would not?"

"I would have a contract prepared. I would purchase a building and the goods needed for your operation, and I would sign them all over to you as a gift of good faith. You would own them in full. That way I could never take them back and leave the poor without your help."

He wasn't making this any easier. Abrianna felt herself being edged closer and closer to allowing for his request. She drew a deep breath. "Very well. I have another question. If on the remote chance that I did fall in love with you and we were to be married, then what? What would become of my ministry to the poor? Surely you could not have a wife performing such a service for the community. What would society say?"

"If you know me even a little, Abrianna, you know that I care very little about what society says or thinks. I'm a businessman. A rather wealthy one, and I find that allows me to move beyond the fetters that some create for themselves in this age of rules and regulations. I would allow you to continue serving the people in whatever way you felt necessary. I'm not a harsh taskmaster. I would be a most loving husband, supportive of your charitable endeavors."

His answer was hard to believe and even harder to find fault with. "How could I be assured of that?"

"Again, I could put it into a contract. Many married people have contracts between them that have nothing to do with the wedding ceremony. Women come into marriages with vast fortunes that they wish to keep. Contracts are made. It's not unheard of, I assure you. Now, to my way of thinking, you are out of arguments."

"I suppose I am." She looked at the man and tried to imagine her life with him. He wasn't bad looking, although she could not call him handsome. Still, she couldn't fault him for that. He was, after all, just as God had made him. It was hardly his doing that his ears were rather large and his eyes were very dark. To his credit he shaved daily and smelled good. His clothes were always in good order, and he did attend church regularly, although she had no real understanding of his spiritual standing with the Lord. That thought brought to her another question.

"You do know that I am a woman of God. I will not be dallied with. Purity is important to me, and you would have to honor that, as well."

He nodded. "Rest assured, Abrianna, I highly value purity. You can be assured I will not take liberties with you . . . until, of course, we marry."

His smile caused a shiver to run down her spine. "*If* we marry."

"Then you'll allow me to court you?"

She shrugged. "I suppose I have no choice. The poor have their needs, and if I am to truly sacrifice myself for them, then so be it."

He roared in laughter. She'd not expected such a reaction, but it gave her a chance to sidestep the man and the tree to put a bit of distance between them. She didn't know exactly what she'd gotten herself into, but she would definitely speak to Kolbein and have him draw up the details of any contract. Mr. Welby might believe he had the upper hand in this matter, but Abrianna would see that he held to his part of the bargain.

Sobering, Welby extended his arm to Abrianna. "Shall we go speak to your aunts? I want to make certain this is handled to their satisfaction. I would not wish to offend them, not now after I've worked so hard to get you to say yes."

Hesitating for a moment, Abrianna reminded herself that this was for the poor and needy. And, after all, she had prayed God would send someone to help her accomplish more. Even Wade wanted her to be mindful of a future that might include a husband and children. With a sigh, she took hold of his arm. This wasn't at all the answer she'd presumed God would provide, but who was she to refuse if this was His way of providing? Aunt Miriam said that often God's answers looked nothing like you thought they should. Apparently this was one of those situations.

15

I don't believe it." Abrianna pulled on Militine's apron. "Look who just arrived. No doubt he felt the need to see firsthand what we've been doing here."

Militine turned and saw Pastor Walker carefully walking among the men who were lining up to receive the noon meal. He looked very uncomfortable and shied away when one man reached out his hand.

"He doesn't seem too friendly, does he?"

"Of course not. He's probably afraid they'll get dirt on his pretty new suit." Abrianna muttered something Militine couldn't quite make out. "Forgive me." Abrianna patted Militine's arm. "I'm afraid that man just gets my dander up."

Pastor Walker crossed the room, avoiding any entanglements with the patrons. He even went so far as to hold a handkerchief up to his nose as he passed by several particularly smelly fishermen.

When he reached Militine and Abrianna, he lowered it. "I had to see for myself that the situation was just as bad as I had suspected."

"Yes, these people are truly without the common needs of life." Abrianna moved to ladle some more soup into bowls.

"That's not what I meant." Walker moved closer to where she was working. "I meant that this is just as bad a situation for you as I presumed it would be. I am certain your aunts have no idea of how exposed you are to foul language and ill tempers."

Abrianna lifted her head and smiled. Militine watched as her friend moved from behind the table to draw closer to the line of men. "What are my rules about eating here?"

"No fightin', no cussin', no drinkin' of liquor, or smokin'." The man at the front of the line smiled, revealing several missing teeth. "And we offer grace for each meal."

Abrianna turned to the pastor. She had the look of a woman prepared for battle. "Any other concerns, Pastor Walker?"

"Of course I have concerns. The biggest being that you are risking your reputation . . .

dare I say your very soul by disregarding common sense and the wisdom of your pastor."

Militine bit her lip and did her best to focus on cutting the bread. Bossy, ill-tempered men were nothing new to her, and she knew from experience it was best to make herself as inconspicuous as possible. Thane and Wade had stepped outside for firewood, and there was no telling when they might return. If she said anything to encourage Abrianna, things might turn truly ugly. It wasn't easy, however. She'd listened to Abrianna rant on and on the night she'd come home from dinner at the Booths' home.

"Pastor Walker"—Abrianna squared her shoulders—"if I felt that you had any wisdom to offer, I might be inclined to listen. However, all I've heard from you is criticism and belittling. This is the first time you've even seen this place. Why not take off your lovely new suit coat and roll up your sleeves to help. I believe the men might like to know more about you and our church."

He sputtered in protest. "I . . . I am not a . . . God did not call me to serve soup, my dear woman. I am a man of the cloth. Furthermore, when you insult me, you insult God."

"Now, hold on there a minute, Preacher." Jay Bowes left the line to come to Abrianna's defense. "You got no call to be treating her so rudely. Miss Abrianna has done nothing wrong. She's shared the gospel with us and given of her heart and time. I'd say she's a lot closer to God than you think."

"Stay out of this. If you knew anything about the Bible, you would know that women have no place in the pulpit or in teaching men."

Jay narrowed his eyes. "Seems to me that she was just doing what decent, God-fearing preachers like you wouldn't do. She don't just live by words—she lives by deeds."

"She is living in sin by disobeying. I try to have some sympathy for her, given she has never had a God-fearing man in her home to direct her life. However, she refuses counsel and direction, and you, sir, are only serving to encourage her behavior. I must demand that you stay out of this. You have no right to interject yourself in this affair."

"I have every right." Jay stepped closer to the pastor. "We all do, as far as I'm concerned, but me more than the rest. I'm her pa."

Abrianna's head snapped up at this. Militine watched the color drain from her face and hurried to Abrianna's side. She put her arm around Abrianna's waist. "Breathe," she whispered.

The pastor looked as shocked as Abrianna. "You would lie to a man of the cloth?"

"I tell no lie. I'm her father. I've long been

absent from her life, but that doesn't change the fact. It also doesn't change the fact that I'm escortin' you from this place. I have plenty of help here to see the job done. Don't I, boys?"

"Yeah," nearly the entire group of twenty-some men declared at once. Those who'd been sitting got to their feet, and those who were standing in line moved out to back up Jay.

"Come along now, Preacher. I believe you've overstayed your welcome." He took hold of the man's coat. "Oh, sorry that my hands aren't so clean as yours. I suppose a little dirt won't hurt you none." He pulled the shocked pastor down the aisle and out the door.

Abrianna continued to stare at the door. Militine moved her to a chair and forced her to sit. Some of the men jumped into action. One brought a glass of water and another took up a newspaper and began to fan her.

"Drink this." Militine handed her the glass from Hairless Mike. She held it to Abrianna's lips and waited until she'd obediently swallowed a sip.

Just then Jay Bowes returned with Wade and Thane right behind him. They all had a look of concern on their faces, and Militine could clearly see that any gathering of wood for the stove had been temporarily forgotten.

Jay came to kneel beside Abrianna. "I'm sorry for breakin' the news to you in such a poor manner. I couldn't bear the way that man was treating you."

Abrianna turned to look at him. "Is it true?"

A smile broke across the man's face. "It is. I wasn't sure at first. God knows I've spent the last year searching."

"Just the last year?"

"I'm afraid it's a long story. See, when you were just a babe, I got caught up in one of those situations you warned me about. You know, hanging with the wrong folks. I was looking for work in California. There was some killing, and I was accused of murder. They sent me to jail, and I'd be there still had another man not confessed to the deed. I guess there was a lot of evidence, too."

"But you . . . Mama never knew." Abrianna looked more confused than ever.

"No, sweet girl. She didn't know. I couldn't shame her like that. I knew if word got back to her that her husband was jailed as a murderer, folks would most likely turn away from her. I figured if they just thought me dead or, even worse, that I'd abandoned the two of you, they might have more sympathy and lend a hand. I'm glad to see that my sacrifice did just that."

Wade came to where Abrianna sat, and Militine stepped back to let him have access to her. She moved back to the table, and Thane joined her there. He leaned down to whisper in her ear.

"He just told us outside. We figured we'd better get in here."

Militine nodded. "I'm glad you did. You can see for herself she's in a state of shock." She looked at the growing number of men. With her most authoritative voice she called out, "If everybody will line up, we'll begin serving as soon as someone offers grace."

No one moved. They were all transfixed. It was as if they were caught up in a theatrical production and didn't want to so much as cough until the act ended and the curtain fell.

Jay took hold of Abrianna's hand. "I'm so sorry. I didn't want to tell you like this. I wanted to find a way to make it easier for you."

"You told me your name was Jay Bowes." She looked at him and shook her head. "Not Cunningham."

"My name is James Bowes Cunningham. I figured it best to go by Jay Bowes in case anyone had read about me in the California papers. My release was something of an affair down Stockton way. I know I've given you an awful shock, darling. That was never my intention. Not that it matters now."

"Why don't you give Abrianna a little time to think," Wade suggested. "I believe she's had enough for one day."

Jay stood and smiled. "I'm sure you're right." He turned back to the rest of the men. "Soup smells mighty good. I believe I'll offer grace."

The men bowed their heads, and Jay Bowes offered a simple prayer of thanks for the food and for finding his daughter. Militine could see the happiness in the old man's face and knew without a doubt that he was telling the truth. She thought of all her fears that someone might show up who knew her. Funny how that had never bothered her here at the food house, yet if anyone from her past were to show up, it would most likely be someplace like this. Her throat went dry at the thought.

The men reluctantly lined up for their soup, and Thane stepped up beside Militine to help. Meanwhile, she could see that the men were still glancing toward Abrianna and Wade. He said something to her and Abrianna nodded. Militine couldn't help but wonder at their exchange, but when Abrianna got to her feet she presumed Wade had encouraged her to leave.

Abrianna took two faltering steps, however, and promptly sank to the ground in a faint. Militine watched as Wade scooped her up.

"Thane, I'm going to take her home. Can you handle this?"

"I can. Militine and I can take care of everything."

"We'll see to it that things get taken care of, as well," Jay told him. "Just see to her." His expression darkened. No doubt he wanted to go along with Wade but knew it wasn't the right time.

But was there ever a right time for the past to return?

Wade sensed Abrianna rousing and paused at the wagon. "Abrianna? Abrianna, open your eyes."

She did and looked at him as if she were in a dream. She glanced around and then shook her head. "Goodness. Why ever are you carrying me? I must be a terrible burden. Put me down."

"The way you burden a man comes in other forms. Are you sure you won't faint again?"

"I fainted?"

"You did."

She let go a heavy sigh and then the event seemed to come back to her. "Mr. Bowes says he's my father."

"Yes, I know." He motioned his head to the wagon. "I'm taking you home for a rest. I don't want to hear any of your protests about how you have to be here at the food house. Everything has been arranged. Now, I want you to get up on the seat." He lowered her to the ground and then all but pushed her up the side of the wagon to take her place.

Afraid she might bolt, Wade didn't bother to walk around the wagon, but instead climbed up and maneuvered to take his place beside her. He picked up the reins and released the brake. "Move on, horse." With a flick of the reins the horse began to walk.

Much to his surprise, Abrianna remained silent. Wade couldn't remember a time when anything had kept her without comment for such a long time. He smiled, and when they hit a hole, his smile deepened as she let herself lean against him.

"You've had a pretty big shock today. Just rest. In no time at all we'll be back at the house."

"I should be happy."

He waited for her to say something more, and when she didn't, he felt compelled to offer his thoughts. "Give it time. News like this, coming all at once, is never easy."

She straightened and Wade immediately missed her presence. "Do you think he's telling the truth, Wade?"

"I don't know. Not for sure. He didn't seem like he was making it up. Besides, why would a man lie about something like that?"

"I don't know." She shook her head. "I can boast knowledge about many things but not about the workings of a man's mind." She looked up and met his eyes. "To me, the way men think and the actions they put behind those thoughts make little or no sense at all."

He laughed heartily at her comment. "I know quite a few men who feel the same way about our female counterparts."

16

Sorry to disturb you like this," Wade announced, holding tight to Abrianna despite her protest, "but Abrianna has had a pretty big shock. She fainted back at the food house and I thought it best to bring her here."

Everyone at the bridal school had been enmeshed in chores, but the chaos came to a standstill at Wade's announcement. Mrs. Madison dismissed the others girls who'd been cleaning the downstairs and ordered they gather the others upstairs and go to the ballroom to practice their dance steps for the upcoming bridal ball. Clara was instructed to play the organ to give the girls some music to dance by and Virginia, the most proficient of the students in dance, was appointed to assist any of the others in their steps.

Miriam Madison wasted no time after the girls were gone. "Poisie, please fetch some tea. Selma, we need a cold, damp cloth." She turned on her heel toward Wade and Abrianna. "Now, I think it's best we get to the bottom of this situation."

Wade looked to Abrianna and nodded. He squeezed her hand. "Go on. It is best to get it all out."

Her gaze latched onto his and for a brief moment, Wade hoped she might one day feel love for him; after all he knew no one would ever care for her as much as he did.

She broke eye contact and took a deep breath. In a matter of moments she had spilled out all the details of Pastor Walker's visit to the food house. Wade watched Abrianna's ire rise again as she recounted the man of the cloth's words and then humble Jay's surprising declaration.

"And just like that," Abrianna told them, "he said he was my father."

Miss Poisie bustled into the room. "Oh, do tell me I haven't missed anything."

"It would seem a man has come to Abrianna declaring himself to be her father," Mrs. Gibson replied before anyone else could.

Miss Poisie's eyes widened. "Her dead father?"

Her sister shook her head and raised her chin. "Not so dead, apparently."

Miss Poisie brought a cup of tea to Abrianna. "I'm sorry, Mr. Ackerman, did you wish to have tea, as well? I'm afraid seeing Abrianna so upset caused me to forget my manners."

"No, I'm fine."

Miss Poisie brought him a cup of tea anyway. "I must say this has been such a month of shocking news from our Abrianna. I shall always remember May of 1889 as such. Goodness, but when Abrianna announced she was going to allow Mr. Welby to court her, I very nearly fell out of my chair. Just imagine it, our Abrianna courting and perhaps even married before the year is out."

Wade blinked several times. His ears must have deceived him. Miss Poisie didn't just say . . . no . . . she couldn't have. "What?" He looked to Abrianna. "Mr. Welby? Why?"

She shrugged as if the matter were completely immaterial. "It's a long story, but suffice it to say I thought hard about what you had said. I had been praying for answers and help for the poor, and it all just seemed to come together when he asked to court me."

"What could I have possibly said that suggested you should court *that* man?" His question came out much louder than he had intended.

"There's no need to raise your voice, Wade. You were the one who posed the questions about whether I wanted a husband and children. I had taken this subject to prayer, as I was sure God wanted me to serve Him, and I wasn't at all certain I could do that and marry. And then there was the terrible burden of seeing those homeless people without a place to sleep. I knew we had to do something, especially before another winter set in.

"I didn't know for sure how God would provide, but then Mr. Welby approached me, and one thing led to another."

"But I never meant . . . not Priam Welby." Wade ran his hand through his hair. What had he done? Could he even fathom losing Abrianna to that . . . that . . . snake? This day couldn't get any worse. He opened his mouth to say his piece, but no words came out.

"We are often surprised by God's answers." Apparently Mrs. Gibson didn't have any trouble finding words. She sat down and shook her head. "I know in dealing with Mr. Gibson—"

Miss Poisie perked up. "God rest his soul."

"Amen," Mrs. Madison and Mrs. Gibson declared.

"He had many misgivings about God. I prayed for God to make him see the truth, and Mr. Gibson suffered a stroke. Now, that didn't look at all like I thought answered prayer would look, but it was clear that I could take the opportunity to spend my husband's last days reading the Word of God to him. In doing so he would have the chance to make his soul right before God. At least that was my prayer."

"It's true," Miss Poisie said, bobbing her head. "I have had many answers to prayer look different from what I thought they would look like. Sometimes that makes it very sad, as in losing my dear Captain."

"God rest his soul," Mrs. Gibson murmured.

The other three women nodded. "Amen."

"That very well may be," Wade interjected, "however I never meant to imply that Abrianna should court Mr. Welby. I think this needs greater consideration. The man is a scoundrel."

"You've experienced this firsthand?" Aunt Miriam questioned.

He shook his head. "Not exactly."

Abrianna set aside the cloth and picked up her tea. "We can talk about all of this another time. It's not like I'm in any hurry to spend time with him." She looked to her aunts. "Do you think it's really possible Mr. Bowes is my father? He says he is James Bowes Cunningham."

"That was indeed your father's name," Mrs. Madison said, giving a slow nod.

"I always thought it a rather complicated name for a man of lesser means," Mrs. Gibson added. "It seems that the poorer folk should have simpler names."

"I agree," Miss Poisie said. "Ink costs good money, and if you had to write your name very often, a lengthy name would cost you a great deal in ink."

Wade wanted to scream but remained silent. *Lord, what do I do?*

Abrianna wasn't sidetracked, however. "Did you have any idea my father might be alive?"

"No, none at all," Mrs. Madison assured her. "We were quite certain he had died. Why would a man otherwise not be in touch with his family?"

"Especially a man with such an expanded name," Miss Poisie added, looking to Mrs. Gibson for her approval. The old lady nodded and Miss Poisie looked back to Abrianna and Mrs. Madison with a satisfied smile.

Abrianna didn't seem to notice or care. "He said he was falsely accused of murder and thrown into prison for twenty years."

Miss Poisie sat down hard, as if the news were too much. "Murder? How very awful."

"I thought so, as well," Abrianna continued, "but was determined to consider that matter another day. After all, the issue of whether or not he's my father is the one foremost in my mind."

"We will have to have him here to tea," Mrs. Madison said.

"Oh, Sister, is that wise?" Miss Poisie looked to Abrianna. "Was he falsely accused of murdering a man or a woman?"

Wade rolled his eyes. Once the snowball started rolling with these women, it could only grow.

Without waiting for Abrianna to reply, Mrs. Gibson offered a suggestion. "There is one way we might be able to ascertain the truth. Your mother's pin."

"God rest her soul," Miss Poisie murmured.

"Amen. I had all but forgotten it," Mrs. Madison said without pause. "That might shed some light on his identity. He gave the pin to your mother on their first anniversary. Your mother told us it was something he had saved up for and surprised her with. He was quite proud of that gift."

"Indeed. According to your mother it was the only thing he ever gave her. They couldn't afford a ring when they married."

"I will wear it when we have him to tea."

"A murderer to tea," Mrs. Gibson murmured. "My, we are quite the sophisticates."

"Falsely accused," Abrianna added. "Although I have no proof of that, either."

"I suppose we should host him outside," Mrs. Madison said thoughtfully. "I wouldn't want him to worry about his attire. He's obviously without means if he comes to have soup with the others."

"And he did shorten his name," Miss Poisie offered.

"Yes, that would suggest he thinks as we do." Mrs. Gibson got to her feet. "The shorter name is more befitting his lowly position in life."

"I have no idea of his financial condition. He could be as wealthy as Mr. Welby, for all I know. After all, he managed to keep his identity a secret all this time." Abrianna sat up with a start. "Goodness. We left Militine and Thane to run the food house. We should get back and help them."

Wade shook his head. "No, you stay and rest. I'll head back and see to the cleanup. I think you've dealt with quite enough for one day. Possibly for one month."

"It's true. Our Abrianna has been full of shocking information this month," Miss Poisie agreed. "It's a wonder we have been able to properly digest our meals given all this uproar."

Wade said nothing more, feeling his own stomach sour. If he opened his mouth, he very well might say the wrong thing. For now, he would hold his peace and deal with the entire Welby matter at a later time. But if he had his way about it, Welby would never have an opportunity to pursue Abrianna.

With the last of the men finally shuffling out the door, Militine felt her resolve give way. Without warning she burst into tears and hid her face in the folds of her apron. The shock of Abrianna's father and the realization that anyone, but anyone, could walk in at any given moment left her feeling completely exposed to the past. What if her father appeared?

Thane came to her almost immediately and took her in his arms. She had no strength to fight him off, nor did she want to. He held her close and whispered in her ear, but the words didn't make sense in her head. Her thoughts were overwhelmed with visions of a life lived before Seattle. A hopelessly ugly life that Militine hoped never to experience again.

"Please don't cry so. I don't know what's troubling you, but you must surely know that I love you, Militine."

His words broke through her tortured memories. She looked up, tears still streaming. "You what?"

"I love you. You have to know that. I realize there are a great many things about me that you don't know, but I want to make certain that you hear this one thing. I love you."

"Stop saying that." She pulled away, hating the look of hurt on his face. "You're right about not knowing things, but it's equally a problem on my part. There is so much of me you have no knowledge of, and believe me, you won't feel the same once you do."

"I don't believe you. Nothing could make me stop loving you."

She put her hands on her hips. "Oh really? Well, I can think of at least a handful that will. I suppose I should have been honest from the beginning, but I came here hoping I could forget the past and everything associated with my life back then." The tears yielded to her anger. "God knows there is nothing but pain to remember."

"You aren't the only one who feels that way about their life. I've been trying to tell you that for months." He moved a few steps to the right and took up a chair. Setting it backward he waved his hand. "So shock me. I suppose you will tell me that your father used to beat you. I've already guessed that part. Mine did likewise. I suppose you might also tell me that he punished you in other cruel fashions—starvation, isolation, humiliation. So did mine."

"I ran away," she threw back at him. "I knew I could never get away from him without a good head start, so I drugged his coffee.

Then I took all the money I could find and I ran. I'm a poisoner and thief."

She turned away, not willing to see Thane's face. If his expression held a look of disgust or even pity, she would never be able to face him again. Why did this have to happen? Why had Abrianna's father ever come back? Just his very presence stole any sense of peace that Militine might have known. There was nothing left to do but move on. She'd have to leave Seattle and the friends she'd made. She'd have to go on the run once again.

Thane touched her shoulders and turned her to face him. "It doesn't change my heart, Militine. Like I said, there is nothing you can say that will make me feel otherwise. As much as I love you, I hate your father for hurting you. You only did what you had to in order to survive."

Forcing herself to look up, Militine saw only love and acceptance in his expression. He tenderly touched her cheek, and she tried to pull away. Tenderness was perhaps the cruelest thing he could offer. To experience such an emotion only to lose it would no doubt be the death of her.

"Tell me anything else you need me to know, and then I will tell you my story. After that, we will bury it away and have nothing more to do with it."

"It's not that simple, Thane." She shook her head. "By all of society's beliefs and rules, I am unacceptable."

"I don't care about their beliefs or rules. I only care about you."

She bit her lower lip. There was no way around this. She would have to tell him everything. "My mother and father never married. My mother was his kept woman, a heathen by the standards of this world. She was Crow Indian. That makes me a half-breed. My skin is lighter, more like my father's, and I even share some of his facial features, but my eyes and dark hair are gifts from my mother."

"And I love them, just as I love you." He took her by the hands and led her to a chair. "Sit." He pressed his hands gently against her shoulders. "Sit, and I will tell you why none of this matters."

He drew his chair up and sat directly in front of her. "The world can have its prejudices and social mores. God knows I've suffered at the hands of such people. None of that matters, Militine. The only thing that matters to me is whether you can love a man who is the son of a murderer. A man who saw his father kill countless times and said nothing. A man who, as a boy, saw his father kill for nothing more than sport." Thane drew a deep breath and let it out slowly. "A boy who watched his mother be killed because she happened to be nice to a farmhand."

"You had said she was murdered."

"But I never explained that my father did the deed. She had taken pity on our farmhand and allowed him to come into the house and warm himself by the fire. It was a vicious winter day. A blizzard had been raging for hours. They were sharing a cup of coffee and laughing when my father found them. He believed the worst, and without allowing either of them to explain, he drew his gun and shot them both."

"And you were forced to witness this?"

"Yes. I was home from school sick. I was just across the room when my father stormed into the house. He didn't care about the truth. I tried to tell him after he'd killed them, and he still didn't care. He was never remorseful. Never. Not even when the townspeople hanged him."

It was Militine's turn to reach out. She touched his cheek. "I'm so sorry. It would seem we both know what it is to have violence in our lives."

Thane shook his head. "I blame myself. If I'd just had the guts to confront my father or turn him over to the law for all those other murders he committed . . . but I didn't."

"And who is to say that anyone would have

listened if you had?" Militine asked. Hadn't she herself tried to elicit help from others? It either served to get her into worse situations or the person didn't care. After a time, she stopped trying. "But to answer your question, yes. I can and do love you. Your past . . . the things done to you . . . do not keep me from feeling what I feel."

"Then you can believe me when I say that your past doesn't matter where my heart is concerned?"

She nodded. "For the first time in my life, I think I can."

"We're both going to need help, however," he said. "Wade has gotten me to thinking on God quite a bit lately. I'm afraid I've not given God much of a chance in my life."

"Abrianna has gotten me thinking, as well. I've tried to see God as my mother taught me, as a loving Father who wants only good for all of His children." The memory of her mother's tender words brought her image to mind, something Militine hadn't allowed for in years. "I wanted so much to hold on to her view of God. When I first came here, I pretended I believed so that I would be accepted at the school. No matter how hard I tried, I just kept coming back to the fact that if He loved me so much, He sure had a poor of way of showing it."

Thane's expression told her that he completely understood. "Maybe together we can try again. Maybe together we can find the strength to bury our anger and learn to trust Him. I think He is a good and loving God. I don't think He liked what happened to either of us any more than we did. But most of all, I don't think He wants either of us to give up and spend the rest of our lives in the past. Maybe that's why He's brought us together. He knew we'd need each other in order to learn to forgive."

"And to forget," she added. Especially to forget.

17

Priam Welby lost little time in pinning Abrianna down to a specific day and time. A card came for her only a week after she'd agreed to court. She had thought to deny him. After all, it was the end of May, and the ball would be in a little over a week. Surely he could wait until after that. But no. The invitation was for a night at the theatre and late supper with the inclusion of the chaperone of her choice. Aunt Poisie was the logical one to accompany them and was delighted when she heard that the theatre was involved. It seemed a pity that Mr. Welby couldn't court Aunt Poisie instead.

Abrianna dressed in a gown chosen for her by Aunt Miriam. For her first outing with Mr. Welby she would wear a watered silk print, white with sprigs of lilacs. The gown, Lenore had told her, had cost a small fortune but had never fit her right. It seemed as though the piece had been made for Abrianna, however.

"This should be appropriate and modest," her aunt declared, giving her a critical inspection.

The sprigged silk bodice was overlaid in a V, with several rows of white lace and lavender tulle. White lace trimmed the top all the way to Abrianna's slender throat. The last thing either of them wanted was a gown that would have men ogling, as Aunt Selma pointed out. Abrianna seriously doubted Mr. Welby needed any encouragement in that department.

"I still don't quite understand this sudden willingness to court Mr. Welby," Aunt Miriam declared.

Abrianna wasn't at all certain she understood it herself. "I just feel like this is something God brought to me. I don't really believe romance or marriage will come out of it."

"Then why court him?"

Her aunt made a good point, but to try to explain the promises Mr. Welby had made would only cause her aunt to worry. She had never liked Abrianna getting involved in risky ventures, and this was perhaps one of the biggest she'd participated in to date.

"I'm trying," Abrianna said, choosing her words carefully, "to be open to whatever God's will is for my life. I don't want to be so stiff-necked that I turn aside . . . something . . . clearly in His plan."

"Well, at least you are properly attired," Aunt Poisie said.

Turning to view herself from every angle in the mirror, Abrianna shook her head. "Goodness, but I do not understand the fascination with bustled backsides. Why would a woman want to draw attention to such an area of her person?" She studied the lavender fringe that trimmed the material covering the bustle. It was lovely, but she would have preferred it be on the front of the gown, if at all.

"Do wear the long white gloves," Aunt Selma instructed. "And clasp this silver bracelet around your right wrist. I have read that this is a most sophisticated way to decorate the glove."

She nodded and took the bracelet from Aunt Selma. It was a beautifully etched piece of polished silver and would make a lovely accessory for her attire.

"Will you wear a hat?" Aunt Poisie asked.

"No," Abrianna replied. "Lenore said it isn't a necessary fashion for an unmarried woman of my age. Instead she suggested I wear that lovely lavender ribbon on the dresser with a tiny spray of white baby's breath."

Aunt Poisie bobbed her head. "That will look wonderful in your honey-auburn hair."

"Speaking of which, you should hurry to arrange it," Aunt Miriam said, pointing to the clock on the mantel. "Mr. Welby will be here soon."

With her aunts satisfied that her attire was acceptable, they left her to finish her hair with Militine's help and went downstairs to await Mr. Welby's arrival.

Moving away from the mirror, Abrianna picked up a brush and tried to form some kind of order out of the tangled curls of her hair. "I cannot make my hair do as I want. There's just too much of it, and it will not obey my direction. Although, I do thank God that it isn't frizzy like Mrs. Bunker's." That poor matron often arrived at church on Sunday mornings with her entire head swathed in a turban-style hat to hide her terrible hair.

Militine took the brush from her and carefully fashioned Abrianna's hair into ringlets. "You are just nervous. I really don't know why you ever agreed to this in the first place." She pinned a knot of hair on the top Abrianna's head and left the remaining ringlets to fall in an orderly fashion around her shoulders. "That man positively makes me shudder."

"Actually, I am given to second thoughts myself." Abrianna twisted to see the result of Militine's work. "You make me look like a Grecian goddess. I should have you around me always, but you would tire of attending this mess. I still wonder why it is so acceptable for a man to wear his hair either long or short, but a woman must leave hers to grow and grow."

"Long hair on men is hardly the fashion at this time. I think you would find more than one person offended should any such man appear on the street, just as they would if you were to cut yours short."

"I'm certain you are right, but it grieves me nevertheless. Will you secure the ribbon and flowers?"

"Of course." Militine gathered both and went to work. She drew the ribbon around Abrianna's head and pinned it and the sprig of dainty white blossoms with two concealed hairpins. "That should complete your hair."

"It's quite amazing," Abrianna said of the results. "I don't think even Aunt Miriam can fault my appearance tonight."

Militine took hold of Abrianna's arm. "But why are you going with him?"

"I have my reasons." She frowned. "I have never cared for Mr. Welby, but I suppose I have also never really given him a chance. Now he has put before me a proposition that I find difficult to ignore."

"What proposition?"

Abrianna felt it would be best to keep the details to herself. "It's just a proposition that involves Mr. Welby wanting the chance to woo me. He's convinced he can make me fall in love with him."

"*Make* you? Should anyone ever have to be made to fall in love?"

"That was exactly my thought. But despite that, I thought perhaps it was God's direction for me, and I don't want to be so caught up in my own will that I miss His."

Militine appeared to consider this for a moment and then, to Abrianna's relief, she dropped the subject. "You should probably get your gloves on and go downstairs. I'm sure Mr. Welby is already waiting. I thought I heard the door knocker nearly twenty minutes ago."

"Then he was twenty minutes early. The height of rudeness, if you ask me. I shall have to tell him so once we are seated for dinner." Abrianna laughed at her comment. "There, do I sound like a proper young woman of society?"

"How would I know? Life in this school is as social as I've ever lived."

Abrianna looked at her for a moment, then reached for her gloves. "You've never said much about where you grew up or what your father did for a living."

"He ran a trading post north of Vancouver. It was a very remote place, and I had little schooling. It was why I was such a mess when

I came here. My mother taught me to read, only because missionaries had taught her." Militine frowned and immediately changed the subject. "I think maybe you need more flowers. I can go pick another spray."

"No, don't bother. We needn't let Mr. Welby think he's so important as to merit an abundance of flowers. After all, I am wearing this massive bustle. That should hold his attention. Not that I want it to. Land sakes, I do not understand this fashion at all." She tried to crane her head around to reevaluate the beast. "Does it look all right?"

"It looks perfectly fine. Now stop fretting. You look quite beautiful, freckles and all."

"Oh, I'd nearly forgotten about the freckles. Aunt Miriam wanted me to powder them out as best I could, but honestly, the man knows I have freckles. Although I will say he's been good enough not to mention that fault of mine." Militine handed her a fan, and Abrianna shook her head. "I would only lose it. I'll do well not to lose the bustle."

This sent Militine into a peal of laughter that did Abrianna's heart good. Her friend had been far too serious of late, despite Thane's courtship and obvious adoration.

Making her way to the stairs, Abrianna licked her lips and tried to calm her nerves. She had no idea what to expect from the evening.

This was truly her first escorted affair with a man as far as courtship was concerned. There were far more rules to this type of outing than simply working at the food house to feed the poor. She was bound to forget everything she'd been taught, especially if Mr. Welby irritated her by saying something controversial.

She paused at the top of the stairs and only then noticed that Priam Welby and her aunts were awaiting her at the bottom. The man had the audacity to look her over as if she were a prized pig, and truly that was what she felt like. He grinned, no doubt satisfied with his accomplishment. Why was it that men could be so smug when they got their own way? Even Wade was guilty of that flaw.

You're getting something out of this, too.

Abrianna tried to push that thought aside as she descended the stairs. Of course this was benefiting her, otherwise she would never have submitted to courting anyone. Welby stepped forward to take hold of her hand as she reached the final step.

"My dear Miss Cunningham, you are ravishing."

"Mr. Welby, that seems a rather vulgar statement," Aunt Miriam said. "Perhaps you could simply say she looks lovely."

"But that would be far too simple. Look

at her. She's is more beautiful than any other woman in the world."

Abrianna sighed. "If we are to start the evening with lies and exaggeration, I know this courtship is doomed. You will not induce me to fall in love by using such comments. The fact that I am a woman with red hair and freckles has been a burden I've had to bear all of my life, but you needn't suggest them an asset."

"But my dear Miss Cunningham—if I may call you dear?" he said, looking to the older ladies. Aunt Miriam nodded but looked dubious. "I happen to like red hair and freckles. You must surely allow for my perception of beauty. Can you not concede that one man enjoys the pastel colors and fashion of a Monet painting, while another abhors it and would favor the darker tones of a Rembrandt? Isn't it possible that not everyone sees beauty the same way?"

Her aunts moved to the door en masse in preparation of seeing the couple off. Abrianna sighed. She had to accept his logic or otherwise listen to him further try to persuade. "Very well. I yield. Your compliment was sincere."

He smiled and lifted her gloved hand to his lips. "Thank you." He bent over her hand but didn't kiss it. Instead, he glanced up and whispered, "I hope you will yield on many occasions."

She felt her face go scarlet but knew better than to rebuke him, for her aunts would then demand to know what he'd so inappropriately said.

He straightened and smiled, as if understanding her dilemma. "My carriage awaits."

Abrianna took a fine silk shawl offered her by Aunt Selma. The day had been warm, almost hot, and she doubted seriously she would have such a need, but it was always wise to have one just in case. Mr. Welby in turn took the piece and draped it over his arm.

"If you are chilled, you have but to tell me."

Abrianna nodded, knowing there was no need to remind him that she'd been seeing to that need for many a year. Surely this was just more of the game to be played. Goodness, but when she thought about all the bread she could be helping Militine to make for the poor, this outing seemed such a waste. Of course, she had made the deal, and there was nothing to be done but accept her fate.

Please, God, don't let me get stuck anywhere with this bustle, and please let the evening pass quickly. Amen.

Mr. Welby retrieved his top hat and gloves. He made a dashing figure, Abrianna had to admit that much. She watched his gentle care as he helped Aunt Poisie into the carriage.

She could find no fault there, either. He then turned to her.

"Milady." He made a quick bow and then handed Abrianna up, as well.

She struggled a bit to sit just right so the bustle would properly collapse. How much easier to be her aunt's age. No one forced such contraptions on the elderly. The old women could even wear their corsets loose and eat whatever they wanted. She sighed.

Mr. Welby climbed in and took the seat opposite her and Aunt Poisie. It was difficult to see him now that they were enclosed, but Abrianna imagined him sitting there quite content, rather like the cat who managed to steal the cream. He tapped the ceiling twice, and the driver put the carriage into motion.

They were very quickly delivered to the theatre, where Abrianna noted dozens of elegant patrons lingering in the lobby. While it was a nice diversion to attend the theatre, it was even more important for one to be seen enjoying such a social event. The newspapers would report on the more esteemed guests, while lesser knowns hoped to be commented on merely by association. It was all a lot of stuff and nonsense.

Mr. Welby doffed his top hat and gloves, handing them to an awaiting attendant. Next he offered her aunt one arm and bid her take the other. Abrianna had no desire to be paraded around, but Mr. Welby seemed to find associate after associate who was enthralled to make her acquaintance.

"My, but you are quite the lucky man, Welby. I do believe you have the two loveliest women in all of God's creation to accompany you. You should be ashamed of keeping them to yourself."

"Ah, but that is my good fortune and your loss," Mr. Welby told the man with a laugh. "Are you here alone?"

"Goodness, no. I was dragged here by my wife and daughter-in-law. My son had the good sense to be previously engaged with a business meeting. One that I'm sure involves cards." The men chuckled.

Mr. Welby turned to Abrianna and Aunt Poisie. "Let me present Miss Poisie Holmes and Miss Abrianna Cunningham." The ladies gave a brief curtsy. "This is Arthur Delecort."

"Of the New York Delecorts," the man added. "I am most happy to make your acquaintance, ladies."

What Abrianna could only describe as a herd of other friends and associates came to pay their respects before ushers called for everyone to take their seats. Abrianna found herself seated between Welby and her aunt without delay. She had to allow that Mr. Welby smelled quite nice.

"I do hope you are enjoying the evening as much as I," he whispered against her ear.

Abrianna wanted again to rebuke him, but to do so would cause a scene, and the play was already starting. Instead, she shot him a glare. He smiled. No doubt he knew exactly what he was doing. Apparently this was how he thought he would woo her into love. How silly.

The play was one with which she was well familiar. *The Merchant of Venice*. The cast performed it admirably, and Abrianna honestly found herself sorry when the play concluded. Welby had behaved himself throughout the evening and only once, when he stretched his leg and accidentally, or not so accidentally, pressed too close, did Abrianna find fault with him.

However, there wasn't time to worry over that matter, either. Mr. Welby reclaimed his hat and gloves, and just as quickly as they were brought to the theatre, they were whisked away to a late supper.

"I thought we might try a new place called Danover's," Mr. Welby said. "It promises the most elegant dining."

"I did hear about that restaurant," Aunt Poisie answered.

"Yes, it's been open just a short time. I've heard the food is exceptional, due to a renowned French chef who prides himself on being the best in all of America."

"I find that boasting often leads one to disappointment," Aunt Poisie replied. "Boasting is hardly necessary if one truly is the best, for word will surely travel about, based on the experiences of those involved."

"That makes good sense, Miss Poisie. You are both a handsome and knowledgeable woman."

"Why thank you, Mr. Welby." She giggled and patted Abrianna's arm. "Isn't he charming?"

Goodness, but now he was sweet-talking Aunt Poisie. What next? Abrianna forced a smile. "He is."

Encouraged by Mr. Welby's praise, Aunt Poisie continued the conversation by telling him that she had sampled excellent French cuisine once while in Philadelphia. "I thought it strange to have a French restaurant in the City of Liberty, but it was quite perfect."

Abrianna relaxed a bit. Aunt Poisie continued to take charge of the conversation, giving Abrianna time to think. She was anxious for Kolbein and Mr. Welby to draw up the contracts. Kolbein said he wanted to handle the matter carefully, which Abrianna interpreted as meaning it wouldn't happen overnight. Still, she didn't want to have to bear these outings with Mr. Welby if there wasn't something to be done in return for the poor.

They reached the restaurant nearly ten minutes later. Welby alighted the carriage quickly and then assisted Aunt Poisie with such grace and gentility that the woman actually gave him a brief curtsy. It would seem Welby had won her over. Just then, however, Aunt Poisie spied a display in the lighted restaurant window and moved to better inspect it.

Welby reached up for Abrianna, and she allowed him to take her gloved hand. "You are an abominable rascal, I must say."

He looked at her in shock. "Me? What have I done?"

She rolled her eyes and said nothing. If her aunt didn't mind his attention, why should she?

The golden glow of burning lights outside the building beckoned them, while the ornate appeal of the building and lovely arched windows suggested an evening of lavish indulgence. Aunt Poisie hurried back to join them.

"There is a wondrous display of desserts in that window. I must say it will be difficult to choose."

"Then why bother?" Mr. Welby replied. "I shall order them all, and you may sample to your heart's content."

Aunt Poisie again giggled like a schoolgirl. "You are much too kind, Mr. Welby."

Abrianna couldn't help but wonder how much money he would spend on this evening. All just to impress them. Surely the money could be better spent on the poor. He was a man of means and as such no doubt had more than enough money to do both, but still Abrianna felt it wasteful. That feeling continued as they were escorted into the restaurant and seated at a beautifully arranged table.

The lovely damask tablecloths were immediately approved by Aunt Poisie, as were the swan-shaped napkins and elegant silverware. All twenty pieces per person. Abrianna counted eight knives, eight forks, three spoons, including a delicate and tiny salt spoon, as well as a butter pick. And that was just what was set before them. No doubt there would be other pieces to come. Goodness, but it would be a tiresome task to wash all of that silver.

In addition to this were a bevy of fine gold-rimmed white china plates, four crystal goblets of varying sizes, and a beautiful flower arrangement set in a crystal bowl atop a beveled mirror. The latter reflected the light from the beautiful crystal chandeliers.

The service was impeccable. They were given a small finger bowl of warm water to refresh their hands. The steward then handed them a fresh napkin on which to dry them. He removed this and returned with a single card menu of a prearranged supper.

"This will do nicely," Mr. Welby declared, and the man went quickly to work to see them served. Welby offered her a smile. "I do hope you are enjoying the evening. I am trying very hard to impress you."

"I can see that. There truly is no need, however. This is far from my normal fare, and if you knew me very well, you would know that I am more content with a quiet evening than one full of fanfare."

He smiled. "I would like to imagine quiet evenings with you." He looked to Aunt Poisie. "I hope that was not too bold a statement to make."

She seemed to consider it for a moment and then shook her head. "I think it acceptable. Although, the hour of the evening would be important."

Abrianna wanted to giggle at the look on Mr. Welby's face. He seemed perplexed at the comment but said nothing.

The first course, a fine foie gras on toasted bread, was served instead of oysters, given it was not the right month for such things. This, Aunt Poisie announced with great authority. Never a fan of foie gras, Abrianna gave the pretense of tasting it but then set it aside. If

Mr. Welby noticed, he said nothing, having downed his with seeming pleasure.

Next they were served a creamed onion soup, then came a consommé. The meal quickly continued with additional courses and more conversation.

Mr. Welby was good to include Aunt Poisie, but Abrianna could see that the older woman was growing tired and spoke less and less, leaving the discussion to the young while she focused on her meal.

"I hope you realize how happy you've made me. Especially in light of our contract not yet being finalized. It shows that you have faith in me."

"I suppose it does, although I really have no reason to. Still, it seemed to be unavoidable. I wanted to say no to the invitation, given that the ball is just next Friday, but I was afraid you might think me unwilling to keep my word. However, if you knew me, you would know I'm a woman of my word."

He smiled. "And a good many words. Although that doesn't trouble me in the least. I am glad you are a woman of information and opinion. I think society has disregarded the intelligence of the fairer sex for far too long. You, Miss Cunningham, and your aunt, have proven to me that women can be most enlightening."

She tried not to take encouragement at his declaration, but he did seem sincere. "I'm afraid my aunts have long thought my willingness to speak out most inappropriate. But honestly, I see no reason to remain silent with my thoughts. Especially if the thought pertains to an ongoing discussion. Why shouldn't a woman be able to speak her mind?"

"Indeed. Any man who tells you otherwise is, in my opinion, a fool."

"I wish Pastor Walker could hear you say that." She hadn't meant to bring the man up in conversation. In fact, she had hoped to forget about him altogether. It was bad enough that the elders and deacons still had done nothing to remove him from the church, but given he had until the end of August for his trial period, she supposed there was little to be done.

"Why do you worry yourself with what he thinks?"

Abrianna shrugged. "I suppose I shouldn't. Wade tells me that constantly. But it bothers me that anyone should judge me so inaccurately. Had I been faulted for speaking too much or running on the street or even singing off-key, I would have accepted such criticism graciously. God knows I do not sing well, and if you need a wife that does so, you should end this courtship here and now." She gave him no chance to answer but continued. "But the man faults me for answering the call of God. He tells me I have no place in ministries of any kind. I cannot abide that judgment."

"Well, he is simply wrong," Mr. Welby said with a warm smile. He lifted his wine goblet. "I suggest we drink to an evening free from such burdensome thoughts. Instead, let us reflect on brighter and more promising things, such as our courtship."

"I do not drink liquors of any kind, but I will toast such a thing with water, if I might."

"But of course," he said. "I want you to be comfortable. I want you to be yourself."

The very thought that Mr. Welby would say such a thing gave Abrianna hope that perhaps they could make a go of the courtship. He was wealthy and willing to help in her endeavors and ministries, and his kindness and gentility proved him to be a gentleman. Perhaps the things Wade had heard about him were wrongly said. After all, people did lie about others, and it was easy enough to make incorrect judgments. Hadn't Pastor Walker misjudged her?

18

Sunday afternoon Militine and Thane walked hand in hand around the grounds of the Madison Bridal School. Their new closeness offered Militine a comfort she'd never known. Since their mutual disclosures of the past, she'd had no more nightmares. She wasn't foolish or even hopeful enough to believe they wouldn't come on occasion, but for now it was enough. More than that, she knew Thane was a completely different man from the men she'd been exposed to at the trading post. He cared about her well-being and wanted to protect her from the ugliness of the world.

"You're awfully quiet," he said in a hushed voice.

She smiled and squeezed his hand. "I'm

still in disbelief. I keep expecting to wake up and find this is just a dream."

"It's no dream. This is our new life—together. Or very nearly. How long do you suppose we must court before Mrs. Madison will approve our marriage?"

She looked at him for a moment and shook her head. "Are you asking me to marry you?"

"Haven't I made clear my intentions?"

"It might be nice to be asked. It seems most all of my life no one cared about what I wanted. No one ever asked."

"Then let me be the first." He knelt in the grass and took hold of both of her hands. "Militine Scott, will you marry me and be my love forever?"

She burst into tears with unexpected emotion. She had never thought it possible that she could have such happiness in her future. "Yes. I will marry you . . . and be your love forever."

He rose and touched her wet cheek. "Don't cry."

She smiled. "They are tears of joy and a few of surprise that something so wonderful could happen to me."

"I feel some of that same surprise." He glanced toward the house. "So you will marry me right away?"

This made her laugh. "The sooner the better."

"Then I must speak with Mrs. Madison. It seems to me these bridal balls are held for just such a purpose. Would you mind so terribly if we were to marry next Friday night at the ball?"

She shook her head. "I would like that very much."

For a moment he looked as if he'd changed his mind. "You do know that I haven't much to my name. I have a very small apartment that I lease. I have little of value and cannot promise you I will ever be a man of comfortable means."

"I don't care. I've never had anything. Not even love. Now I have that, and it makes me feel rich. I can do a great many things and am not afraid to work. If you aren't ashamed of having a wife who holds employment, I shall be more than happy to seek a position. Then, perhaps if your apartment is too small, we might get something a little larger. However, I cannot imagine a small space uncomfortable if I'm sharing it with you."

He pulled her close and Militine glanced toward the house. "You'll get a severe reprimand if Mrs. Madison or the others catch sight of you holding me like this."

"It would be worth that and more." He pressed her lips with a kiss that she thought might be nothing more than a brief peck.

Instead, he pulled her closer and held her tighter, kissing her until she felt light-headed from lack of breath. When he released her, she could see he was just as affected by the kiss as she.

"I'll go . . . now . . . and talk to Mrs. Madison," he said, the words seeming to stick in his throat.

"I'll come with you. That way there will be no mistaking whether I am in agreement." Militine began to walk away and then looked back over her shoulder. "Because I am definitely in agreement. As far as I'm concerned, Friday cannot come soon enough."

"I have to say that I'm much obliged to being invited to share tea with all of you. I'm just sorry I didn't have anything fitting to wear." James Cunningham attempted to brush some dirt from his well-worn suit coat, casting a glance at Wade's immaculate coat.

"You have no need to apologize," Aunt Miriam said, looking down her long straight nose at him. She had once been a schoolteacher and knew how to take command. "We are enjoying a casual afternoon, and there is no need to concern yourself."

Abrianna picked at the folds of her pale

blue muslin dress. How very awkward the entire affair was to her. She knew this man as Mr. Bowes. She'd offered him food and encouragement, never even suspecting that he could be more to her than one of her charity cases.

They were sitting on the front porch of the bridal school sipping the tea that Aunt Poisie had served before joining the group. The entire purpose of the visit was to determine whether this man was who he said he was, but something inside told Abrianna it was all true. She could see something in his eyes that reminded her of her own reflection. Was it real, or was she just imagining it, hoping that her deepest desires had been answered at least in part? For, of course, her mother could never be returned to her.

Abrianna watched her father handle the cup and saucer with discomfort. It was clear to her that he was out of his element, and the fine china only served to drive home that point. At the food house they had mugs for the men to use. Perhaps she should offer to trade his cup and saucer for one just now.

"Miss . . . Abrianna," he said, turning his attention to her, "I am very sorry for the start I gave you. It was wrong of me not to break the news in a more gentle fashion. I'm afraid, however, when I heard that man being so rude to you, I couldn't . . ." He fell silent. His face paled just a bit as he pointed to the small seed pearl pin she was wearing at the neck of her lacy bodice.

"I gave that pin to your mother." He shook his head. "I never thought to see it again." The shock seemed to wear off, and he smiled. "I worked for over six months doing odd jobs and extra hours at the lumber camp just so I could afford to give her something special for our anniversary."

Abrianna couldn't stop the flow of tears that came. He truly was her father. It wasn't a cruel joke or a case of mistaken identity. Wade reached over and gave her arm a squeeze. She looked at him and smiled. Only he knew how much this meant to her. She hadn't even discussed this with her aunts, for fear of hurting their feelings. They had been such dears to adopt and raise her, and in spite of their often trying to thwart her plans, Abrianna knew how much they loved her. But this man *was* her father. Her own flesh and blood.

"I didn't mean to make you cry, sweetheart." Her father extended a rather dirty handkerchief.

Abrianna didn't give it a second thought. She took the cloth and dabbed at her cheeks. "I can scarcely believe this has happened."

"Well, now that it has, and we know for

certain you are who you claim to be," Aunt Miriam began, "what is to come of it?"

The man looked to her aunts and then back to Abrianna. "I don't know. I guess that depends on Abrianna. I don't want anything from her, if that's what you're thinking. I just wanted to see her again, to know her. She takes after her mother in size. But I'm afraid that red hair comes from my side of the family. Her grandmother had the same red curls.

"Goodness, at least we now know where that came from," Aunt Poisie declared as if an important mystery were finally resolved. "We have pondered that red hair for many years, and at times it has quite vexed us."

"It's true," Aunt Selma added. "We knew her mother had curls, but of course she was not a redhead, and she said nothing of your hair."

He reached up to touch his thinning gray-brown hair. "What's left of it is the same color as my pa's. There's a bit of curl to it, or at least there used to be. My ma and pa were always glad I took after him, but I secretly wished I had red hair like my mother. She was a real beauty, and Abrianna looks a lot like her."

Hearing her father call her a beauty like her grandmother caused a strange sense of pride to rise up in Abrianna. There had been some people who had told her she was pretty, but she'd never believed them. Hearing her father speak of his mother, however, allowed her to believe that perhaps, just perhaps, there were those who could appreciate her type of beauty. As Mr. Welby had mentioned regarding art, she could very well be someone's Rembrandt or Monet.

They talked for over an hour before Aunt Miriam finally stood. Abrianna's father rose immediately, as did Wade. They were men of great respect, and Aunt Miriam had a commanding presence.

"Mr. Cunningham, I cannot see you returning to whatever dockside home you have managed to find. I would like, with the approval of my sister and dear friend, to offer you the room in the carriage house. We have not yet taken a groomsman, and you would be most welcome to the space."

"I could handle your horses for you," he offered. "Earn my keep."

"We haven't any as of yet," Aunt Selma explained. "We do have a large omnibus ordered. Mr. Ackerman is making it for us."

"Rather slowly, due to helping Abrianna every day but Sunday at the food house," Wade explained. "I hope to have it to them by the end of the week, maybe sooner."

"We thought to wait on getting a team of horses until we actually had the wagon for them to pull," Aunt Miriam explained.

"I used to be a good judge of horseflesh. Perhaps you'd allow me to help you pick out a team," Abrianna's father told the ladies.

"Why don't we retire indoors and discuss it? I'm afraid the warmth of the day is leaving me rather uncomfortable. We have a parlor that maintains a very cool temperature, even on days like this." Aunt Miriam looked to Aunt Poisie and Aunt Selma. "Shall we?"

"Indeed, Sister. I was about to succumb to the vapors myself." Aunt Poisie stood and bobbed a smile in Wade's direction. "You are more than welcome to join us." She looked quickly to her sister, as if suddenly concerned she had overstepped her bounds.

"Of course you are welcome."

"I think I'll just sit here a bit longer with Abrianna," Wade replied. "But thank you for the offer."

The older folks departed for the coolness of the parlor, and Abrianna took the opportunity to let out a sigh. "Can you believe it? It's like something out of a novel. I could never have hoped that my father was alive after all this time."

"It is a wonder, to be sure."

"Goodness, I know nothing about his likes and dislikes. I don't know where he grew up or spent his boyhood years. I don't know if he likes white bread or dark. I don't have any indication if he expects me to call him Papa or go on with Mr. Bowes. Oh, surely he wouldn't expect that, do you think?" She looked at Wade but gave him no chance to answer.

"I must say these last few weeks have had my head spinning. The ordeal with Pastor Walker caused me such grief and the courtship of Mr. Welby left me positively questioning everything I'd known up until now and then comes my father." She shook her head. "I don't believe I could stand for any more surprises."

"Speaking of Mr. Welby," Wade said in a cautious tone, "I understand you two had an outing the other night."

She nodded, uncertain if that was disapproval in his tone. She knew he had misgivings about Mr. Welby. She'd had plenty herself. He had behaved like a gentleman, at least for the most part, on their outing, and so she was determined not to speak against him.

"He escorted Aunt Poisie and me to the theatre and then to a late supper at a very fine restaurant—the name escapes me now." She struggled to remember, but the name wouldn't come. "It was all a lot of stuff and nonsense, and I couldn't help thinking the money could have been much better spent in helping the poor. However, it was a lovely evening, and Mr. Welby was a perfect escort."

"You do know that he has been known for

a great many underhanded dealings around town, don't you? I mean, I have tried to mention some of my concerns to you prior to this."

"I remember, but I don't want to misjudge him. Those stories could be false, and even if they are true, perhaps he has changed in the last year."

Wade's eyes narrowed. "Do you have feelings for him?"

"Goodness, no. He tells me he's quite besot with me, but I cannot conjure up even a decent feeling of friendship, much less of ardor. He tells me he will convince me in time, that he has the ability to woo me and win my heart, but grief, Wade, I simply haven't the heart to tell him that he . . . well . . . I just don't believe it will happen."

Wade looked relieved. "I don't, either. He's not at all the type of man you could be happy with. He is power hungry and desires to have a name of importance here in Seattle."

"Well, I suppose having a respected name is not something I can fault him for. Aunt Selma is always saying one's name is important and one should do whatever one can to keep it held in high regard. Although I will say having a name like Priam doesn't conjure up regard in my mind. Where do you suppose such a name comes from?"

"I have no idea. Neither do I care. I care

about you, Abrianna. I don't want to see you hurt or . . . compromised. If he were to try anything untoward, I'm afraid I might well break his neck."

His words first shocked and then amused her. "Oh, you are so silly. You wouldn't do something so awful. I've known you far too long to believe you capable of anything so base."

"Just know this, Abrianna. I care very deeply about you." His voice seemed edged with emotion, but for the life of her, Abrianna couldn't understand why he was so worried. "I promise you that I will always be here for you should you need me, even if it's just to talk."

She popped up from her chair and placed a customary kiss on his cheek. "Stuff and nonsense. I know that. You are my very best friend in all the world. I am so blessed to have you in my life. You are kind to me and gentle in your rebukes. Well, most of the time." She smiled down at him and touched his cheek. "I care very deeply about you, just as you do me. God gave us to each other for comfort and assurance, encouragement and support. I cherish that, Wade, and want nothing to ever come between us—even my ill temper." She paused. "Or when I disobey and you think me foolish, or when I sneak out to tend to business that you find less than important. I didn't mention it, but just the other night—"

Wade got to his feet and put his finger to her lips. "Enough. You've already aged me a dozen years with this food kitchen endeavor and your courtship of Mr. Welby. Pray do not bring up your hidden deeds to further my worries, otherwise I might be tempted to do something we would both regret."

She pushed away his hand and raised her brow in question. "Like stop being my friend?"

"Hardly. I was thinking more of giving you a spanking."

And in truth, Wade couldn't help but wonder if that was exactly what was needed. The old ladies had never laid a hand on her. Punishment was meted out in sending Abrianna to her room or denying her something that was important to her. Unfortunately for them, Abrianna easily adjusted and never seemed overly put upon no matter what was taken from her. Objects didn't mean that much, while her freedom was everything. That and her notion of what God wanted from her.

Wade kept mulling this over and over as he made his way back to his shop and the quiet little room near the docks. It was the Lord's Day, so he wouldn't work on any of his projects, but perhaps if he spent some quiet time in prayer, he might come up with some answers as to why he felt like he'd just fallen off a cliff.

To his surprise, Thane stood leaning against his door awaiting his arrival.

"I thought you were spending the day with Militine."

A grin spread from ear to ear as he pushed off from the door. "I asked her to marry me, and she said yes."

"What? So soon?"

"It's never too soon when you know you're in love."

Wade unlocked the shop and stepped inside before asking, "And how can you be so sure it's the right kind of love, a marrying kind of love?"

Thane followed him inside and laughed. "Because she's all I think of these days. When I'm at work I think of how wonderful it will be to leave and go help out at the food house, because then I'll see her again. When I'm with her, all I want is to go on being with her. And when I kissed her this afternoon, I felt I might well explode in joy."

"Abrianna makes me want to explode, but not necessarily in joy," Wade muttered, not really wanting to discuss it with his friend but also not able to remain silent on the subject.

"That's because you're in love with her," Thane said directly.

Wade looked at him and shook his head. "I can't be in love with her." It was a hard lie to speak, but he feared if he said otherwise, Thane would only encourage the matter.

Thane grinned. "It's a good thing you don't perform on the stage. You're terrible at lying."

Wade pushed back his hair. He knew Thane could see right through his protests. "She's courting Priam Welby, of all creatures. So it matters little what I feel for her. She's not in love with me."

"Then perhaps you should persuade her to be. Why hand her over to Welby? We both know he will only hurt her in the long run. If you love her as much as I think you do, you will fight for her. Maybe you should marry her."

Wade felt a rush of confusion and fear. What if she could never love him that way? Love him the way a wife would love a husband, with a heart of devotion and desire. He did his best to shrug off the emotions. He wasn't about to let this control him.

"There are a lot of kinds of love, Thane. I do love Abrianna. She's precious to me, and I intend to keep her safe if I can. But just because I love her doesn't necessarily mean I should marry her."

Thane shook his head, as if not believing a word of it. "Well, maybe, my friend, you need to reconsider what it does mean."

19

Thursday, June sixth, found the bridal school in a flurry of activity. “No one has retrieved the trunk of costumes,” Aunt Miriam declared. “I must say that with all these affairs of Abrianna courting Mr. Welby and the reappearance of her father, I had quite forgotten about them, and the rosettes we need are surely to be in that trunk.”

“Oh dear.” Aunt Poisie shook her head in a most sad manner. “We are doomed to failure.”

“Nonsense, Sister. Not failure, but it will spoil some of my plans. I recall that those large rosettes of red, white, and blue are also in that trunk.”

Aunt Poisie continued to shake her head. “A tragedy.”

“Don’t fret so. I will attend it after feeding

the poor," Abrianna told her. "I'll have Wade walk us over, and Militine and I can bring back the trunk on the streetcar."

Aunt Poisie put her hands together, her expression changing to glee. "We are saved!"

"I suppose I will have to allow for it," her aunt replied. "We must not ask Wade, however. He is busy finishing our omnibus and plans to deliver it this afternoon. And your father is off with Selma looking at horses up north." She went to her purse. "Here is the fare. Pray do not tarry and, Militine, you will go with her. Perhaps once you find the trunk, Mr. Welby can drive you both home. If so, I would prefer that. I do not like the thought of you on the streetcars like common . . . common . . . well, unescorted females on the streetcar can be dangerous."

Abrianna kissed her aunt's cheek. "We will be back before you know it. Oh, and I've already told the men that there will be only bread and cheese tomorrow. Wade said he would go down and hand it out so Militine and I might stay here and help with the last-minute touches for the ball."

"That's awfully good of him. He is such a dear man. I keep thinking one of our young ladies might do for him, but he never shows any interest."

"And why should he?" Abrianna laughed. "He has all of us."

Aunt Poisie interjected, "Yes, but a man needs a wife, and Wade looks quite lonely sometimes, much as my dear Captain once looked. God rest his soul."

"Amen, Sister. Now really, we must be about our business. Sister, go and see if the table decorations have been completed." Poisie scurried off in her manner, seeming delighted to have a task to perform.

The idea of Wade needing a wife momentarily threw Abrianna into a state of confusion. Wade? Lonely? She'd never really given it much thought. He was at the school often enough that it seemed impossible he could be lonely.

Aunt Miriam continued. "Poisie is right. The Bible says it is not good for man to be alone, and frankly, I believe Wade would benefit from a wife and family. Since he is closest to you, Abrianna, perhaps you could suggest one of the girls. Clara, for example, is coming along quite well. She will be ready to dance at next year's ball, and that would give them time to court."

The thought of Wade marrying and no longer being able to work with Abrianna and the others at the food house made her uncomfortable. In fact, the very idea of Wade giving all his time and attention to another woman made her feel very nearly cross. Not understanding the feelings of perplexity, Abrianna picked up a basket with ingredients for tomorrow's lunches and, without commenting on her aunt's suggestion, headed for the door.

"We will be back as soon after two as we can."

Militine followed her outside, bringing a large basket loaded with bread. Wade hadn't yet arrived, but Abrianna knew it would only be a matter of minutes.

"I'm so nervous about tomorrow," Militine said, shifting the basket to her left arm. "Just think, after the ball I will be Thane's wife."

"It is a wonder," Abrianna said, trying hard to push aside her irritation. "I do wish you would reconsider and wear one of Lenore's gowns." Her words sounded harsh and critical. "Oh bother. I'm sorry. You are entitled to wear whatever you'd like to your own wedding."

"Thank you, but I appreciate that you want to make everything perfect. However, Thane and I aren't at all worried about appearance. Your aunts helped me earlier in April to make my dress for the ball, and it's a lovely piece. I rather like that I made it with my own hands."

"I know you will be beautiful." Abrianna craned to see if Wade's wagon was yet approaching. It wasn't, and for reasons beyond her, that just irritated her all the more.

"What about you? Will tomorrow be

perfect for you with Mr. Welby coming to share the evening?"

"Bah! I'd just as soon he stay home," she admitted. "I told him I would be busy helping to see that things ran smoothly. He said he didn't care, that he intended for us to have several waltzes, even if he had to bribe Aunt Miriam." She shook her head at the thought. "The man can be positively exasperating, and once Aunt Miriam found out that he was willing not only to come, but to pay the admission, she has been at me since. She tells me I must look my best and dance as much as possible so that I might get to know him better."

"What about Wade?"

"What about him?"

Militine shrugged. "Will he get any waltzes with you?"

"You do ask the silliest questions. If I'm to dance all the time with Mr. Welby in order to know him better, I'll have no time to worry about anyone else. Besides, Wade will probably be enamored with one of the other young ladies. I saw him having a deep conversation last Sunday at the dinner table with Clara. I think she's sweet on him." Abrianna frowned. Again, such a thought caused her uneasiness, and her stomach tightened. Perhaps she was coming down with a summer cold. Yes, that would explain a great deal.

"I don't think he's sweet on her," Militine replied.

Wade's wagon appeared down the street. The single chestnut horse clip-clopped at a slow pace, as if they were both out for a summer ride to take the air.

"Goodness, I wish he'd put the horse to a trot. It's very nearly ten, and I need time to cut the bread for today and tomorrow."

"Good thing you put the soup together yesterday."

"Thank goodness for the icebox. It's a wreck of a piece, but it does the job." Thane had managed to round up an old icebox for them to keep foods from spoiling. Better still, he'd found some ice to put inside. It made things much easier for them to have the next day's soup cooking while feeding the poor their lunch. Abrianna had already decided she would press Mr. Welby first thing to provide a very large icebox for the new facility.

Finally the wagon drew even with them, and Wade set the brake. Militine and Abrianna hurried to put the food in the back. Militine surprised them both by jumping up to seat herself on the back of the wagon.

"I'm just going to ride here today. Mind the holes in the road so I don't fall off."

Wade laughed. "I don't think Thane would appreciate it if I lost you in one of those pits."

He turned to Abrianna. "May I assist you in taking your seat?"

He didn't look so lonely. Instead, he looked quite happy, and he was clean-shaven and smelled good. She smiled. "I would be thankful for the help. Although I have donned my serviceable clothes, I would hate to have my skirt catch and tear," she said in a sophisticated manner and then broke into laughter. "Help me or not, Wade, I'm sure I can manage either way."

He smiled and handed her up before taking his seat. "Just look. There isn't a cloud in the sky. I recall your aunt Miriam saying that the ball might be moved outdoors to the gardens if the weather stayed nice."

"It's been nice for so many days that she has decided it will last at least one more. Already she has the girls setting up decorations in the garden, and every table that was in the house has been dragged outside."

"She should have waited for Thane and me to help."

"My father—goodness but that's still hard to get used to—my father helped a good deal, and most of us gals are as strong as oxen, and you well know it.

"Still, I'm glad. I think it will be cooler outside. It always feels so warm with formal clothes and so many people stuffed into one room."

Abrianna cast him a sidelong glance. “Wade, can I ask you something?” She lowered her voice as they moved into traffic. She hoped the activity around them would muffle her voice so that Militine wouldn’t overhear.

“Sure. What do you want to know?”

“Do you find yourself . . . well . . . interested in any of the girls at the bridal school?”

He looked at her in surprise. “What a question. Tell me first why you ask.”

“Well, it’s really not important. Someone mentioned that one of the girls might be sweet on you.”

“Really.” He sat back with a cocky grin. “Is that so? Which one?”

Abrianna frowned. He wasn’t helping matters. “It’s not important. Forget I asked.”

He laughed. “You are a funny creature, Abrianna Cunningham.”

After the rush of lunch and cleanup at the food house, Abrianna was more than ready to return home. First, however, there was the duty of retrieving the costume trunk. “Aunt Miriam wants us to get that old trunk of costumes that we left behind at the Madison Building.”

“I can’t take the time just now,” Wade said, looking worried. “I promised her I’d deliver the wagon, and it’s just about ready.”

"You needn't worry. We already discussed that very fact. Aunt Miriam gave us fare for the trolley but suggested that if Mr. Welby wasn't busy, he could bring us home instead."

He looked unhappy. "She honestly said you two could manage it on your own?"

"Yes. I wouldn't lie to you. If I were of a mind to do something underhanded, I certainly wouldn't announce it to you. You know me well enough to realize that."

"I suppose I do. Well, I can at least walk you over. It's only a couple of blocks."

"That would be exactly as my aunt wished it." Abrianna grinned. "However, I wasn't going to tell you that part, just in case you were too busy. Speaking of which, when are you headed up to deliver the wagon?"

"I'm attaching the sign, and then I'll head up. It'll probably take me about forty minutes or so. I hope to be there by three, and then I'll be staying to help with the decorating. Your aunt even invited me to share supper and stay the night. They're to set me up in the carriage house with your father. I thought it all rather easy, since they have taken the care to ready all my formal clothes."

"Wonderful. I can hardly wait to see the wagon. I've wanted to sneak over to your shop several times just to have a peek. Will it really seat ten?"

"It will."

Without thinking, she reached up and pushed back a lock of his brown hair. Goodness, but he looked so handsome. No doubt Aunt Miriam was right. Someone, somewhere, would want him for a husband. "You need a haircut and—"

He grabbed hold of her wrist as if it were reflex. Abrianna met his gaze, but for the life of her she couldn't remember what else she was going to say. Her stomach tightened again, just as it had on the trip to the docks. Whatever was wrong with her, Abrianna could only hope it wouldn't interfere with the ball.

"We should go," he finally said, dropping his hold.

Abrianna nodded and headed for the door. Her confusion seemed to double. "I promised Aunt Miriam we would hurry home. We might beat you there."

The walk took only a matter of minutes, and once they were at the doors to the building, Wade made his excuses and turned back toward his shop. Abrianna couldn't imagine what had gotten into him. He'd scarcely said a word on their walk.

"Oh bother." She wasn't going to worry about his moodiness. "Let's go." She opened the door and held it for Militine before following her into the building.

When they reached Mr. Welby's office on the first floor, Militine made way for Abrianna to enter first. A man looked up from a typewriter and seemed confused.

"May I help you?"

"Is Mr. Welby in?"

"He is not."

Abrianna moved toward the still-open door where Militine stood. "It doesn't matter. I know my way around. We're just here to retrieve a small trunk from the basement." She started for the basement door, but Welby's right-hand man again appeared out of nowhere.

"You can't go down there. I told you it was being reconstructed. Besides, I searched and didn't find anything."

She didn't believe him. He had that look about him that suggested he would say anything to rid himself of their intrusion. "Well, thank you. I suppose I shan't bother further."

His leering smile made her uneasy as his gaze traveled the length of her body. "It's never a bother to talk to a beautiful woman. The boss is lucky to have you."

"He doesn't exactly have me. Now, if you will excuse us." After enduring his perusal, all she wanted was to go home and take a bath.

They exited without another word. Abrianna could feel Carl's gaze watching her every move. She headed down the walk with Militine at her side, then paused when they reached the busy intersection. Instead of crossing, however, she turned left and skirted the Madison Building.

"Where are you going?"

"I know a way in."

"Don't you think they'll have the back door locked?"

"I'm not heading for the back door." Abrianna glanced down at her gown. The apron had protected her from food stains, but what she was about to do would ruin the skirt and blouse for good.

"Then where?" Militine took hold of her arm. "What are you going to do?"

"The coal chute is just big enough for me to get inside. Hopefully, the coal will neither be too high nor too low, otherwise it will be difficult to hand that trunk back up to you."

"What?"

Abrianna laughed at her confusion. "When I was a little girl I learned early on all the various ways I could get in and out of the building unseen. The coal chute was just one of those." They came to a metal flap positioned at the bottom of the brick wall. She lifted it and pointed. "Down the chute, as they say."

"I'm not going in there." Militine backed up.

Abrianna sighed. "Very well. I'll go and you stay here. When I have the trunk I will lift it up to you. I hope it won't be too big, or we'll have to take the costumes out and carry them separately. And Aunt Miriam is certain the rosettes will be there, as well."

"Abrianna, you'll be covered in coal dust. Your aunt will know what you did."

"I'll worry about that later. I'm sure I can slip in the back unnoticed while you take her the costumes and rosettes. She'll be so delighted, she won't even notice I'm not there."

Without waiting another minute, Abrianna sat on the ground and wrapped her skirt around her legs. "Hold the flap open."

Militine did as instructed, and Abrianna wiggled her way down the chute feet first. It wasn't as easy as when she'd been a child. Goodness, but she'd gotten fat over the years. Her aunts had installed a small slide for the coal. It didn't reach to the ground, however, so there was a bit of a drop when the coal was low. Fortunately, that was not the case. Abrianna maneuvered down the sharp chunks of coal and got to her feet. She dusted off as best she could, thankful that the open flap held by Militine allowed her a bit of light.

"I'll be right back. It isn't all that big down here. I should be able to search it all in just a few minutes."

"Please hurry, Abrianna. I'm frightened."

"Silly mouse. I'm the one risking discovery."

Abrianna crept toward the closed door of the boiler room. She hoped no workmen would be around to question her arrival. She opened the door with great care and listened. To her surprise, there was no sound at all. She slipped into the open area and glanced around. There wasn't much light from the windows. Most were boarded over. She could see that Mr. Welby had made serious use of the room for storage, but there wasn't much in the way of repair, with the exception of one walled-off area that appeared to have a locked door.

She looked around the room and behind numerous crates. She startled when a mouse ran out from one of the straw-packed wooden boxes. Weaving around the stacks, she looked high and low for any sign of a trunk. Nothing. Perhaps Mr. Welby had heard of their search and found the piece for them. Maybe he had even intended to deliver it but had forgotten.

Abrianna was just about to return to the chute when she heard the unmistakable sound of someone crying. It was muffled, but sounded like a child weeping. She moved to one side of the room, but the sound faded. As she crossed toward the locked room the sound increased. She could hear whispers and more crying. At the door she tried the lock, but it was secure. The crying stopped immediately.

"Hello? Is someone in there?" Surely she was just hearing street sounds. "Hello?"

"You go. Plenty in here, but big danger for you." The broken English answer was clearly delivered by a woman.

"Who put you here?"

"You go. Those men come and put you here, too."

Abrianna tried the lock again. "I won't leave you. I will get you out of here. What men did this? I will see them jailed."

She wondered if this was Carl's doing. Worse still, did Mr. Welby know anything about it? The lock wouldn't give, and she tried to figure out what to do next. "I'll be right back. Stay quiet."

Abrianna hurried to the coal chute. "Militine?" she called in a whisper. Nothing. She tried a little louder. "Militine."

This time her friend's face appeared in the opening. "Hurry up. We need to get out of here."

"I can't. There are some women—I think Chinese—locked in a room down here. There is a big lock, and I can't budge it. Go to the Post Building. It's just a couple blocks away. Matt got a job there stacking papers. Tell him he must come right now and bring his lock-picking tools." Militine looked at her as if she were crazy. "Hurry, we don't have much time, and I fear Carl will come down here to check on his hostages."

"This is much too dangerous, Abrianna. Come up and let's go for the police."

"The police won't care what happens to a handful of Chinese. Please just do as I say."

She could see that Militine was torn, but finally the young woman nodded. "I'll go." She lowered the flap and the room grew dark.

Abrianna didn't know whether to go back to the girls and risk discovery or just close the boiler-room door and wait. It was abominable to think that Priam Welby had anything to do with keeping these women locked up in the basement. But it was his building. Surely he had to know what was going on. Still, by his own admission and her experience, he was seldom here. It was just as likely this entire matter was something his man had done, but for what purpose or perversion Abrianna couldn't imagine. Nor did she want to.

20

"This is the finest omnibus ever created," Mrs. Madison declared.

Wade stood back, quite proud of his accomplishment. "One of the city councilmen saw it and told me he was going to suggest I be hired to build the new trolley cars. That kind of job would give me enough money to relocate. I've already set aside a good bit for such a thing."

"That would be a wonderful thing indeed." Mrs. Madison ran her hand down the side of the painted sign.

The Madison Bridal School had been painted in burgundy letters against an ivory background. The wagon itself had been painted a muted yellow on the bottom and burgundy on the top and the driver's seat. It sported three windows on either side. Mrs. Gibson had wanted more, but Mrs. Madison feared it would look too garish.

"Well, come inside, Wade, and I will give you the balance on this magnificent carriage. Mr. Cunningham, would you unhitch the horses while we tend to business?"

"Happily."

Wade looked over his shoulder. "I'm staying the night, so if you want to just put them in the carriage house, I can return them to the livery tomorrow."

Cunningham nodded and began to lead the team away. "I'll secure the omnibus in the carriage house, as well."

"Thank you, Mr. Cunningham," Mrs. Madison called from the porch.

Wade followed her into the house. Glancing around, he wondered where everyone had gotten off to. "Seems awfully quiet in here. I've never known that to happen too often."

"Oh, the girls are out in back decorating the gardens and tables. We are ahead of schedule, I'm happy to say. Having Mr. Cunningham around has proven quite useful."

"How is Abrianna adjusting to the idea of having her father here?"

They entered the tiny room that Mrs. Madison used for an office. "She seems happy enough. Of course, only time will tell. Mr. Cunningham seems to be the good sort, and

I haven't any complaint except for his lack of proper clothing. Sister suggested we take him shopping, but I find it an uncomfortable situation."

"I could take him if you fear he'll run off with the money or not buy something appropriate."

"That might be a wise way of handling it. After all, you would have better knowledge of the shops that might carry the appropriate clothing. That way he need never know there was any mistrust." She sat down to her desk and drew out her cashbox. "I had thought to give you a draft, but since we were out to the bank yesterday, I decided to get the money for you."

"That was very considerate, Mrs. Madison, though I've never known any of you ladies to be otherwise."

She counted out a large sum in twenty-dollar bills. "This is the balance of our agreed-upon price."

Wade didn't tell her that he'd quoted her a price nearly half of what most people would pay. He knew the old ladies had no idea what the cost of such things would be, and he liked sharing his talents with them. They had been good to him over the years, especially after his parents moved to California. Even so, with all they had given and done for him, they wouldn't like thinking he was giving them charity.

"Thank you. Could I impose upon you to hold the money for me in your safe for the time being? I really have never trusted banks."

"But of course." She wrote him out a receipt and then put the money in an envelope and sealed it. She added his name to the envelope and then stood. "It will be here whenever you need it." Moving to a small safe in the corner of the room, she quickly maneuvered the lock and opened the door. "As safe as the bank but not as large. Although Abrianna said it is a great risk to have one these days."

"I hadn't considered it, but I suppose she's right. Should anyone learn that you have a safe, they might be compelled to steal it."

"I had thought of that." Mrs. Madison closed the safe. "Abrianna said if we were to have one, we should install one of those wall units so that a thief couldn't just load it up and take it away. I suppose I should have you build me one."

Wade considered it a for moment. "It wouldn't be that hard to do. It would require I cut into the wall, but I think we could manage it. Speaking of Abrianna, did she and Militine get back safely?"

"Goodness, I'd all but forgotten about them. I've been so busy. My guess is that they would be in the garden with the others." She paused a moment. "You care very much for Abrianna, don't you?"

Wade knew there was no use denying it. "I do."

"I would even venture to say that you . . . love her."

He nodded. "I do. I suppose I should have realized it sooner. I guess it just seemed she was always there and underfoot like an annoying little sister. But now . . ."

"Now you're in love with her and consider her in a completely different light."

"Yes," Wade admitted. "Am I that obvious?"

She smiled. "Not to everyone, but I've seen it coming for some time. I knew, however, that if it were meant to be, God would bring it about."

"But now she's courting Welby."

Mrs. Madison laughed heartily. "And you intend to sit by and just let that happen? If so, you're not half the man I believe you to be."

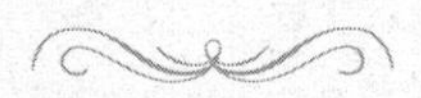

Matt slid down the chute without trouble. "I'm here, Miss Abrianna, but we're gonna have to hurry. There's some big fire going on around here. The air is smoky, and bells are ringing out all over town."

"I know. It won't take you but a moment," Abrianna said, leading him to the locked room. "I'll keep watch." She leaned against the door and spoke to the girls. "We're back and we're going to get you out. Don't make any noise."

"We be quiet" came the same voice from earlier.

Abrianna maneuvered herself so she could watch the basement door. The stairs were clear across the large basement, and there was plenty to hide behind should someone start down. Even so, her heart raced.

Matt had no trouble with the lock. It popped open, and he hurried to free it from the door. Abrianna left her perch and came to help the victims. To her amazement there were several small Chinese women—very young and obviously terrified—all stuffed into the tiny enclosure. The smell of urine almost overwhelmed her. She motioned to them to come out and asked who could speak English.

"Please to be sorry, I speak very bad," a girl who looked to be maybe as old as fifteen answered.

"That's all right. How many of you are in here?"

"Ten."

"Ten? Oh my goodness." She took a brief moment to gather her thoughts.

"Tell the others that we're going to get

them out, and they need to follow us and be very quiet." The others barely moved from their places.

"We not eat. We not drink but sometimes, and then it taste very bad and make us sleep."

They had been drugged. No doubt to keep them quiet, but why were they here? Her rage began to burn at the injustice. Was this Priam Welby's doing or that of his man, Carl? She would get to the bottom of it, no matter what.

"Matt, they're going to need our help. You take one and I'll take another. Let's get them all to the boiler room, and then we can help them outside."

"We're gonna need help, Miss Abrianna. They're little enough, but I don't know that we can get them up that chute."

She nodded. "I'll have Militine go fetch Thane and Wade."

Abrianna hurried to the boiler room and called out for her friend. "You must get Wade and Thane. There are ten Chinese girls down here, and they are too weak to move on their own. We'll have to have help to get them out."

"Thane may be busy with the fire," Militine said. "There must be a big blaze nearby, because the air is getting thick with smoke."

She hadn't considered that they might be in peril from the fire until that moment.

"You have to hurry then. If the fire spreads, we might be trapped."

"I'll run," Militine promised. "I'm good at running."

Abrianna turned as Matt brought the first of the girls into the boiler room. It was the one who could speak a little English. Abrianna went to her and pulled her over to the chute. "Stay here. We have help coming, but there's a fire outside, and we don't know how close it is."

"Fire here?" the girl questioned, her eyes growing wide.

"I hope not." Abrianna didn't want to frighten the poor child any more than she had. She smiled. "Stay right here. Do you understand?" The girl nodded.

Matt and Abrianna worked together to get all the girls into the boiler room. She had no idea when Militine might return or how bad things might be outside, but Abrianna knew they couldn't wait. Even if the fire proved to be no threat, they could still be discovered.

"Matt, I think I will be better at pushing than pulling. You climb back out, and then lie on your belly. I'll help each girl get up to the chute flap and then you pull them out. Agreed?"

"Sure, Miss Abrianna. I can do that." He scurried up the pile of coal and then the metal chute as if it were no more difficult than climbing over a chair. Once he was in position he called back. "Miss Abrianna, I think the fire must be close. I can't even see down the alley if someone is coming."

"Don't worry. We'll get out of here quick enough." She looked at the ten souls who were watching her and waiting for their salvation. No matter what it took, she would see these girls to safety.

"Has Militine returned?"

"I don't see her," Matt replied. "Come on, hurry up. We gotta get out of here."

Abrianna motioned to the smallest girl. "We'll start with you." The girl looked at her with large black eyes. She had no idea what she was to do, so Abrianna took hold of her hand and smiled. She pointed to the chute and Matt. "You go up there. I will help." She looked at the girl who had acted as interpreter. "Can you tell them what we're doing?"

"Some I can talk for. Some I cannot."

Abrianna frowned. She hadn't thought about all the different dialects of Chinese. She knew a little of Liang's language and tried it on for size.

"We will go now," she said, hoping that the words were correct. Three of the girls perked up and nodded. They understood. At least it was a start.

She pulled the small girl up from the floor and all but carried her up the coal and to the slide. Abrianna put her hands together and motioned the girl to step into them. The girl did so, though it seemed to take forever because of her weakness. Abrianna began to hoist her up, and the girl finally seemed to understand and took hold of the metal to pull herself upward. At the top, Matt took hold of her and quickly pulled her through to freedom.

Abrianna sighed. Only nine more to go.

Wade grew worried when he saw that Abrianna and Militine weren't back. It was clear there was a major fire somewhere in town. He climbed to the top floor of the bridal school and could see great billows of smoke. It looked to be in the area of his shop.

"I'm going to go back to my shop and see what's going on," he told Mrs. Madison. He didn't want to mention that he would also look for Abrianna and Militine.

He didn't need to. "Will you find the girls? I'm sure they're delayed due to the trolley, but I would rather they be safe at home."

"I will," he promised. He made a run for the carriage house, where Mr. Cunningham was still currying one of the horses.

"There's a fire downtown, and Abrianna

and Militine haven't returned. I don't like the looks of it." He took up the rope that Cunningham had used to tie up the horse and jumped on the gelding's bare back.

"I'll come, too," the older man declared.

"No. Stay here. The ladies here may need you. I'm sure it's not all that bad of a situation, but you know Abrianna. She's probably standing with the bucket brigade to help douse the flames."

Cunningham laughed. "I'm sure she is."

But Wade didn't laugh. Instead, he shook his head and urged the horse toward the road. "Oh, Abrianna, where are you and what have you gotten yourself into now?"

21

Out of breath and feeling light-headed from the smoke, Militine found Wade at his shop. At first he didn't seem to notice her. He was busy throwing his tools and belongings into the back of a wagon. And she didn't have enough air to say anything. But if she didn't hurry, what would happen to those girls? And Abrianna?

"Wade!" Her voice pushed through heavy breaths.

He stopped and glanced around. "Where's Abrianna?"

"I'm sorry, but we need your help."

His shoulders slumped. "I was afraid of that when I couldn't readily find you. What's she done this time?"

"She's trying to rescue a bunch of Chinese

girls from the basement of the Madison Building. We don't have time. Please, we need your help."

"What? That's not far from the fire." He moved toward her.

She choked back a sob. What would she do without Abrianna? What if some awful person caught her in that basement? And to think she had to bear such news to a man so obviously in love with her friend. "We went there for the costume trunk, but they wouldn't let us in. She went down the coal chute and found these girls locked up." She took hold of his arm. "We have to hurry. Even if the fire doesn't cause trouble for her, they could be discovered."

"Welby ought to be hanged for this." Wade pushed her toward the wagon. "Come on."

Wade attempted to maneuver the wagon out from behind his shop and onto the street. The borrowed gelding wanted no part of the chaos that had become Front Street.

"I was supposed to get Thane, too," she said and then tried to explain further above the noise.

"He's probably at the fire. Look, I don't know if I can get to the Madison Building with this wagon. Let's leave it on the docks and come back for it. Hopefully folks will be too busy to start looting it." He set the brake and jumped down. He pulled Militine to the ground. "Now, where did you leave them?"

"The alley behind the Madison Building."

Just then a man broke from the stream of people and joined them. "Thane! Glad to see you."

Militine rushed to him. "Are you all right?"

"It's a bad one. The whole block is burning." He put his arm around Militine. "I thought you and Abrianna would already be home by now."

"Abrianna apparently is on one of her fool crusades," Wade told him.

"It's not foolish at all. We went to the Madison Building to get that trunk Mrs. Madison wanted, and when they wouldn't let us in"—Militine barely took time to breathe—"Abrianna decided to go down the coal chute."

Thane rolled his eyes. "Of course she did. Is she stuck?"

"No! Listen to me. Both of you need to come with me. Abrianna and one of her young orphan friends are trying to rescue ten Chinese girls who were locked up in the basement. We don't know why they are there or who put them there." Steam whistles from the waterfront began to blast along with the ongoing clang of bells.

"But we can guess it was Welby, since it's his building," Wade replied sarcastically and in a barely audible voice.

They kept step with Militine, although it was becoming more difficult to work their way against the flow of people. Militine feared for their lives as people, animals, and wagons flooded the streets. It seemed everyone had the same idea—get their possessions to the docks for safekeeping.

"Fire's outta control," one man yelled as he passed them. "Better not go that way."

"We pulled the Gould steamer to the wharf," Thane said, "but it's low tide, so we can't get water to pump. That's going to limit them to the water mains and hydrants, and we already know those don't have the capacity we're going to need to put out this blaze."

Militine coughed and ducked her face into the top of her blouse. Thane handed her a handkerchief. "Use this. It won't do much but ought to help a bit."

They rounded the corner where the Madison Building stood. Militine quickly pulled them out of sight. Numerous people were carrying crates out of the front door of the building, and she didn't wish to be questioned. "They may already be on to Abrianna. Hurry."

They skirted around to the alley and found Abrianna and Matt with the Chinese girls. One by one they were moving them away from the building.

"I'm sure glad to see you," Abrianna declared. "We're in a pickle here."

"When *aren't* you in a pickle?" Wade asked. He took hold of the girl Abrianna was trying to move.

"They're really weak from lack of food and being drugged. I think if we each take two, we can get them out of here and down to your place," Abrianna said, looking to Wade and then Thane.

"That's not going to help," Thane told her. "The fire is spreading that way."

Abrianna coughed and wiped her eyes. "Then we can at least get them to the wharf."

"That's probably all we can do," Wade admitted. He went to help another girl to her feet and wrapped his arms around two of them. Thane did likewise with two of the larger girls, while Matt took up two that were closer to his size. Militine and Abrianna followed suit. It wasn't going to be easy, but Militine knew that if they didn't try, those girls would die.

"Let's just head down the alley," Thane suggested. "I don't see any flames, so we ought to be okay." He stumbled and quickly righted himself. "Smoke alone can kill, though, so keep moving and try to stay low."

Militine lost sight of Abrianna. They were staying close to the wall, but the smoke worsened, and it was impossible to see much but their own feet.

God, I know I haven't always been faithful, but Thane and I are trying hard to trust in you, and right now we need you more than ever.

Her prayer seemed like such an ineffectual thing, but Militine remembered Abrianna saying that God heard every prayer. She didn't have to have flowery words or know all sorts of Scripture in order to pray.

As they came to the end of the alley, Thane called back to them. "Let's meet at my shop if we get separated. It's a little farther from the immediate path of the fire."

Militine saw a rush of people moving like a tidal wave toward the docks. Most were carrying possessions and store stock. Some were crying, many were cursing, and others looked stunned out of their wits.

The smoke had risen in this area, and Militine could see a bit better. Down the street the fire brigade was prying up planks from the sidewalk at the north end of the block. Without warning, flames burst from the open area and drove the firemen backward.

"It's spreading from building to building," Thane declared, "via the basements. So many are connected by thin wood walls."

Even as he announced this, flames began to break through the wooden structures and explode out open windows. The warm breeze fanned the blaze.

"We gotta get out of here," Wade yelled. "I've got the wagon and horse at the dock just outside my place. Provided they're both still there."

"Sounds good. Let's go."

The group worked into the flow of people on Front Street. Screams and cries mingled with the smoke and flames. Never had Militine seen such pandemonium. It was like watching the city come apart at the seams. This, along with the cacophony of bells and whistles, made it all so surreal.

Her arms ached from the stress of all but carrying the two small figures. They couldn't have been all that heavy, but Militine struggled nonetheless. Hurrying to keep up, she felt someone or something plow into the back of her. The force sent her and the girls to the ground. She knew she would have to act fast. The ground was the most deadly of places to be in a stampede of panicked people. Without thinking, Militine forced herself upward with a strength she didn't know she possessed. The girls seemed to sense their death was imminent unless they helped, so they, too, fought to regain their feet. Together they stumbled to the other side of the street, where Wade and the others were waiting.

"Are you all right?" Thane asked, leaving his victims long enough to help Militine to safety.

"I am now." The smoke choked out her breath. "It's getting worse, isn't it?" She met his eyes and could tell it was true without his even needing to answer.

Behind her something exploded, and she couldn't suppress a cry. The girls began to weep. "Come on," Thane encouraged. "We're almost to the wagon."

"The opera house is on fire!" someone yelled from behind them.

Militine turned to look down the street, but the smoke had thickened, settling lower than it had earlier. Her eyes burned and teared at the constant barrage of soot that moved through the air. Her lungs ached for clean air, and her throat had grown sore and dry. Would they ever manage to get out of this nightmare?

They finally reached the docks, only to see people chalking out sections where their belongings were to be placed. The few ships in Elliott Bay were taking on goods as fast as they could be moved up the gangplank. Wade's horse and wagon were still there, but the animal, spooked by the commotion, was trying to pull against the brake to escape.

"I need to get back and help with the fire," Thane said when they finally reached the wagon. He gently lowered the girls to the ground, then went to Militine and helped her with hers. Once free again, he took Militine in his arms. "Stay with Wade and the others and get back to the school. I'll come as soon as I can."

"Please come back to me, Thane. I can't bear the thought of losing you. There is nothing else left."

He smiled. "We have God. That's more than we started out with."

He kissed her firmly but briefly. He tasted of ash, and Militine felt her eyes tear up all the more. He was going to put himself in the thick of it. He might even be killed. She wanted to hold him in place, but he broke her grip and moved away. As he disappeared down the street, Militine had to fight to keep from running after him.

"The wind is picking up," Wade said. "Let's get everyone loaded in the wagon. Matt, help Abrianna get the girls in." The boy nodded and did as he was told.

He lifted one of his girls into the wagon to sit atop the other things already gathered there. The horse whinnied and stamped. A man rushed up to Wade and took hold of his coat. "I'll pay you a hundred dollars to come with your wagon and help me load up my merchandise."

"I'm sorry. I'm transporting these ladies."

The man shook his head. "They're just a bunch of Chinese. Please help me."

Wade pushed the man away. "Get out of here."

Once all the girls were in the wagon, Wade motioned to Abrianna and Militine. "Get up on the seat. Matt, you sit at the back and keep an eye out for anyone who might try to commandeer this wagon. Abrianna, take the reins while I stay down here and try to guide the horse through the crowds."

She nodded and climbed up to the driver's seat. Militine followed her, turning once she'd claimed her seat to see if there might be a glimpse of Thane. There wasn't.

The horse inched forward. It wouldn't be easy to get him away from the docks and north to safety. Militine held her breath as Wade fought the people to maneuver even a few feet. Curses were hurled at them, as well as a few threats. Even more people begged Wade to come help them. The crowd was getting ugly in fear. Militine took hold of Abrianna's arm for comfort. Her friend turned and gave her a weak smile.

"I'm sure he'll be fine," she said above the din. Militine wasn't as sure, but she nodded nevertheless.

What little progress they made was soon

halted by a collection of firemen who were hustling another pump to the bay. Militine could see the tide was still out. She had no idea if the men could reach water with their hoses or not, but it looked to be an awfully far distance.

"You won't get far this way," one of the firemen called out to them. "Everything in that direction is on fire."

Militine looked at Abrianna. "What are we going to do? We're trapped."

Priam Welby hadn't expected to be so long at his meeting. As he emerged from the Third Street offices, he could finally see what all the commotion was about. A runner had come to tell them that there was a large fire near Front Street, but there were always fires, and usually no one seemed overly concerned.

He stopped a policeman who seemed to be in a rush to join the fracas. "How bad is it?"

The man shook his head. "Everything is going up from Marion to Union. It's coming this way, thanks to the winds. I fear we're all doomed." He said nothing more and ran off in the direction of the fire.

Welby looked in the direction of the Madison Building. A moment of panic washed over him. He had thousands of dollars of merchandise housed in the basement. Would his men have taken the time to get that stuff out and to safety? Then there were the girls. Pity that. There would be no way to get them out and keep them from being seen. Carl would no doubt try, but most likely they would have to remain where they were.

He thought for a moment, wondering if he should attempt to lend his assistance. If the fire was as bad as the officer claimed, it would spread fast and out of control. There was probably nothing any of them could do. He gave a shrug. Perhaps it would be best to go back to his home on Denny Hill. The fire would never spread that far, and from that vantage point he could watch the affair in comfort.

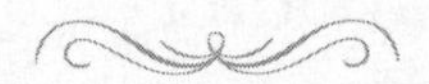

Abrianna gripped the reins tighter. Her hands ached and pain shot up her forearms. She gasped for breath but found little air in the black smoke. Getting the girls out of the basement and moving them this far had taken a toll on her energy. Fear ran through her like the flames that rushed from building to building. Everything around them was now burning, and the intense heat made it impossible to move away from the bay. At least the tide was starting to come back in. That would give the firemen some much needed water.

"We're going to set off some dynamite," a man told them, coming to where Wade stood. "You're going to have to stay right where you are for the moment. Hopefully this will stop the fire's spread. It shouldn't take long and then you should be able to move on up and past the worst of it."

Abrianna couldn't imagine that dynamite would help. It seemed foolish to start another fire to put out a fire. She looked to her left and watched as frantic men scurried up and down the gangplanks of a ship called the *Alameda*. A man was fighting to pull a pump organ up the gangplank even as the ship was leaving the dock. He quickly lost control and the organ plunged into the bay, while the man barely managed to jump back to the dock. People were losing their minds in this madness.

Time seemed to stand still. There was no way of telling whether an hour had passed or if it had been two. She looked around for something to give her an idea, but even the sun overhead was darkened out by the thick billows of smoke.

An explosion shook the ground around them. "They've dynamited the White Building across from the Reinig Building," Wade told her. "They're hoping it will slow things down, if not stop it all together."

The girls behind her were growing hysterical. "Wade, we have to do something. I don't know what, but we have to get these girls out. Wait, what about Thane's shop? Might there be a boat there? There are usually several tied off around there and even some in storage. We could load everyone up and push off into the bay. That way at least we won't catch fire." She didn't want to tell him, but the scorching air and flying embers terrified her to the bone. It wouldn't take much to set the wagon on fire.

"That's worth a shot. I think I can maneuver the wagon down that far. Let off the brake." He went back to the horse and took hold. "Come on, horse." He pulled the straps, and the horse danced a bit but turned.

It seemed to take forever to reach Thane's, and even there, Abrianna could see they weren't much better off. Flames reached as high as the tallest buildings. Walls of orange, yellow, and red devoured everything in their path. The roar intensified, like a horrible hungry beast. She handed the reins to Militine and jumped to the ground.

"Wait with the girls, Militine. I'm going to help Wade find us a boat—or something." She ran to catch up with him, but her legs felt like heavy weights, and it was a struggle just to move.

"I think other folks had the same idea."

Wade looked over the rail of the high dock. "There's not a single boat tied up below."

She looked around, assessing the situation. "There's a small rower over here," Abrianna declared. They both went to inspect. "It looks seaworthy." But she could immediately tell that it wasn't big enough for all of them.

Wade nodded. "I'll lower it down to the water. Make sure the oars are inside."

She did as he instructed and waited while he cranked the craft inch by inch to the water. Next they went back for the girls. One by one they managed to get them down the weathered steps to the water's edge. Wade helped each of them into the boat. Thankfully they were small. To Abrianna's amazement he managed to fit all ten of the girls into the vessel, with two of them sitting on Militine's lap. Abrianna was waiting for him to say what she already knew. There wasn't room for another three people. They'd be lucky if they could squeeze in one.

"Matt, you're going to have to row. Between you and Militine you should be able to at least get out far enough to be safe." Wade's voice was calm and strong.

"What are you and Miss Abrianna going to do?" the brave young man asked, his voice cracking.

"Don't worry about us. We'll swim for it, if we have to. Just get going."

The teen was in no way put off. "I don't want to leave her here. You neither. We can just squeeze you in."

"Look at the boat. You'rc already overloaded and may start taking on water if you're not careful. Now go." He untied the vessel and gave it a push. "When you are able to get to safety, arrange to get everyone back to the school."

Matt nodded and began to work the oars. Abrianna saw the concern in his expression, but it was certainly no more than her own. For all her bravery over the years, she had never faced a moment quite like this. Exhaustion and the feeling of being trapped didn't suit her well at all.

"What are we going to do, Wade?"

He shook his head. "I'm not exactly sure. We can take up some of the planks off the dock and use them for keeping us afloat. The fire brigade did that down by my place to make fire breaks."

"It's getting closer, so we'll have to do something soon." She tried hard not to let her emotions get the best of her. Goodness, but a woman had to keep her head at times like this, even if she was scared down to her stockings. She wasn't going to let Wade see her as a weak little mouse.

They climbed back up to the wharf only to

realize that while they'd been below, the fire had spread to their location. Wade pushed her back toward the stairs. "Go. We're not getting out this way."

All of the ships, schooners, sailboats, rowers, and liners had pulled far out into the bay. For a moment Abrianna could make out the bigger vessels through the smoke, and then they too were swallowed up. She and Wade were completely alone.

"Good thing I taught you to swim," Wade said, pulling off his boots.

"We're really going to try to swim to safety?" She tried to show her bravery by untying her own high-top boots. Even that took a colossal effort.

"It appears to be our only choice."

She paused and looked at him. Gone was all of her bravado. "Wade, I'm scared."

He stopped unbuttoning his shirt and pulled her into his arms. "I know, but we're gonna be all right. I already promised you I wouldn't let harm come to you. Do you trust me?"

She pulled back and nodded. "I do, but I don't trust these circumstances."

The roar of the fire seemed to grow, and Wade released her. "Get rid of that skirt."

Abrianna looked at him and then to the serge skirt blackened by the coal and soot.

She supposed there was nothing else to do. She unfastened the button at the waist and let it drop. Her single petticoat left her feeling bare to his gaze.

"You'll have to take off the petticoat, too. It'll just get tangled around your legs in the water."

"That would be highly inappropriate. I'm already in a state of undress, and to lose my petticoat would leave only my . . . drawers. Goodness, but my aunts would faint dead away from shame if they or anyone else found out. I'd be forever known as a . . . foolish ninny."

"Better than being known as dead. I think even the old ladies will allow for it, since it's probably going to save your life." He threw his shirt aside and turned his back. "Hurry up. I won't pay a lick of attention."

Feeling completely ill at ease, Abrianna slowly untied the string that held her petticoat in place. Just then something crashed up above, sending a rain of sparks and embers down upon them. She kicked out of the petticoat and, without waiting for Wade's instructions, jumped into the water.

He followed into the bay and motioned to move further out. "That's all going to collapse behind us, and we need to be well away from it before it does."

The water was cold, much colder than she'd

figured, what with the warm days they'd been having. It wasn't worth worrying about. She prided herself on being able to swim. Wade had taught her when she'd been a young girl. If only her muscles weren't already so over-stressed.

Behind her, Abrianna could hear the fire and destruction of the pier. She tried not to think of what might have happened to the horse or to Wade's wagon. She hadn't reset the brake and didn't know if Militine had thought to do so. Maybe the animal would manage to get to safety. It was doubtful, but she prayed it might be so. And what was one horse compared to hundreds of people who might perish.

Oh, Father, please save the people of Seattle from death. The prayer gave her marginal comfort as she continued to stretch out her arms and stroke the water. Her feet felt like lead weights as the cold permeated her legs. She was grateful Wade had forced her to disrobe, knowing she'd have been pulled under by now from the weight of her skirt and petticoat.

She couldn't feel her hands, and her arms were growing heavier by the minute. Apparently one needed to practice swimming a great deal to be very good at it for very long. She felt herself slowing, her strength giving out. She stopped and rolled onto her back to let her body float for a moment. Wade had taught her this, as well, as a way to rest should she get a stitch in her side.

"Abrianna, come on. I see a schooner not far."

She shook her head, gasping as a wave of water washed over her. "Ca . . . can't."

Wade swam back to where she was floating and treaded water. "I'm not going to let you give up, you little hoyden. You're always pushing everyone else to their limits, and now I'm demanding the same of you."

"I . . . can't. My arms wo . . . won't move. I'm t-too cold."

"Quitter."

She gave a weak laugh. "Yes."

"I won't let you." He grabbed hold of her arm. "I suppose I shall have to drag you to safety, like usual."

She tried to think of something witty to say but was unable to think of anything. She opened her eyes, and Wade began to pull her through the icy water.

Behind them, Seattle burned.

22

Ahoy there!" came a voice. It was like being in a dream. Who was it? Captain Jack? Hairless Mike? Maybe old Charlie. No, he was dead. Murdered last year and they never discovered his killer. Abrianna tried to speak, but only a moan escaped from her mouth.

"Permission to come aboard," Wade said in a jovial tone. "Look, Abrianna, the navy has come to rescue us."

She could hardly make sense of his words. With no strength left to her, Abrianna allowed herself to be dragged and pulled out of the water. She heard one of the men order another to get a blanket. The next thing she knew she was wrapped into a scratchy wool blanket and nestled down between Wade and Hairless Mike.

"Where are we?"

"Captain Jack took . . . borrowed this here boat," Hairless Mike told her. "We thought to do our part and help them what couldn't escape the fire."

"Like us," Wade declared. "We were trapped and had to swim for it. God was looking down on us when he sent you boys."

"Ain't nothin' we wouldn't do for Miss Abrianna. She's cared for us like nobody else. She was never uppity to us, always offered us her kindness."

Abrianna smiled. Her eyelids felt so heavy. She had once read an account of someone freezing and how they started to fall asleep. Was that happening now? Could someone freeze when a fire was burning down the town on a warm June day?

"Don't go to sleep," Wade ordered. He reached over and shook her hard. "You have caused me far too much trouble to let you get off scot-free." He began to rub her arms. "I've spent a lifetime getting you out of one predicament and then another. The least you can do is be grateful and obedient."

"You're . . . so . . . bossy." Despite the pain of his massage, Abrianna wanted nothing more than to sleep.

"Give her this," Captain Jack said.

Wade put something to her lips. "Drink."

She nodded in obedience. At least she could do that much. White-hot fire burned down her throat, and her eyes snapped open as if she'd been slapped. She coughed and gasped to get her wind, but the harsh liquor very nearly choked her.

Wade pounded her on the back until she could regain her breath. "What was that?"

"Whiskey." Captain Jack held up a flask.

"You told me you would never take another drink," Abrianna accused, her head beginning to clear.

"It was merely with me for medicinal purposes."

"And it helped to rally you around," Wade declared. "Now stay awake and try to keep warm." He looked to the sailors. "I think she'll be all right. Can you get us up the coast a bit closer to her home?"

"Certainly," Captain Jack said, tucking the flask into his pocket. He barked out several orders, and the men went to work.

Abrianna shook her head. "You are a bad influence on me, Wade Ackerman. Why, today I've done things that I've never done before and hope never to do again. You've quite compromised my good name by having me strip down to almost nothing and giving me whiskey."

"You weren't down to almost nothing."

"I was close enough, and I'll be surprised if my aunts don't faint dead away. Especially once they smell liquor on my breath." She could see the worry in his expression begin to fade. She smiled and continued. "However, I'm sure that once they realize how the rest of Seattle has fared, they won't be giving me much thought, so I suppose I should thank you, instead of being upset with you."

"Yes, you should, as well as all your old sailor friends."

She pulled the blanket close. How would she ever be able to face those men at the food house again? The food house! It was probably burned to the ground. The thought sent her spirits spiraling downward.

"Oh, Wade, it's all gone, isn't it? Your shop. The food house. Thane's apartment, and the boat shop." She heaved a sigh.

"Yes."

The single word drove her sorrow deeper. "I've been so selfish."

"You saved those girls." He shook his head. "Honestly, Abrianna, I don't know how you found them or got them out. It's a sure bet Welby didn't try to save them."

She shrugged. "I don't know if he even knew they were down there. He said he was seldom at the building, and his man, Carl, seemed awfully suspect to me. He was the one who didn't want us to go down in the basement."

"Welby's too much in charge not to know what was going on."

"You're being awfully judgmental, Wade. We haven't even asked him about it yet. You should reserve your judgment until then. I agree that it would be normal for a man to know what's going on at his place of business, but Mr. Welby has many places of business, and I feel we should give him a chance to explain."

"Because he's courting you?" Wade asked. "I didn't think you even liked him."

She stiffened. "It's not a matter of liking him or courting him, Wade Ackerman. I'm trying to be a good Christian and not judge him falsely." She pushed away his hold. "I just want the truth."

Wade's expression grew rigid. He crossed his arms against his still damp chest and leaned back against a wooden crate. "Sometimes you can't see the truth of what's right in front of you, Abrianna."

The fire proved impossible to stop no matter how hard Thane and the others worked to contain it. They first planned to keep it from moving farther than Front Street and the docks. They failed. The wind and weather offered no help, and the water-main pressure was very nearly exhausted. Thane couldn't see how anything would stop this blaze but the grace of God.

He prayed, but the words seemed hollow in his ears. He'd spent so long refusing to seek God that now he felt hypocritical. He'd barely gotten himself right with his heavenly Father and already he was pleading for divine intervention. Suddenly he felt helpless again. Helpless like when his father bullied him. Helpless like when he witnessed his mother's murder.

God, you know I'm no good, but some of these folks are. He thought of Militine and the school, of Abrianna and Wade. Would they ever come out of this alive?

Around five o'clock Thane felt the wind shift. He looked up from where he'd been ripping up planks of sidewalk in hopes of creating a firebreak. "Look, the wind. It's blowing the fire back onto itself," he told the man working at his side.

All of the men around him were strangers. He'd not been able to find his company, so he'd set to work with those nearby who needed him. Everyone stopped what they were doing to assess the situation.

"God be praised," one of the men murmured. "Maybe this will be our salvation."

They continued their work, ever hopeful, until the wind again shifted and began blowing from the northwest. It gave the flames new momentum, and the earlier encouragement faded. Thane saw how the fight had gone out of the men. He felt the same.

By six-thirty one of the company chiefs came to tell them they were needed at Third and James Streets. "Third?" Thane asked, thinking surely the man was mistaken. Had the fire really spread that far?

"Third," the man replied. "It's moving fast up James. We're going to tear down all those shanties along the street and hope the fire won't jump the gap and set fire to Skid Road. Places along there are nothing but kindling, even on a good day."

The men gathered all of their tools and hurried in the direction of the newest concern. Along the way Thane could see the extensive destruction. Buildings were ablaze from Front Street to Third. The heat was such that many of the firemen had been burned without ever coming in contact with the flames. Explosions sounded from the numerous hardware stores as ammunition and dynamite were ignited by the fire. Debris flew through the air, and brick facades collapsed as buildings gave way to the intense heat. It felt as if they were in the middle of a great war with death flying at them from every angle.

At Third Street they turned on James and crossed over to lend aid to the workers already there. The smoke was thicker there, with intense fire at their backs. The Occidental Hotel, the finest in all of Seattle, suddenly exploded and roared into flames just a short way behind them. The temperature became unbearable, and the firemen were forced back.

"It's melted the fire hose," someone announced. "There's no hope for us now."

Men pulling one of the pumps hurried past them toward the fire. Even so, by the looks on the faces of the weary men, Thane knew they didn't think it would do any good.

"We've been at this for almost four hours," the man at Thane's right said, shaking his head. "Ain't saved much of anything."

"The way I see it," another man said, stopping long enough to wipe a sooty handkerchief across his sweaty neck, "we might as well let the fire have it."

Thane couldn't give up that easily. He was just as worried and just as tired as everyone else, but some things were worth dying for, and this was one of them. Militine came to mind. He found himself praying again that she was safe and well away from the fire. They were to have been married tomorrow night. Now that would be impossible. Who knew if they would even survive this night?

"I think it's God's punishment," the man at Thane's right added. "Just last week it was Johnstown, Pennsylvania, getting wiped out in a flood, and now Seattle is burnin ' to the ground. Seems like maybe it's the end of all time and God's takin' back the earth a piece at a time."

No one challenged the man's thinking. Thane had no way of knowing if there was any truth to what he said. He hadn't read the Bible, and short of listening to sermons in church and Wade's occasional teaching, he hadn't even known about God's return. What if the man was right and God was taking back the earth a piece at a time? What would happen to the people? It was thought that over two thousand had died in the Johnstown flood. Had God taken those folks back, as well? Would He take some from Seattle? Maybe take them all?

"Oh dear. Oh dear." Miss Poisie was flitting about like a little bird. "Oh, Wade, what are we to do? We've packed as much as possible, but there's only so much a person can take with them."

Wade tried to appear a pillar of strength for them, but in truth he was exhausted. The worry and fears he'd had for himself and Abrianna had taken their toll, just as the waters had.

"Sister, calm down," Mrs. Madison ordered. "Right now we must see to it that Abrianna is dry and comfortable."

"Oh, dear Abrianna, forgive me. This is all quite beyond me. I would take a bit of Dr. Dremer's Syrup for calming nerves, but I'm afraid I might be of no use to anyone then."

"Well, do try to make yourself calm, Sister. There is nothing to be gained by fretting. We are all very worried about the fire and what we should do, but we must be strong. The ladies are counting on us to offer leadership."

Wade glanced over to see the older woman towel drying Abrianna's curls. He tried not to worry about whether her time in the water would take some further toll. She looked very pale and small. He was so used to Abrianna being full of energy and life, willing and able to battle all kinds of giants who threatened to tear apart her perfectly ordered kingdom. In so many ways she was still such an innocent. At least she was, until today.

Once she had time to think through why those Chinese girls were locked up and what Welby no doubt had in mind for them, she'd have a difficult time ignoring the evil generated by men like him. And certainly Welby had to have had a hand in all of it. Abrianna might be willing to question him first and listen to whatever story he chose to tell, but Wade knew otherwise. He'd once seen Welby on the docks with his men. There was also a small woman who had tried to run from them, but she'd been caught and put into Welby's carriage. Those women in his basement were not there by mistake.

"All right. Take her upstairs, Selma, and get her dressed. I want a word with Wade and Mr. Cunningham, and then we will decide what is to be done."

Before she could address her concerns, however, Lenore and Kolbein Booth were ushered into the house by Liang, the Chinese house girl.

"Oh, Mrs. Madison, we wanted to come and check on you. Kolbein came from the city and everything is afire," Lenore said, moving to the older woman's side.

"We know. Wade has just returned with Abrianna. They were there and very nearly consumed. They had to jump into the bay and be rescued in order to keep from being burned alive."

Kolbein stepped forward. "Are you all right?"

"Abrianna got too cold, but I think she's all right now," Wade told him.

"You must have had quite a shock, as well."

Kolbein nodded to the shawl one of the ladies had put around his shoulders. “Why don’t you come back to the house with me and I’ll get you some dry clothes.”

“First we need to know what is to be done,” Mrs. Madison said. “Do you suppose we should flee?”

“The fire is moving this way,” Kolbein replied. “I have no way of knowing whether it will continue in this direction or not. The wind is against it, but that hasn’t stopped it from spreading in all directions.”

“Oh dear. Oh dear.” Miss Poisie popped back up on her feet. “It’s like the fires of hell. Oh, Sister, I’m quite distraught. Where are Miss Muffy and the others?” She began searching behind the settee.

“Miss Muffy?” Kolbein asked.

“The cat. One of three, actually,” Mrs. Madison replied. “We all are distraught, Poisie, but you must remain calm. We have to think of the girls here who depend on us. They are awaiting our decision and watching the fire from upstairs.” She turned back to the men. “Do we go or stay?”

“I don’t think it would hurt to be overly cautious,” Wade said. “We could at least go up the hill and wait it out in the park. It will give us a good vantage point, and it seems that others are doing likewise.”

"He's right," Kolbein said. "I've already sent my household staff away. Look, I have two carriages that we can use to get everyone out of here."

"And Wade just this afternoon brought us our new omnibus," Mrs. Madison added. "Goodness, but it seems that was years ago. I'm afraid this fire has taken a great deal of my energy."

Wade thought she might well collapse and went to her side. "Why don't you sit a moment."

She nodded and allowed him to help her to a chair.

"Then it's settled." Kolbein turned to his wife. "Lenore, you stay here and help the ladies gather their things. Wade will come with me and change clothes, and then we'll be back."

"We need horses if we're to take the omnibus," Mr. Cunningham said.

"I'll bring all I have," Kolbein said. "After all, we can't leave them to the fire. Just wait for our return, and we can help you."

Abrianna and Selma rejoined them. Abrianna had donned another of her old skirts and a well-worn blouse. Her hair was pulled back and tied with a ribbon, and Wade could see her color had returned. She was holding the cat Mrs. Madison called Buddy in her arms.

"Oh, you found one of them," Miss Poisie

exclaimed, clapping her hands. "Now, if we can find Miss Muffy and Mr. Masterson." She went to Abrianna and took the cat. "I shall put her in the laundry hamper, although I daresay she will not like it." Miss Poisie paused, looking most perplexed. "Do you suppose she would prefer a wooden crate?"

Abrianna ignored her aunt's dither as she caught sight of her friends. "Lenore! Kolbein! Oh, have you seen the great tragedy?" She rushed into Lenore's arms. "Wade and I were nearly taken by the flames. We had to swim to escape, but I was overtaxed after we helped those girls."

"What girls?" Lenore and Abrianna's aunts questioned.

"It's a long story." Abrianna threw a quick glance Wade's direction.

"Welby was up to his old tricks, but this time he's going to have to answer for it." Wade wasn't about to let the man get away with what he'd done. "Apparently he had ten girls he was holding hostage in the basement of the Madison Building."

Abrianna nodded. "Someone held them hostage. Suffice it to say we helped some Chinese girls get away, and they will join us later."

Wade all but growled at her comment. Would she defend Welby even after all they'd gone through?

"They will find us departed," Mrs. Madison declared. "The men believe we should move to higher ground, farther from the fire, and I agree."

"We can't leave them without hope," Abrianna said, looking to Wade as if she expected him to intervene on her behalf. "Militine is with them and plans to bring them to this house. I'll leave them a note."

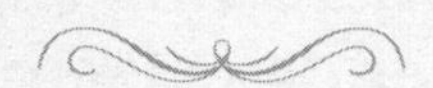

Militine and Matt found themselves aboard one of the ships in Elliott Bay. The Chinese girls were huddled in a group just behind them, but Militine refused to leave the railing. She watched the glow of the city fires and thought only of Thane. Somewhere out there, he was fighting to save lives with no thought of his own. She knew he would never think twice about risking himself for another. It was a self-imposed price to pay for all those lives his father had taken. She had heard him say as much once. Fear tore at her from every side. What if tonight all claims came due?

As the night wore on, the ship's crew brought buckets from their fresh water supplies, as well as bread, cheese, and baked potatoes. Those who had either sought refuge on the ship before it sailed or who had been rescued in the harbor, as had Militine and the others, offered their gratitude, but most of the food went untouched.

"Do you think Miss Abrianna and Wade made it out?" Matt asked.

Militine felt ashamed that she hadn't given those two much thought. She looked at him and nodded. "I'm sure they did." She turned back again to the burning city. "They must have."

It sickened her to imagine that she could lose all three of her dear friends. These people were the most important in her life. *Oh, God, how can I go on if they are taken? Please hear our prayers. Let the fire be put out and please, please, Lord, don't let a single life be lost.*

23

Militine had never been so exhausted in her life. She arrived at the bridal school with the Chinese girls in tow later that evening only to find the place deserted. There was a note to let her know where everyone had gone and why. Apparently Mrs. Madison was worried that the fire might spread and claim the school, as well.

Glancing around the dark neighborhood, Militine found the silence eerie. It would seem everyone had abandoned their houses.

She turned to the young woman who spoke a bit of English. "I believe the others left in case the fire came this far, but I think we're safe. I'm not sure where Mrs. Madison would have me put you all, but I'm going to just take my chances." The girl looked at her oddly. Clearly she couldn't follow Militine's words.

"Come on." Militine motioned to the house. "We go inside."

By three in the morning, it was clear that the fire had finally been contained and would be no threat to the school. Much to Militine's relief, the others returned.

"Oh, you are safe!" Abrianna cried, embracing her. "I was worried about whether you'd found refuge."

"A schooner captain picked us up. We were later put off on a dock nearby. We walked the rest of the way. Matt was kind enough to watch over us until we got here." She turned to Mrs. Madison as Abrianna let go of her hold. "I didn't know what else to do, so I gathered blankets and had the girls bed down in the spare room off the ballroom."

"That was good thinking, Militine. We will go check on them. I would suggest the rest of you get to bed. We will of course cancel our festivities. I believe it would be reasonable that you all sleep in for as long as needed."

The students of the school dispersed while Abrianna went with her aunts. "If any of them are still awake, I'll introduce you so they won't be afraid."

With her responsibilities discharged, Militine made her way upstairs. She crawled atop her bed fully clothed, still filthy from her ordeal. Her mind struggled to find peace. On the boat they had heard hideous rumors of hundreds of firemen killed, as well as victims who were trapped in the raging inferno. And then at the docks a great many people had gathered, and with each newcomer came a new dreadful rumor. The tales were so disheartening that many stood in a numb state of shock.

But I'm not numb. The pain I feel is acute and will not be relieved until I know Thane is safe.

Militine gritted her teeth and closed her eyes tight. She tried to keep from crying, but tears seeped out all the same. There was a certain kind of despair that came in not knowing the truth one way or another. The waiting and watching left her emotions raw. Over and over the image of Thane being burned alive came to mind. Over and over she fought it off with pleas to God.

She wandered around the house until she could no longer stand the confinement and then slipped into the gardens just as dawn broke. The world around her was uncanny in its silence. Even the birds were quiet, as if they knew cheerful noise was uncalled for. A smoky haze still hung over the city.

Militine looked at the abandoned preparations for the ball. Her wedding was to have taken place that evening at the party. She would have married Thane and moved with him to his little apartment. They would have set up housekeeping together and been happy.

"I know we would have been happy."

Stop this. He's not dead. He's not.

She sat down on one of the metal garden benches and began to sob. Her faith was so weak, so fragile in its newness. Did God understand how hard this was? Did He know how much she hurt? How frightened she was?

She had endured a heinous childhood full of violence and beatings. She'd watched her mother lose the will to live—had lost it herself. She had prayed for death so many times but found herself abandoned even in that. Why would God give her a taste of happiness only to tear it away from her? She buried her face in her hands. It was all so unfair.

"Militine."

At first she thought she'd imagined Thane calling her name, but then she felt his arms enclose her. And he was there, holding her. Just holding her. He smelled of sweat and smoke, but he was there, and she never wanted him to let her go.

"Don't cry, my darling. I'm here."

She tightened her hold. "I feared the worst."

"As did I. And then I knew I had to trust my life to God or go mad." He stroked her hair until she calmed.

Pulling away just the tiniest bit, she looked into his face. His skin was blackened with soot and ash, and even his red hair was matted and dark. But none of that mattered. She gazed into his eyes, so thankful that God had brought him back to her.

"Is it as bad as they said? Hundreds dead—everything gone?"

"I don't know about the people. The town is burned to the ground. If we hadn't had the help of the Tacoma Fire Department and others, we might still be fighting the flames. As it is, everything is still smoldering." He stood and pulled her to his side. "What about Wade? Abrianna and those girls?"

"Everyone's safe."

Thane pushed back her hair and took hold of her face. "You were all I could think about. I just knew that God would keep you safe. When I thought my strength might give out, I remembered you would be here waiting."

"I kept praying, but I wasn't even sure I was doing it right." She shook her head and finally offered him a smile. "I guess in times of trouble maybe God doesn't need us to have certain words or to be on our knees. He just needs us to trust Him."

"I think you're probably right." He kissed her then. It was a long and slow kiss, sweet and gentle, just like his spirit. Militine lost herself in the moment and hoped—no, prayed—there would be many more to come.

A knock sounded at the parlor door a little before ten-thirty. Thane had tried to sleep on the floor, but his concerns for the city weighed heavy on his mind.

Kolbein stuck his head in the doorway. "Thane, I came for Wade, but learned you were here, as well. I realize you were probably fighting the fire all night, but there's going to be a meeting of all Seattle businessmen who lost their places—some six hundred, as I hear it. The meeting is being held at the armory. The governor will be there, the mayor and the council, too. I figured Wade would want to be there—you too."

"I'm definitely coming along." He had slept only a few hours, but it was enough. He needed to return in the light of day and see what was left of Seattle.

"Will you come back and tell us about the meeting?" Mrs. Madison asked. "I want to know if there is anything we might do to help."

"I will learn what we can do," Kolbein assured her.

Thane and his companions were stupefied by the scene that unfolded as they drew nearer the city.

"I thought it was bad seeing it all in flames," Thane murmured. The burnt remains of telephone and telegraph poles still smoldered. They were like tall charred sentinels standing guard amidst the rubble.

"Someone may get hurt if those brick walls come down," Wade said, pointing to a precariously balanced wall that stood amidst the rubble.

For over twenty-five city blocks—a hundred twenty acres—nothing but destruction and lost dreams remained.

"I've never seen anything like it," Wade murmured. "Never."

"Me either," Thane admitted. Kolbein remained silent, though Thane could see he was just as disturbed.

The closer they came to the devastated downtown area, the more people they found wandering around in a daze. The National Guard had been assigned posts and guarded the remains of the town from looting and did their best to instruct the lost as to where they might find help.

"How in the world can we hope to come back from this?" Wade shook his head.

"It will no doubt take years." Kolbein's words echoed Thane's thoughts.

Years and years of work would be necessary to clear the debris and rebuild the town. And where would all the money come from?

As they approached the little church they attended each week, Thane was surprised to see the structure still standing. Pastor Walker was standing on the church's doorstep preaching to a gathering of victims. Kolbein drew the carriage to a halt.

"The fires of hell have been unleashed on this sinful generation. God has released His wrath upon you and demands that you turn from your wickedness. Like Sodom and Gomorrah of old, this den of liars, thieves, and murderers has been called to account for its sin.

"I stood last night at this doorway—this sanctuary of God—and demanded that the fires not touch one stone, and as you can see not one stone has fallen. I stood toe-to-toe with the Devil himself and called him down. I single-handedly saved this church, and now I am calling you to repentance. Repent before it is too late! Repent before God sends another disaster to get your attention."

"The way I see it," Kolbein murmured, "God is the one who saved the building, not Walker."

"Is that how God really works, Wade?" Thane wasn't sure he could abide a god whose idea of grace and mercy was such utter and total destruction. "Is this God's punishment?"

Wade seemed to think on the question while Kolbein urged the horse forward. "I know there were times in the Bible where God took a heavy hand with the people. I can't really say one way or another why this fire came about. The truth is we live in a world that is full of sin and sinners. But I will say this much, the Bible shows that God is love. I believe He loves His children in a never-ending way."

"But this isn't love," Thane said, sweeping his arm toward the blackened landscape.

"Sometimes love comes in unexpected ways," Wade replied. "And sometimes God's answers come in ways we don't recognize. I'm not saying this fire is that kind of thing. I'm not saying it isn't. I won't try to second-guess God. What I do know is what the Word of God says. 'That if thou shalt confess with thy mouth the Lord Jesus, and shalt believe in thine heart that God hath raised him from the dead, thou shalt be saved.'

"Confessing Christ means we have to take a hard look at ourselves first and see what's alienating us from Him. Our sin nature wants nothing to do with His purity and goodness, but He wants us to repent and be reconciled to Him."

"But if God is good and is love like you said, why would He ever let bad things like this happen to us?"

"He let His own Son go to the cross for us. And Jesus said we'd have a hard time of it here on earth. Most of His disciples were killed for sharing the gospel. Many of His followers, too. These terrible things will go on happening until He returns. All we can do is trust Him and believe."

"And still we suffer His wrath?" Thane asked.

"No. Ephesians five says, 'Let no man deceive you with vain words: for because of these things cometh the wrath of God upon the children of disobedience. Be not ye therefore partakers with them. For ye were sometimes darkness, but now are ye light in the Lord: walk as children of light.' We're children of light, Thane. God's children. Therefore His wrath isn't on us and . . . furthermore . . . I believe that verse says that the wrath of God is still to come. All through the New Testament we can see evidence that if we are in Christ, we are no longer to fear God's wrath."

Thane fell silent. It was easy to blame God because He was . . . well . . . God. He had the power to do anything—and to stop anything.

"This looks like the place," Kolbein said. People were swarming the area around the armory, and it was almost impossible to get the horse and carriage within a block. Finally Kolbein gave up and tied the horse off. He motioned to a boy of about ten.

"Will you watch my horse and carriage while we attend the meeting? I'll pay you a little now and more when I return."

The boy's eyes widened at the sight of a quarter. "Sure, mister. My pa is in that meeting. He told me to stay right here. I ain't doing nothing else."

Kolbein handed him the coin. "Good. Then we will count on you."

They worked their way through the crowd and found a place where they could stand. Once gathered with the others, Thane listened to Mayor Robert Moran read a proclamation of disaster.

"All persons found on the streets of this city after eight o'clock p.m. without the countersign will be arrested and imprisoned. All persons found stealing property or otherwise violating the laws will be promptly arrested, and if resisting arrest will be summarily dealt with." He paused and looked out over the people gathered there and then lowered his face to read.

"All saloons in this city are hereby ordered to immediately close and remain closed until further orders, under penalty of forfeiture of their licenses and arrest. No person will be allowed to sell or dispose of any liquor until further orders. Any person found so doing will immediately be arrested and imprisoned.

"Officers and members of the militia and all policemen are strictly enjoined to enforce the foregoing orders."

Next came the governor and his announcement. "I have called out the First Regiment of the Washington National Guard. They will patrol and maintain order to keep the city remains from looting. I'm proud to say that these men took their post only three hours after the start of the fire and will continue until such time as they are no longer needed."

Cheers and applause arose from the crowd.

The mayor reclaimed the podium, and the meeting continued with him posing several important questions. "We will not waste our time on pointing blame on how or why this fire started. That information will come soon enough. Instead, we are a people known for our strength, and we will build again."

Thane couldn't help but get caught up in the enthusiasm of the crowd. The mayor continued. "Therefore, the questions that come first and most important: Do we permit the erection of wooden buildings within the area burned by the fire? And two, should the streets in the burned area be newly platted before rebuilding begins?"

The room erupted in opinions. Most favored widening and replatting the streets. It had long been a source of frustration to the growing community. Representatives from the fire department declared that wider streets would help considerably in getting to fires more quickly. However, unless the city could do something to improve the waterlines, it wouldn't matter.

The issue of brick versus wood buildings set the people arguing for quite a while. Many held that the fire would not have been nearly so devastating had the buildings been of brick or stone. Others argued about the high price of brick, but the price, someone pointed out, had been paid in last night's fire.

"I don't know that I even plan to rebuild," one outspoken man declared. A good number of his companions agreed.

"Might as well leave it to someone else."

Many of the businessmen stated that they were through with Seattle. Leaving seemed to be a better alternative to starting over. Obviously distressed, the former governor, Watson C. Squire, rose to offer words of encouragement. "Let me say first that I believe a committee should be formed to look after the poor and suffering. Furthermore, I will start a subscription drive with a donation of five-hundred dollars."

The crowd clapped wildly, but the former governor motioned them to calm.

"That said, I recognize there is a great deal of discouragement among some here, and they would give up on our fair city. However, let me say that although I have only a few hundred dollars in the bank, my credit is good, and I'll rebuild on every foot of my ground that was burned." He took his seat amidst a roar of enthusiasm while another man came to the podium.

It was time to put their thoughts into action. G. Morris Haller began, "I move that the fire limits remain as they now are, and that no wooden buildings be erected therein by permit or otherwise. All in favor?" The *aye*s rang out in a thunderous confirmation. Only a few protested.

Additional appointments for relief committees and one to help the council replat the city kept the crowd buzzing. It seemed that most everyone agreed with the thoughts of their council, including ideas to raise Front Street by building over the wreckage of the fire. The steep grade had always been an issue, and by burying what had once been there and erecting new buildings atop, they would reduce that grade considerably.

As Thane wearied of the meeting and thought to excuse himself, the last order of business was declared. The president of the Board of Trade, George B. Adair, was introduced. "Many of you know that I was the chairman of the committee to collect funds for the sufferers of the Johnstown, Pennsylvania, flood that took place last week. As you also know, the flood caused over two thousand deaths and left many homeless. The good citizens of Seattle raised over five- hundred dollars for this cause, and I now ask if this should be kept for local sufferers? Or should we send it on to the folks in Johnstown?"

The immediately response spoke volumes of the spirit of Seattle. "Send it away! Send it to Johnstown!"

Thane smiled despite his exhaustion. Sometimes the goodness of folks amazed him. He had known so much ugliness and selfishness throughout his life that to see the love and giving of these people was humbling. Maybe there was hope for this world after all.

24

In the week that followed, activities at the bridal school did not change much, except the production of goods focused on benefiting the homeless of Seattle rather than making sales for the school. Abrianna loved the chance to minister to so many people. God had called her to this work, and she answered. Aunt Miriam declared they would supply as many blankets and articles of clothing as could be made by the school. They would also furnish food from their gardens and animals and other supplies. So long as they had anything to their names, they would help the homeless of Seattle.

"Just look at what the paper has to say today, Sister," Aunt Poisie announced. "The

U.S. Army has sent a hundred fifty four-man tents from Fort Vancouver and Fort Walla Walla. The Tacoma Relief Committee has provided cots in two large downtown tents, where people will sleep at night and eat during the day. I find that quite industrious." She looked to Selma and Abrianna. "Don't you?"

"Oh, indeed," Aunt Selma replied. "I never had much good to say about Tacoma. They have often been a thorn in the side of our good city, but their help in our time of need has been quite amazing. Perhaps they aren't the rapscallions that we were led to believe."

"Perhaps they have had a change of heart," Aunt Miriam commented. She looked up from her sewing. "After all, it could just as easily have been their city."

"It's true," Aunt Selma said. "The mayor said that the fire was started because of a glue pot being neglected. A Swedish man was involved, as I understand it."

"Oh, a Swede. That may explain a great deal," Aunt Poisie said.

"Goodness, Sister, whyever would you say that?"

Abrianna found herself curious at this. Aunt Poisie looked rather remiss, as though she had committed some kind of social faux pas.

"I was thinking of the language barrier. Perhaps the man spoke only Swedish. Perhaps he was new to this country and the job." Aunt Poisie cocked her head to one side and looked thoughtful. "Do they even have glue in Sweden? Perhaps he was told to attend it and hadn't been trained properly."

"I am certain they have glue in Sweden, Sister. However, no matter that, the paper said the glue ignited and then water was thrown onto it." Aunt Miriam shook her head. "That only served to spread it."

"Well, Swedes do have all that water surrounding them. He might well have thought it the cure."

Aunt Selma put aside her knitting. "I hate that everything is in ruins. Nothing looks right or smells right. The days have been so dry and warm. Nothing like they should be. I fear we may well see additional fires, and then what will we do? What if this place were to burn?"

"I could not live in a tent with other people." Aunt Poisie looked quite disturbed. "I would be most uncomfortable. After all, what if a man . . . were to . . . take advantage?"

Abrianna suppressed a giggle. Her aunts were always worrying about the strangest things. At a time like this she doubted very seriously that those poor souls wandering the streets were overly worried about anything but finding a place to rest and a hot meal.

"Sister, you needn't be afraid. I do not believe you will have to live in a tent anytime soon."

Liang appeared at the door to the sitting room. "Mr. Welby is here."

Abrianna tensed. She knew she would have to receive him. She had already decided she would confront him regarding the girls. Wade was certain he was to blame for their imprisonment, but Abrianna felt it was only right to give the man the benefit of doubt. After all, even though she had no intention of marrying Mr. Welby, she did say she would give him a fair chance to prove himself.

"Show him into the front parlor." Aunt Miriam set aside her sewing and looked to Abrianna. "I suppose you will want to speak to him about the girls?"

"Indeed. The truth must be found out." She rose and set aside the blanket she'd been hemming. "Although I do not relish this moment in time. I sometimes wish I'd never gone down that coal chute."

"I have also wished it on many occasions," Aunt Miriam murmured.

Abrianna looked at her aunt in surprise. "You knew?"

"Of course I knew. You did a poor job cleaning up afterward."

"But you never said anything." Abrianna

looked to her other aunts. "Did all of you know?"

"Certainly we did," Aunt Selma said.

Aunt Poisie merely bobbed her head and smiled. Her eyes seemed to dance in amusement. Abrianna felt certain her aunt would have liked to have commented on the matter, but already her sister was guiding the conversation.

"How will you confront him, Abrianna?"

She sighed and smoothed the skirt of her mauve gown. "I've given it a great deal of prayer. I plan to tell him the truth of what I did and what I found. I believe we will know if he is lying by the way he reacts. And we can bring the girls to confront him. If he had charge of this situation and dealt with the girls in person, they will recognize him, and that will be that."

"Will we need the police?" Aunt Poisie asked, her eyes growing wide. "I daresay that would be most scandalous to have them come here to the house."

"I think we can probably avoid that," Aunt Miriam replied.

"If they do need to come, we shall offer them refreshments. Then we could tell our neighbors that we took tea together—if they asked." Aunt Poisie leaned back in her chair and smiled, as if proud at her clever thinking.

"Then no one would need be wiser about the real reason."

To Aunt Poisie it no doubt seemed a master plan. Abrianna couldn't help but smile. She loved these dear old ladies with all of her heart.

"Well, let us join him." Aunt Miriam moved toward the door. "We will let Abrianna take charge of the conversation regarding the young Chinese women."

"Oh, agreed," Aunt Poisie declared. "Quite agreed."

"She is best to confront him." Aunt Selma got to her feet.

The comments surprised Abrianna. Perhaps her aunts were now starting to see her in a different light. Rather than treating her like a young child who had little or no sense, maybe they were seeing her for the sensible young woman she'd become. Of course, sensible women probably did not slip down coal chutes.

The front parlor had been arranged in a most welcoming way. The decorating had been a labor of love by the three older ladies, and most visitors agreed that it was one of the most pleasant parlors they'd yet encountered. However, Priam Welby did not look at all comfortable as he paced the beautiful Oriental rug.

"Mr. Welby." Aunt Miriam and the others

entered ahead of Abrianna. They nodded their greeting and took their places.

Mr. Welby smiled. "Ladies, I am relieved to know that you are well." He looked past them to meet Abrianna's scrutiny. "And you, I am most relieved to see that you are well, too. I feared you might have been at your little food house when the fire broke out."

"I was indeed downtown." Abrianna swept into the room like a regal queen, the satin merveilleux gown rustling like a whisper. She held herself as precisely as Aunt Miriam, hoping her formality would indicate her maturity. She sank gracefully onto a French corner chair, which had recently been reupholstered in a dark hunter green silk. "Please sit."

He did so but still looked uneasy. "I thought to come here today and invite you and Miss Poisie for a carriage ride. There are already many people coming from far and wide to see the remains of Seattle, and I thought perhaps you might desire a closer look."

"I cannot agree to any carriage ride just now," Abrianna said. She folded her hands together. "We need to talk first."

He looked from her to the older ladies. "Is there something amiss?"

"Perhaps." Abrianna tried not to sound condemning. The fact was she couldn't bring herself to believe him guilty of such a horrible thing. He might have big ears and be a ruthless businessman, as Wade suggested, but holding people hostage in his basement seemed beyond anything she could imagine him doing.

Welby looked to Mrs. Madison. "First, let me say that I felt great sorrow at the loss of your old building. It was a grand place and suited my needs so well. However, I was greatly relieved to know that you had long since moved from it to the safety of this house. I believe that to be divine providence."

"We quite agree, Mr. Welby," Aunt Miriam answered for them all. "We were just speaking of that yesterday. God certainly blessed us in bringing us to this place. I was never easy in leaving my husband's legacy, but it is clear that God provided safety and provision for us."

"Yes. That's exactly what I was telling some of my men."

"Will you rebuild, Mr. Welby?" Aunt Selma asked in such a casual manner that they might well have been taking tea.

"I will. I had insurance on the building and its contents. I have been informed of where to file my claim and plan to do so Monday."

Abrianna couldn't resist a blunt question. "Will that insurance extend to human loss?"

He looked at her and shook his head. "I don't know what you're asking. There were no deaths at the Madison Building."

Abrianna felt her resolve to be calm and meticulous fade. She couldn't bear to think that he could so easily talk about insurance and replacing what had been lost if he knew that human life might have been lost, as well.

"I went to your building the day of the fire."

Everyone stopped and looked at Abrianna. Mr. Welby appeared confused. "But why would you go there? You knew I was seldom in my office."

"Yes, I knew that. However, we needed to search for a trunk full of costumes that we feared had been left behind in the basement."

His expression didn't change, and Abrianna took this to be a good sign. "Your man, Carl, wouldn't let us go and look. He said there was danger there, and that some repairs were being made."

Welby rubbed his chin. "I do recall he said something about that. Surely he offered to look for the trunk himself."

"He told me that he had, but the trunk wasn't there." She narrowed her eyes, watching him closely. "I could tell he was lying to me."

"But why would he lie to you?"

"That's what I wondered. It seemed harmless enough to go look for the trunk or even to escort me to look for the trunk. It wouldn't have been inappropriate, because Militine was with me. However, he simply refused. He was quite rude."

"I am sorry about that, Abrianna. I will speak to him and ask that he treat you in a gentler fashion in the future. I suppose the trunk was lost in the fire, and I assure you that I will happily replace it and the contents if you let me know what was inside." He looked to the older ladies and gave a slight nod. "I would feel completely remiss if I were to do anything less."

"I didn't find the trunk down there." Abrianna watched him for a reaction, but he only looked puzzled.

"I thought you said Carl wouldn't admit you."

"I did, but you know me well enough to know that I'm not easily put off. I grew up in that building. I know, or rather knew, other ways to get inside. I let myself in through the coal chute."

He laughed out loud. "You didn't. Oh, but what I wouldn't have paid to see that."

"Sir, I am speaking on a most serious matter and would appreciate it if you would refrain from laughter." She had heard Aunt Miriam use similar words on her more than once. "What I found in that basement was most appalling."

He sobered. “I do apologize. Whatever are you speaking of?”

“Chinese girls. Ten to be exact.”

He shook his head. “What have they to do with my basement?”

“They were being held hostage there. Locked in a room that had been built, I suppose, for just such a purpose.”

“Girls in my basement?”

He clearly appeared stunned by the information. Abrianna relaxed a bit now, more convinced that he was innocent. Aunt Miriam rang for Liang. When the girl appeared, Aunt Miriam looked to Abrianna.

“Would you bring the girls, please?”

She turned back to Priam Welby, but his expression suggested that he still had no idea what she was up to. In a matter of minutes, Liang returned with the ten young Chinese women. They lined up near the door, and Liang spoke to them in hushed Chinese.

“Do you know these young ladies?” Abrianna asked Welby.

“No.” He shook his head and looked from one face to another. “I’ve never seen them before now. Who are they?”

“These are the women who were held hostage in your basement.” She looked to Liang. “Please ask them if they know Mr. Welby.”

Liang again spoke and three girls shook

their heads. One of the three spoke in yet another dialect and a couple of the other girls shook their heads. The one who spoke broken English did her best to translate for the others, but not one of the girls appeared to know Priam Welby. Abrianna gave a sigh.

"You may take them back to their duties," Aunt Miriam declared.

As the girls shuffled out of the room, Abrianna turned back to Mr. Welby. "I did not believe you capable of such a heinous thing, but I had to be certain. Please forgive me if I have offended you. That was not my purpose."

"I am not offended by you. I am, however, offended that someone sought to use my building to further some devious and appalling scheme."

"I am of a mind that your man, Carl, is responsible. After all, he was the one who seemed most upset by my desire to go into the basement."

"Carl does lack certain . . . qualities." Mr. Welby shook his head. "I am fearful that you may be right."

"Sister believes we should contact the police," Aunt Poisie announced.

Abrianna looked to Mr. Welby. "I think we must. After all, those girls were taken from their homes in China and forced to come here.

They were drugged and mistreated, and someone should have to answer for it."

"If it is Carl, and I feel more confident by the minute that it must be, then he will answer for it. I don't believe the police will give us any satisfaction, however. Not with the city in such upheaval. Not only that, but you know very well the attitude they have toward the Chinese."

"I do. I must say that was also my concern."

He stood and looked quite severe. "I promise you, I will deal with the matter. I will see the man dismissed from my service and punished."

"How will you accomplish that, Mr. Welby?" Aunt Miriam questioned.

"I am not quite certain at this juncture, but you may rest assured that it will not go unpunished. I will find a fitting penalty and see to it that it never happens again."

"I suppose, Aunts, that we cannot ask for more than this. At least we have a champion in Mr. Welby." All doubt drained away. Priam Welby seemed to be just as incensed by the situation as they had been.

"I'm afraid, my dear Abrianna, that I will have to postpone our drive. I cannot set this development aside for an afternoon of pleasure in your company. If you will excuse me, ladies." He bowed and moved to the door. "I will show myself out."

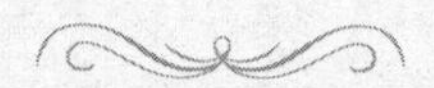

"He was certainly alarmed to learn what had happened," Miss Poisie said later that evening when the men had come home from working on the pier. While Thane had eyes only for Militine and quickly found excuses for them to leave, Wade and Abrianna's father seemed quite interested in what had taken place earlier that day.

"Yes, I believe he was just as startled by the news as we were," Mrs. Madison added. "He did not look to be a man who was bearing guilt."

"And the girls didn't recognize him as their captor," Miss Poisie threw in. "It would seem to me that his innocence was proven."

Wade held his tongue. Welby was a master at deception. Of course he'd been able to fool three old ladies and an innocent young woman. Now, however, he wasn't at all sure how to respond. If he made a scene, it might only serve to alienate Abrianna. One way or another he would need to find proof before he spoke his mind.

"I am relieved to hear that. Although I do find it difficult to believe that a man with his power could be so deceived." Wade tried to be careful with his words. “Did he say what was to be done?”

“Oh yes. He felt confident, as we did, that his man, Carl, most likely had something to do with it,” Abrianna replied. “He said he would handle it himself and see that the truth was learned and Carl punished—if responsible.”

“I see. He didn’t feel the police should be involved?”

Aunt Miriam spoke before Abrianna could reply. “He pointed out that the law cares very little about the Chinese except to get rid of them.”

“And that the police are consumed with the problems brought about because of the fire,” Miss Poisie offered. “The paper said they’ve deputized over two hundred men to help keep everything under control.”

Wade couldn’t argue their points. Welby was no fool. He would know, just as Wade did, that even if the truth were to be told, most likely everyone in authority would look the other way. They had their hands full with more important issues, and the lives of those young women would mean very little because of their race. Not only that, but as he’d heard rumored, Welby had quite a few of the officials taking bribes. They would no doubt defend him.

“I suppose there is nothing more we can

do about it," Miss Poisie said in a dismissive manner.

"We will, of course, tend to these girls," Mrs. Madison declared. "It is my personal desire to see them returned to their families."

"Maybe Mr. Welby will even pay for their transport, Sister." Miss Poisie glanced at Mrs. Madison for her approval.

"Perhaps."

The conversation moved on to other events and concerns. The men answered questions about their work at the pier and what all was being done to get some kind of order back in the city. It was strongly believed that the docks were to be the first to be rebuilt. After all, the city was very dependent upon ships to bring in cargo.

"Here it is just two days after the fire, and goods are coming in from everywhere. People too. I heard today that San Francisco is sending a ship north that is loaded to the brim with building supplies and men eager to hire on in the rebuilding."

"The brickworks around this area are to labor 'round the clock," Mr. Cunningham added. "Now that buildings have to be constructed of brick, they'll need to keep that up for some time."

"There are plenty of bricks to be had elsewhere, but no way to get them here. In time, however, that will change." Wade tried not to show his agitation. He kept looking to Abrianna, who seemed quite happy to go on believing that Welby was a decent man.

Am I misjudging him? Wade shook his head. No, he knew what kind of man Welby was. The real problem would be getting Abrianna to see the truth.

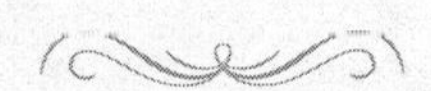

The Sunday after the fire dawned bright and warm. It proved to be a good thing that the weather held. Had it rained, the town would have been reduced to a muddle of ash and mud, making the work of cleanup much more difficult.

Brother Mitchell offered praise from the pulpit for the fact that in spite of tremendous loss of property, not a single life had been claimed by the fire. It was amazing that with all the destruction, no one had died.

"There would have been at least ten deaths if you had not risked your life," Militine whispered in Abrianna's ear. "I prayed there'd be no deaths—not even one."

Abrianna patted her hand and smiled. "God hears our prayers."

Brother Mitchell offered a prayer and then turned the pulpit over to Pastor Walker. The man had something of a wild look to him.

Abrianna narrowed her eyes and tried to figure out what was different.

"Sinners, repent!" He looked hard at the congregation. "We have seen the powerful hand of God—His judgment in fire."

Abrianna quickly lost interest in the man's accusatory tone. She thought instead of the blessings God had given her. She caught a glimpse of her father to the far right in the pew ahead. It was such a miracle to have him back in her life, but with all that had happened, they'd had very little time to talk in private. She hoped to resolve that situation as soon as possible. She wanted to know him better, to see him as a real father and not just one of the needy they had fed.

Pastor Walker ranted on about the judgment that had come down on Seattle. He condemned each and every citizen as having not been right with the Almighty, otherwise this might never have happened. As his voice rose in volume, Abrianna found it impossible to ignore.

"Some of you avoided the wrath of God this time. But there will be other times. God will not sit by while you live your lives in sin. You, even here today, allow for licentiousness and adultery. You might as well be the ones sleeping in the beds of harlots, for the guilt of this town is upon your heads.

"I stood at the door of this church and prayed back those spirits that would have fed on the walls of our building, those that feed upon your very souls. I preach despair today because that is what you are to face unless you turn away from your sin-filled ways."

Abrianna could hear weeping throughout the church. The place was packed to capacity, no doubt due to the fire and the sense of loss felt by so many. She longed to offer comfort and words of hope rather than the harsh and condemning ones their minister was spouting out. Selfishly, she also longed to leave her seat and never return. It saddened her deeply to feel that way about the church she'd grown up in.

"The sins of this congregation are many and must be purged before you can be right with God." He looked straight at Abrianna and pointed his finger. "You women who seek to do the job intended for men—you must cease or face the fires of hell." She felt her cheeks get hot. He continued to shake his finger at her. "You are no less a harlot for the shame you bring upon yourself and this congregation." She wanted to move, to call him down, but Abrianna found it impossible to do anything.

"And you older women—women whom God called to be teachers of the younger—you wallow in sin because you refuse to allow for the male leadership God intended you to have. You honor only your own word and keep company with those who agree. You are condemned to a life of hell unless you repent."

He didn't stop there. He pointed to a group of young men. "You adulterous generation. You give yourselves over to the pleasures of the flesh and bring condemnation down on this city. Repent!"

Pastor Walker had worked himself up into such a sweat that he threw off his suit coat and began pounding his fist on the Bible. "I alone hold the answer for you. I am the only one who can lead you to redemption."

"I think I'm going to be sick," Abrianna said under her breath. Would no one challenge this man? And then out of nowhere, someone did.

"You are wrong, Pastor Walker." It shouldn't have surprised her that Wade would take a stand, but in that moment she'd never been prouder of him. "Jesus said that *He* is the way, the truth, and the life, and no man cometh unto the Father but by *Him*." Wade got out of his pew and started walking toward the front. "You dare to stand as a man of God and deceive these people with words that are not scriptural?" He continued walking slowly forward.

"You are guilty of leading these people astray with your pride and arrogance, saying you alone have the answers. You say that you alone saved this church, but to my way of thinking, that honor goes to God." There were murmurs of amen throughout the congregation.

"Apostate! Blasphemer!" Walker screeched.

Wade was unmoved. He held up his hand and closed his eyes. "Father, I ask in the name of Jesus that you silence this man."

He opened his eyes and stared hard at the preacher. "You are the apostate and blasphemer. You would have these broken and wounded people believe that the fire was somehow their fault, their sin. You are wrong. We live in a world corrupted—that much is truth—but you, sir, are not our savior. That honor goes to Jesus."

Walker opened his mouth and nothing came out but sputters. He looked furious and pounded his fist against his Bible several times before giving up. In fury he rushed from the pulpit and came at Wade with fists raised. In a matter of seconds there were at least half a dozen men at Wade's side. This stopped Walker cold.

"I think we should sing a hymn and conclude the service," Brother Mitchell announced from the pulpit.

Abrianna breathed a sigh of relief as several of the men took hold of Pastor Walker and escorted him from the building. She met Wade's eyes when he turned. She smiled, feeling such a sense of pride and love for him that she wanted to go to him and tell him all that she felt. He smiled back, then took his place back in the pew alongside a giggly Clara, who tugged on his arm and was now whispering in his ear. Seeing her do that robbed Abrianna of her joy. Seeing Wade smile back at the young woman very nearly took her heart.

25

A couple of days later, Abrianna looked at the older man who sat beside her and pondered what it might have been like to grow up with a father in her life, rather than three old ladies. James Cunningham had had no place in her past life, except that of a name. Now as they shared a bit of time alone on the expansive porch of the bridal school, Abrianna found she wanted to know everything about this man.

"I still can't believe you are really here." She met his gaze. "I used to dream this might happen, that you and Mama would come to me and tell me it had all been some horrible mistake. That you were both alive and well and loved me."

"I've always loved you, Abrianna." He

looked across the yard toward the bay. "I loved your mama, too. I'm deeply ashamed that she died without me by her side. Maybe if I'd been there, she wouldn't have died at all."

"Possibly." She knew life was full of what if's, and few ever served a good purpose. "I know Aunt Miriam said Mama loved you and felt certain you had died, otherwise you would have returned to her."

"I'm glad she knew I loved her and never lost faith in me," her father replied. "All those years in prison, paying for something I didn't do, nearly drove me mad. I worried about whether you two were safe. I knew there would be no income for her and fretted something fierce over what she would do to keep you both from starvation."

"She sought help from God's people. The ladies who took her in were strong in the Lord. They still are. My aunts told me that they knew beyond a doubt that they were to see to us and, when Mama died, to go on caring for me. I've had a good life with them, and I love them as dearly as if they were my own blood."

"They are good women," he agreed. "Your mama used to say that God was able to meet our every need. She was the one who helped me see the truth. She was there on the Sunday when I went to the altar and prayed for forgiveness. How I wish I could have back all those years with her and with you."

"We will have to make the best of the years to come instead. I have spent far too many moments lost in sorrow and longing for what could have been." Abrianna smiled and put her hand atop his. "That is behind me now, and I have you. I shall look forward to getting to know what it is to have an earthly father."

He took her hand in his. "I hope we have a good many years."

A carriage came up the long drive, and several well-dressed men stepped from within. The driver sat ramrod straight, not moving from his perch as the men made their way up the stairs of the bridal school. Abrianna got to her feet to investigate, her father right behind her.

"May I help you gentlemen?"

"We are here to speak with Mrs. Madison," one of the men declared. "Might she be in residence?" He handed Abrianna a calling card.

"'Mayor Robert Moran,'" she read aloud.

"Yes, and this is Judge Junius Rochester and former governor Watson C. Squire."

"I'm honored to meet you, gentlemen. I am Miss Abrianna Cunningham, and this is my father, James Cunningham. Mrs. Madison is my aunt. If you will follow me inside, I will announce you."

She escorted them into the main parlor and asked if they would like to take tea. They declined, assuring her that their stay would be brief. Abrianna found her aunt in the kitchen teaching a group of young ladies how to make a proper salmon soufflé.

"Aunt Miriam, I am sorry to interrupt." Abrianna handed her the calling card. "He is in the front parlor, along with a judge and former governor of the state. They said they would be brief."

Her aunt looked appalled. "I suppose this fire has sent proper etiquette out the window when it comes to calling on people. Goodness, but it's not even ten." She dusted flour from her hands and untied her apron. "Ladies, Abrianna will take over."

Abrianna tried not to appear shocked as Aunt Miriam handed over her apron. "You know very well how to make a salmon soufflé." She left Abrianna and the others to attend her company.

Abrianna looked back at the gathering of ladies and shrugged. Even the Chinese girls she'd helped to safety were watching and waiting. She donned the apron and smiled. "All right, let's see where Aunt Miriam left off."

Militine and Thane shared a quick kiss before entering the large informal sitting room where the others were waiting. Mrs. Madison, Mrs. Gibson, and Miss Poisie sat together on the edge of the large sofa, while Abrianna, Wade, and Mr. Cunningham all sat separately.

"Now that we are all assembled," Mrs. Madison said, "I have news to share that will affect each of you. The mayor came to meet with me and has made a request. It seems that he would like us to hold our annual ball as usual. He asks, however, that we consider opening it to everyone as a way of encouraging the citizens of Seattle. He thought it might serve well if we were to hold it on the Fourth of July."

"Although that is a Thursday, and the ball has always been held on Friday," Miss Poisie interjected, as if this were an important point.

Mrs. Madison gave her a nod and continued. "He told me that he and several others who did not suffer loss are quite willing to put up the money to see the event held. I thought since we have only one couple who wish to wed that we refrain from this being a ball and perhaps call it a Fourth of July celebration. However, I wished to discuss it with all involved."

"I think it sounds like a wonderful idea,"

Mr. Cunningham said. "I'll happily do whatever I can to help with the affair."

"Me too," Wade declared. "Maybe we could get some fireworks. Thane and I could handle a display for the party."

"Oh, that would be grand," Mrs. Gibson said, clapping her pudgy hands together. "Just imagine how spectacular that would be."

Mrs. Madison smiled, but her gaze was fixed on Militine and Thane. "I do want you two to know that this needn't interfere with your wedding plans. We have thoroughly discussed the situation, and if you are agreed, we would like to have your wedding here in the garden. It would be a private affair."

Militine looked at Thane and nodded. "I would much prefer a small wedding to a large and formal ball."

Thane smiled. "As long as she's happy, I'm happy."

"We thought perhaps the twenty-ninth of this month. We could have a lovely morning wedding."

"Oh yes, and then a wedding breakfast," Miss Poisie said with great gusto. "I do love wedding breakfasts. They are always such grand affairs."

"I do have one concern," Thane said. "I have no home to take a bride to. Were it not for you, Mrs. Madison, as well as Mrs. Gibson and Miss Poisie putting me and Wade up in the carriage house with Mr. Cunningham, I would be living in the relief tent downtown."

"We did consider that, as well." Mrs. Madison looked to Wade and then Thane. "However, it will involve a little work on your part. Perhaps Wade's, as well."

"What is it? What can I do?" Thane asked.

"Well, as you know, just off the third-floor ballroom there is a large open room that is currently housing our Chinese guests. Prior to this, it hadn't served any purpose other than storage, and we are of a mind that it would be better divided into rooms. I believe two large rooms and a bathroom could easily be fitted in that area. If you and Wade are willing to do the work, I will provide the money to purchase the materials. It seems the entire town is all about building, anyway, and I have it on the word of the mayor that he will personally arrange the supplies." She paused and her expression softened from her usual stern look.

"I know what it is to find true love, and I am quite happy that you and Militine have found each other. Therefore, given the circumstances, I would like to invite you to stay here with us after you wed. Thane, you have been like family for some years, and we have grown fond of Militine. You could call this home for as long as needed."

"Sounds like a pretty good deal," Wade said, giving Thane a wink.

Militine felt herself blush at the thought that so many people were arranging for her to have a bedroom with her husband. It was quite a concession for Mrs. Madison. Never had men been allowed to stay in the house. The Bridal School had always been absolutely proper on that matter.

"I think we'd like that." Thane looked to Militine. She nodded and squeezed his hand.

"Very well. Then we shall make arrangements for the materials, the wedding, and the Fourth of July celebration. Agreed?" Mrs. Madison asked.

"Agreed," they declared in unison.

"And the wedding will be on the twenty-ninth." Abrianna strolled the grounds with Priam Welby and chattered about most anything that came to mind. Although the man had proven to be kind and even pleasant company, she still had no feelings for him.

"Would that it could be our wedding," he said, turning her to face him. "I apologize if that was inappropriate, but I find myself more and more anxious to make you fall in love with me."

She shook her head. "Should a person ever

be made to fall in love? I thought those things were to happen naturally, not to be forced."

"Oh, Abrianna, you are so innocent of life. Many people marry without love and then develop it during their time together. I could teach you much." He tried to pull her into an embrace, but Abrianna moved to the side.

"Mr. Welby, as I told you when this . . . courtship started, I do not love you, nor do I believe that I will fall in love with you. You were the one who drew up the contracts with Mr. Booth, and you know very well why I agreed to see you."

His expression hardened for a moment, and then he looked quite remiss. "I am sorry. I never meant to push you. As an innocent young woman you have no idea the wonder of a love that blooms between a man and a woman."

Wade came to mind. She tried to put his image from her head, but it remained even as Mr. Welby spoke of romance. Thinking back to how Clara had flirted with Wade again over dinner the night before, Abrianna realized in a start that she was jealous. Jealous of Clara. But why? Was it because the girl interacted so easily with men?

But I have never had any trouble speaking to a man—especially to Wade. I have shared my heart with him on many occasions and have had great fun in his company.

"I fear you are no longer listening," Mr. Welby said. "I'm not convinced that you are truly giving me a chance."

Abrianna cleared her mind. "I am sorry. It's just that there is so much to be done. The wedding is in less than two weeks, and we are busy not only with those preparations but also for the Fourth of July celebration."

"Might I escort you to the wedding? Perhaps with me at your side in such a romantic setting, you will find yourself envious of your friend and reconsider marriage."

"I'm sorry, but no. I am to stand up with Militine, and the entire affair is very private." Seeing his look of disappointment, she added, "Of course you are invited to the Fourth of July party. Everyone is."

He said nothing for a moment, and Abrianna feared she had offended him. Goodness, but men were so easily put out. She tried to reason how she might soothe his feelings when he appeared to completely recover and changed the subject.

"I have found a ship that will take the Chinese girls back to their homeland."

"Truly?" It was news most exciting.

"Yes." He gave a chuckle. "I'm glad to see

that at least something related to me brings you joy."

She ignored his comment. "Tell me, when can the girls be returned? Now that they are recovering from their ordeal, at least where their health is concerned, I know that my aunts are anxious to see them where they belong."

"As am I," Welby replied in a most matter-of-fact manner. "The ship leaves next Thursday. I have already told Mrs. Madison that I will make the arrangements."

"Wonderful!" Abrianna clapped her hands together. "That is such joyous news." She forgot herself and reached out to give him a hug as she would have Wade.

Welby took full advantage of the moment, and before Abrianna could offer protest he pulled her close and covered her mouth with his own. Her stomach clenched, and a wave of something akin to anxiety flooded her emotions. Abrianna pushed him away and gave him a most disapproving glare.

"You had no right."

He seemed put out, but his words were apologetic. "I am sorry. I lost my wits." He smiled, seeming to change his mood once again. "I can't help but be overcome with my feelings for you. When you approached me, I lost all reason. Please forgive me."

He sounded sincere enough, but Abrianna

detected something of pride and arrogance in his countenance. He didn't strike her as truly being all that sorry.

"I will forgive you, Mr. Welby. It was in part my fault. I forgot myself. I am used to my friendship with Mr. Ackerman. He has always been a dear friend since we were young, and I find that we are quite comfortable together." A frown came as her thoughts betrayed her. Wade was the only man she had ever truly felt comfortable with. He was always someone she could rely on, trust, and confide in. He was to her all the things Priam Welby wished to be.

Mr. Welby cleared his throat, and Abrianna shook off her thoughts. "I must be going," he said, giving her a little bow. "I will speak to your aunt tomorrow. Tell her I will make all the arrangements for your house guests and bring her the details."

They reached the front porch once again. Abrianna bid him farewell and watched Mr. Welby leave in his fine carriage. Without thought to her gown, Abrianna plopped down on one of the steps and pondered the events that had just taken place. Welby's kiss had meant nothing to her. Instead, it had put her off. She had no desire to be in his arms. She couldn't even conjure up feelings for the man that weren't edged with mistrust and suspicion. There was nothing of the ease she found with Wade.

She placed her elbow on her knee and leaned her head in her hand. And always there was Wade. Day after day she could see that her heart was more tied to him than she'd realized. She had so long thought she would remain single—doing God's work—that to find herself pondering courtship and marriage to Priam Welby seemed at best unrealistic. But when she thought of Wade, those ideas left her with different feelings altogether. For just a moment she allowed her heart and mind to inspect the possibilities more deeply.

"Do I feel more for Wade than just friendship?"

26

Have you ever seen a more beautiful morning?"

Militine glanced at Abrianna and smiled. "It could be pouring rain, and it would still be perfect. It's my wedding day, and I am happier than I've ever been."

Abrianna helped to secure flowers in Militine's simply styled hairdo. "Well, it would not be so perfect if it were pouring rain. That would ruin everything. The garden would be all droopy, and the cake and breakfast ruined. Not to mention these curls would never hold. Instead of looking like a Grecian goddess, you would look like sad wet . . . well . . . you would look bad."

Militine laughed and moved to see herself in the mirror. "But all that matters is that

Thane and I can be together. I never thought I would ever want to marry, but here I am."

She could see Abrianna looking at her strangely in the mirror's reflection. "So what changed your mind?"

"Feeling loved and finding the right man to love in return." Militine studied her appearance. She hadn't wanted to wear frills and silks. She and Thane were simple people, and because of that she wanted to wear a simple gown.

This is truly happening—to me. She thought of her mother, so long gone from her. *Oh, Mama, how I wish you could be here with me.* A tear slipped from her eye.

"You look beautiful," Abrianna told her. "That green is a good color for you."

"I do love it." Militine wiped the tear with her finger and pushed aside those thoughts that would only sadden her.

"I still don't know why women like these bustled backs." Abrianna twisted to look at her own gown of light yellow trimmed in lilac. "I find them such an annoyance."

"No doubt, given time, the fashion will change again, Abrianna. At least we aren't required to wear hoops."

Abrianna stopped her study and nodded. "Yes. You are correct about that, and I should not complain on your wedding day. I apologize profusely and ask your forgiveness. I suppose some of my anxiety has to do with acting as your maid of honor."

"But why?"

She shrugged. "The wedding atmosphere has given me cause to think on my own situation. I found in you a dear friend of the heart, one who understood my ideals and planned to never marry. But now I find that entire ideal disrupted."

"Because I'm marrying? But that shouldn't cause you grief. You aren't the one marrying. You can go on with your ideal."

"I know." Abrianna looked almost confused. "I just don't know that I want to."

With nerves taut, Thane recited his wedding vows. He had watched Militine come down the garden path on the arm of Mr. Cunningham and thought he might well do a most unmanly thing and pass out cold. She was radiant in her attire and beamed at him as though he were a gallant knight who had just saved her from a dragon. But that only served to make him more light-headed. Why women cherished such fanfare was beyond him. Seemed to him a couple were just as married whether they spoke the words in private or before finely clad guests.

They had opted for a judge to marry them rather than a minister, given that the church elders had dismissed Pastor Walker. Thane had never liked the man anyway, and wasn't sorry to see him go.

Wade stood at his side as his best man, and Abrianna stood up with Militine. Despite his anxiety, Thane knew all was as it should be. Now, if Wade could just come to his senses about Abrianna and vice versa.

When instructed to kiss the bride, Thane did so with trembling and awe. All the times he'd kissed her before were special, but this one spoke of a permanency that actually frightened him. What had he done? He was now responsible for a wife, and he didn't have a dime to his name or a home of his own. Had they been completely foolish in this endeavor?

Throughout the wedding breakfast he considered the matter and felt almost guilty for having gone ahead with the wedding. It wasn't a case of cold feet. He wanted to be a husband to Militine more than anything else, but he feared that he'd put both of them in a bad position.

"Do you think I made a mistake?" he asked Wade.

"What?" His friend looked incredulous. "What's gotten into you?"

Thane shook his head. He glanced around

to make sure no one else could overhear. "I have nothing, Wade. I can't offer her anything that isn't borrowed."

"I don't see that she minds," Wade replied. "Besides, it won't be long at the rate we're working for you to put aside a good deal and build your own house or buy one already established. I wouldn't worry over-much about it. I think together you two will do well. You're both sensible and solid in your thinking."

Thane felt his misgivings fade a bit. "I suppose you're right. I just keep worrying that I won't be the husband she needs me to be."

"If you love her with all your heart and stay true to her alone," Wade said, his attention fixed somewhere behind Thane, "you'll be what she needs."

Thane followed his friend's gaze. Abrianna stood laughing about something. "I think," Thane whispered, "that maybe you should follow your own advice."

Militine appeared at Thane's side. "Aren't you weary of this breakfast? I think we should just slip away and leave the others to their revelry."

Thane feigned surprise. "Why, Mrs. Patton, what a scandalous suggestion. I'm only sorry I didn't pose it myself."

The Fourth of July Celebration proved to be a wonderful idea. People flooded the grounds of the Madison Bridal School and danced and ate throughout the day as if the great fire had never happened. Reports came from everywhere that the town was well on its way to recovery. Already there were tents erected for most every purpose. The Methodist church, which had burned to the ground, now held tent services atop the site of their former building. They were well into plans for rebuilding, as were many others.

The mayor announced that over two hundred businesses now operated out of tents, and the new platting of the roads was being worked to accommodate every possible need. The city had agreed to take control of the waterworks and promised new, more efficient waterlines. The Yesler Dock had been repaired so as to receive passengers and freight, and the coal bunkers, where some three hundred tons of coal had burned for days after the main fire had been extinguished, were replaced with new bunkers. The good people of Seattle were reclaiming their lives and in the mood for celebration.

Now, if only I could reclaim my life and figure out my future.

Abrianna placed her plate of uneaten food on one of the picnic tables. She longed to be away from the others in order to think. The extensive grounds of the Madison Bridal School afforded her some privacy as she took herself on a walk.

Abrianna tried to maintain a positive spirit. Mr. Welby had come to the party, bringing her a huge bouquet of flowers. The week before he had taken Aunt Miriam and the Chinese girls to the ship *Northern Star*. Aunt Miriam had inspected the quarters to be given the young girls, as well as the matronly woman who would act as their escort. The woman, it was said, was returning to her work as a missionary in China and would oversee the return of these girls to their families. It was all very efficiently done, Aunt Miriam declared.

Welby seemed quite pleased with himself. Maybe Wade was right and Welby was a cold and calculating man, but at least he'd done right by those poor girls. Mindless of her lovely gown, Abrianna took a seat on the ground under a large cottonwood tree. It would still be a little while before the sky was dark and the fireworks display would commence. Maybe this time alone would help put her mind at ease.

Relieved that Priam had kept his word, Abrianna still wrestled with the conflict in her heart. The more she thought about it, the more his kiss repulsed her. Would she feel that way about all men and their kisses? Would she remain unmarried and become a spinster like Aunt Poisie? The feelings of indecision and confusion overwhelmed her. Whatever God required of her, she would do. No question. But what was He requiring?

"Those look like some deep thoughts." Wade crouched down. "I was surprised to see you leave the party, and now I find you here with a worried look on your face. Normally you're concocting some crazy plan when your brow gets that deeply furrowed." His laughter floated over her.

Her stomach tightened as she looked up at him. Strange feelings in Wade's presence were not normal. Yet here they were, twisting and turning and flipping her stomach into knots. Earlier she'd watched him laughing and appearing quite content in the company of Clara and Elizabeth, all the while suffering through her own emotions that bordered on longing and anguish. Surprisingly, however, she'd had nothing to say, at least nothing she felt she could say.

"You look awfully lonely here by yourself," Wade said, taking a seat on the ground beside her. "Is something wrong?"

"I don't know." Her honesty would, of course, open the subject up for discussion, but perhaps it was time to resolve it. She still couldn't figure out if she wanted more from Wade than friendship.

"That's not like you," Wade replied.

She looked at him. Really studied him for a moment. His brown hair had been sun-kissed from long hours of working outdoors. She'd never known it to be that way before, but then there generally weren't so many sunny days in Seattle. His eyes held her attention the longest. Their dark coloring, a rich brown earthy tone, had always been pleasing to Abrianna. Wade's nose, broad smile, and rugged jaw were well ordered, and his ears, unlike Mr. Welby's, were perfect in size and placement. He was a handsome man.

"Oh, stuff and nonsense." She jumped to her feet. "I find myself quite perplexed. Vexed really, and I don't know how to resolve my confusion."

Wade got to his feet. "Have I done something to disturb you?"

"Yes." She shook her head. "No. I don't know what it is." She paced a bit, always throwing him a glance. Finally, she decided to just have it out.

"Mr. Welby kissed me."

"He what?" Wade's scowl did nothing to give her pause.

"Just hear me out." She put her hands on her hips and faced him. "He kissed me, but

I didn't like it. In fact, I found it to be most unpleasant. Earlier he kept talking about our courtship and how he could make me fall in love with him, but I didn't believe him. The entire time all I could think about was you and how you had warned me against him."

"Well, at least that's something."

Wade sounded sarcastic, but Abrianna wasn't to be dissuaded from continuing. "As he continued to talk, as he has always done in promoting himself, I found his words to appear sincere but unmoving. I kept pondering if I was ever meant for love.

"You know full well that I believe God has called me to serve Him with my life, and Mr. Welby assured me that I could do that as his wife, but it did not ring true. I believe if I married him, he would soon have me planning parties and serving teas to his associates' wives. Can't you see it? Silver service and china cups for twelve or twenty? Ladies in their finest, and all that stuff and nonsense about the latest gossip and who was courting whom and what scandalous event had taken place at the opera?" She shook her head. "I couldn't bear it. I would go mad within a month.

"But," she continued quickly, lest she lose her nerve, "the thing I kept coming back to was that I wouldn't be able to share your company anymore. We've been friends for so very long, but I kept wondering if there was something more between us. Something more personal."

At this he smiled but said nothing. Abrianna felt ten kinds of fool for blathering on about her sentiments, but she knew she might well explode if she left the thoughts unsaid.

"Then I thought again of Mr. Welby and my distaste for his kiss, and I found myself wondering . . . well . . . about kissing you." She closed her eyes. "There, I've said it, and now I can surely let the matter go. I feel so relieved. You can laugh at me if you—"

He wasn't laughing. Instead, without asking her permission or giving her any warning, Wade took her in his arms. Her eyes flew open just as he pressed his lips to hers in a passionate kiss. It was unlike anything she'd ever experienced. Almost against her will, her arms went around his neck. When he pulled away, his expression was quite smug.

"Oh." She could form no other word.

He gave her a most self-satisfied smile. "There. Does that answer your question, you silly hoyden? I've wanted to kiss you for a very long time, but you seemed far too preoccupied with everyone else. I wasn't at all sure there was room in your thoughts for me."

She swallowed hard, wishing very much he might kiss her again. He certainly had addressed her concerns about whether or not she might enjoy the kiss of a man. That moment had proven it only needed to be the right man. Finally, she felt sense returning to her.

"I . . . well . . . yes. I suppose it does answer my initial question. Unfortunately, it brings to mind a great many others. I'm afraid I'm just as confused as I was before."

He didn't seem at all concerned. Instead, he sat back down and patted the ground. "Why don't you come sit beside me, and perhaps we can sort through that busy little mind of yours and figure out a way to lessen your confusion."

She sank down without giving it another thought and gazed in awe at his handsome face. "How do you propose we do that?"

He chuckled softly. "I have a couple of ideas."

Tracie Peterson is the award-winning author of over one hundred novels, both historical and contemporary. Her avid research resonates in her stories, as seen in her bestselling Heirs of Montana and Alaskan Quest series. Tracie and her family make their home in Montana. Visit Tracie's website at www.traciepeterson.com.

You May Also Enjoy...

At twenty, Lenore's deepest desire is to find love. Her father wants her to marry a man who could never capture her heart, but she's running out of time to find a man who can.
Steadfast Heart by Tracie Peterson
BRIDES OF SEATTLE #1
traciepeterson.com

When Marlena Wenger is faced with a difficult decision—raising her sister's baby or marrying her longtime beau—what will she choose?
The Love Letters by Beverly Lewis
beverlylewis.com

Torn between her heart and her family's needs, will nurse-in-training Miriam Hastings choose to remain in Blessing, North Dakota, or return home?
A Harvest of Hope
SONG OF BLESSING #2
laurainesnelling.com